MELTING POINT

MEMPHIS, TN

NEVAEH RYN

Melting Point by Nevaeh Ryn
Royal Harlots MC
Published by Makin Groceries Media
24200 SW Freeway, Suite 402, Box #353
Rosenberg, TX 77471

https://nevaeh-ryn.square.site/

Melting Point
Royal Harlots MC, Memphis, MEM Chapter
By Nevaeh Ryn

Manufactured in the United States of America

ISBN: 979-8-88630-050-5 (paperback)
ISBN: 979-8-88630-051-2 (special color paperback)

Participating Authors

Crimson Syn–The Duchess
J. Lynn Lombard–Calypso's Shield
Roux Cantrell–Heat
Barbara Nolan–Martina
Kathryn C. Kelly–Dr. Feel Good
K.L. Ramsey–Ember
Elle Boon–Belle & Flame Royally Hacked
Via Mari – Pearl
Thetta James–Blaze of Retribution
JA LaFrance–Cuda
Quinn Slater–Femme Fatale
Jena Doyle–Filthy Little Witch
D Williams–Safe Haven
Kris Anne Dean–Katana
Elisabeth N. Harris–Sapphire's Gem

Chelle C. Craze–Lunatic's Asylum
Nevaeh Ryn–Melting Point

Royal Harlots Code

LOYALTY: Stand by your sisters through hell and fire. Blood in, blood out – once you're in, you're family for life. Any betrayal will be punished.

RESPECT: THE PATCH IS EARNED, NEVER GIVEN. HONOR IT, WEAR IT WITH PRIDE AND NEVER LET IT BE DISRESPECTED. RESPECT CLUB LAW. RESPECT THE PATCH. RESPECT YOUR SISTERS. DISRESPECT A MEMBER AND THERE WILL BE HELL TO PAY.

STRENGTH IN UNITY: WE STAND AS ONE. NO SISTER RIDES OR FIGHTS ALONE.

RIDE FREE, RIDE PROUD: THE ROAD IS OUR HOME, AND FREEDOM IS OUR CREED. LIVE

BOLDLY. RIDE HARD, AND NEVER APOLOGIZE FOR WHO YOU ARE.

TAKE NO SHIT: STAND TALL AND UNSHAKEN AGAINST ANYONE WHO THREATENS THE CLUB OR YOUR SISTER. SISTERS DO NOT LEAVE FAMILY BEHIND. CLUB IS FAMILY.

HONESTY: NEVER, LIE, CHEAT OR STEAL.

EARN YOUR KEEP: EVERY SISTER HAS A ROLE TO PLAY. NO ONE RIDES FOR FREE. CONTRIBUTE WITH YOUR SKILLS, YOUR STRENGTH, AND YOUR SPIRIT.

SHOW NO FEAR: FEAR HAS NO PLACE HERE. FACE CHALLENGES HEAD-ON, WHETHER ON THE ROAD, IN A FIGHT, OR IN LIFE.

RESPECT THE ROAD: WE RESPECT THE LAWS OF THE ROAD AND THE FREEDOM IT BRINGS. WE RESPECT OUR ALLIES BUT BOW TO NO ONE.

DEATH BEFORE DISHONOR: BEING PATCHED IN IS A PRIVILEGE, NOT A RIGHT. YOUR COLORS ARE SACRED, NOT TO BE LEFT ALONE, AND NEVER LET THEM TOUCH THE GROUND.

CHURCH IS MANDATORY.

TERRITORY: YOU ARE TO RESPECT YOUR SISTERS' TERRITORY AND FOLLOW THEIR CHAPTER'S CLUB RULES.

TRUST: YEARS TO EARN IT…SECONDS TO LOSE IT.

"The Harlots gave me a place in the world."

32-year-old Denali 'Everest' Bernard has never had it easy. Raised in the gritty streets of Chicago by an abusive father and a powerless mother who disdained her, Denali saw the military as her escape. That dream was shattered into a million tiny pieces when an act of self-defense led to a dishonorable discharge and a decade behind bars. When she's released, Denali finds herself adrift. On the edge of society, the Prez of Memphis's Royal Harlots gives a home. With a new family, she quickly rises through the ranks as their treasurer.

"I write about happily ever afters, but it seems like I'm not destined to have one."

26-year-old Estelle Pratt-Milton thinks she has it all. Raised by a loving mother and stellar stepfather, she used her love of writing to launch a lucrative career in the erotic romantasy genre, creating worlds where love conquers all. Her family is a tight-knit unit, and Aydin, her fiancé, treats her like a queen. At least, he did, before the secrets she didn't know Aydin harbored started coming to light, threatening to unravel everything she holds dear.

Little does he know Estelle has secrets of her own.

Denali and Estelle's worlds collided as children, before life saw them lose contact. Years later, they reconnect at a bar, leading to a night of passion. They go their separate ways, but the strings of fate keep pulling them back to one another, throwing both of their lives out of orbit. The bubbly author easily breaks down Denali's perfectly crafted walls, proving to be her melting point as the two start an affair. The fixation that forms is far from logical and further complicated by Estelle's engagement to an enemy of the Royal Harlots.

Denali's solution? To kill two birds with one stone and hold Estelle hostage, duh.

Dedication

To my mother, whose knowledge on the MC world and editing skills were more helpful than words can express. You continue to be an inspiration and my rock. Natasha, thank you so much for your help over the months. Alegra, my beautiful little sister, your strength is motivational. And last but not least, I couldn't have done this without the help of my psychiatrist. Thank you for helping me through tough times and thank you for always listening without judgment.

Acknowledgments

First off, thank you to Crimson Syn for giving me a chance and allowing me to be a part of her wonderful series. Shoutout to Claire Shaw for being so friendly and helpful, and shoutout to everyone who decided to give this book a chance. To my grandmother for being my secondary editor, thank you so much. And to my big sister, who continues to encourage me, even if you don't read my work. I love you.

Table of Contents

MELTING POINT

Part One

The Past

DENALI

19 years ago…

"Mr. Bernard, thank you for coming," the principal, Mrs. Delroy, said with a smile aimed at my father.

I rolled my eyes when she fluttered her fake eyelashes. Despite being married, her crush on my father was obvious to everyone but him. He and Mama had gotten into more than one argument about the amorous woman, often ending with him beating her.

Why she continuously fought for a man who was the scum of the Earth, I'd never know. If at 13 I knew Daddy was the bottom of the barrel, I didn't know why my 29-year-old mother couldn't see it.

"What did she do this time?" Daddy asked with a sigh, sidling me a glare.

I looked away, my jaw clenching. My infractions always resulted in harsh punishment. With Mama pregnant again, he'd begun turning his violence onto me more and more. I couldn't wait for my latest sibling to be out of her, so I could get a break.

"Beat up my son," Mrs. George said with a prissy sniff, reminding me of her presence.

Her raggedy son was at the nurse's office, his busted lip and black eye requiring attention. I, for one, felt pride that I'd laid out an athletic boy. Granted, he wasn't very good at basketball, but that didn't dampen my satisfaction.

"Not my fault that he can't take a hit," I taunted, shrugging when all three adults glared at me.

"Silence," Daddy said, his expression promising hell when we got home. "Adults are talking."

"She wasn't there. I was, and he—"

"Shut up, little girl," he barked.

This time, I listened, deciding not to push my luck. If I talked back anymore, I might get beaten in the car instead of in the privacy of our rundown Southside home.

"Everyone, let's settle down," Mrs. Delroy said, looking between us, her flirty smile replaced with a disapproving frown.

I'd long ago lost hope that she'd notice any signs of abuse. She was a lost cause, unable to sense the violence brewing. The one time I'd tried to speak to her about my father's treatment, she'd dismissed it as discipline, before going on a tangent about how 'entitled' teenagers are nowadays.

Like everyone else, she just saw me as an angry little Black girl.

Her stare settled on my father. "Mr. Bernard, your daughter knocked a boy out. He's currently with the nurse—"

"But may have to go to the hospital for stitches!" Mrs. George interjected.

"Get to the point," Daddy ordered, growing shiftier with every passing second.

He must've been dipping into his supplies again. I wonder how Curly would react, knowing that his second-in-command was stealing drugs to feed his addiction. He hid it well enough, but I prayed he'd be caught.

A bullet in his head would solve a lot of my problems.

"Denali is being suspended for three weeks. This is her second offense of the semester. Per the school policy, one more, and she may be expelled."

Her words made me wince. I'd vowed to be better than both my parents. If I didn't finish middle school, I'd be worse than them both. At least they made it to high school before they gave up on education. I had to get my high school diploma if nothing else.

"Give me what I have to sign, so we can go," Daddy said through gritted teeth.

He was upset with me. Maybe disappointed, but that was giving him too much credit. He didn't care enough about me to feel disappointment. But whatever he was feeling, the result would be the same: violence.

"Of course, Mr. Bernard," Mrs. Delroy replied, too blinded by her poor taste in men to be alarmed by Daddy's behavior.

Sure, Daddy has some attractive features, but anybody with sense should be able to detect how awful his mere presence was. But Mrs. Delroy must've turned off critical thinking when he was around, stupid fantasies clouding her judgment. I must've done something horrific in a past life. It was the only reason my life was so shitty, and the only logical explanation as to why stupid bitches surrounded me.

The silence in the car was deafening. Daddy hadn't said a single thing to me since we left the principal's office. I'd tried to turn the radio up to distract me from my looming ass-whooping, but he'd slapped my hand away when he noticed me touching the volume dial. The closer we got to home, the more anxious and frustrated I felt. It wasn't fair that I was being punished for defending myself. Jonathan George had been harassing me for weeks. He'd crossed a line by grabbing my ass, and I couldn't let that slide. His behavior towards me was growing worse, and if I didn't act now, I didn't know what he'd do in the future. Maybe if Mama had demanded respect when Daddy had started mistreating her, it wouldn't have escalated to physical violence.

All too soon, we were parking outside our house. I jumped when he slammed his car door shut, my body freezing as he stalked to the front door. No matter how much I tried to become immune to his treatment, his beatings were something I'd never gotten used to. As I watched him fumble with his keys, I tried to will my body to move so I could dash down the street and escape his wrath. Mrs. Milton would let me crash at her place until he cooled down.

However, my body wouldn't fucking obey my mind, and once the door was unlocked, Daddy was returning to the 1992 Cadillac Fleetwood.

"Get out the fucking car," Daddy ordered after he yanked the passenger door open. When I remained still, he continued. "Imma count to three, Denali. One…"

The countdown snapped me out of my stupor. I unbuckled my seat belt just as he said, "Three." That wasn't good enough for him. He snatched me by my bicep, dragging me through the open door and tossing me onto the floor of our living room. A yelp left me, combining with the sound of the front door being kicked shut.

"Get undressed," he commanded, his eyes tracking me as I scrambled to my feet.

The tears that burned my eyes were just as humiliating as his request. There was nothing sexual about his demand. When he was furious, clothes weren't allowed during his beatings, the thin barrier they provided against his fists or the leather of his belt was unacceptable to him when he was in a shitty mood, or high off blow.

"Daddy, just let me explain," I begged, my eyes darting to the kitchen where Mama was cooking as I got to my feet.

The chatter of the twins and '90s R&B flowed to me, familiar after-school noise. Usually, though, Mama came out to greet me. But she must've heard the commotion and decided to mind her own business and let Daddy dish out his punishment. Her silence was an omen.

"I was just—"

"I don't give a fuck about why you hit that boy," he spat, his words infused with venom. "You did it, interrupted my goddamn day to come get your ass, and got suspended."

"That isn't fucking fair!" I exploded, wishing one adult had given me the chance to explain the situation before reacting. "Jonathan—"

He closed the distance between us, backhanding me, sending me back to the floor. My cheek stung, and I swore I tasted blood in my mouth. The stupid rings he wore made the blow more painful. When I staggered to my feet, he grabbed me by my curls, forcing me to look at him.

"Cuss at me again, and you'll spend those three weeks in a coma."

He released me with a shove. My gaze fell to the floor. The bravado I had at school was gone, leaving me unwilling to push my luck any further. His fury was a prelude to a brutal beating, one that'd be nothing compared to a few shoves and a slap. I knew the drill by now, knew how to tell when he'd be more merciless. The foreboding dread before the beating was just as bad as the pain of his fists.

"Strip, girl," he repeated, his voice low and dangerous.

My lips trembled as I continued to fight my tears. I refused to break down, though. Like any predator, showing weakness only emboldened my father.

"Do you want me to be molested?" I blurted, the words spilling from my lips when he began to unbuckle his belt to beat me with. "Because that's what Jonathan wanted to do."

He paused, his hands falling away from his belt and making me relax. "Explain."

"He's been harassing me for weeks, Daddy," I said, forcing my voice to remain steady, though I couldn't meet his eyes. I wasn't allowed to. "Ever since I rejected him. He cornered me today. Grabbed my ass and tried to unbutton my jeans, so I swung. I didn't do anything wrong; I was just defending myself."

The resulting silence was tense. I held my breath as I waited to see what he'd do.

"Look at me," he finally said. I obeyed within a second, and he continued. "You telling the truth?"

"Why would I lie about that?"

"Why wouldn't the principal bitch tell me?"

I shrugged. "Mr. George is on the school board. We're us."

"And you're a troublemaking little bitch, so I guess that doesn't help shit," he said, his words making me flinch, even though they carried no heat, a rarity with my father. Sighing, he rebuckled his belt. "Fine, girl. I'll give your ass a pass this time, but don't do that shit again. Next time, wait until after school, so I don't have to deal with those prissy bitches. Now go help your mama with dinner."

The relief I felt was overwhelming. If it wouldn't piss my father off all over again, I might even do a happy dance.

"Yes, sir," I mumbled, turning to go through the archway that led to the kitchen.

"And Denali?" he called, making me pause and look over my shoulder. Our eyes met, the deep brown of my irises contrasting with the hazel-green of his. "I'm proud of you, girl. I don't want no one taking advantage of you or your sisters."

"Really?" I asked without thinking.

Praise from my father was rarer than a solar eclipse. Though he doted on my six-year-old twin sisters, if he wasn't yelling at or beating me, he ignored me. Both he and

Mama blamed my existence for upending their lives.

His eyes narrowed. "You think I'm a fucking liar? Y'all came from my balls; you're mine. Why would I want a motherfucker fucking over my daughters like that?"

It would be easy to point out everything he'd done that led me to believe he wouldn't care about what happened to me. But to do so would be ignorant, as it'd only reignite his temper and earn me the beating I'd managed to avoid.

"No, Daddy," I said carefully, shoving my hands in my pockets to stop from fidgeting. He hated it when I did that. "Thank you."

He walked to his favorite recliner and plopped down, then jerked his chin toward the kitchen. "Go to the kitchen. I'm hungry."

Grabbing the remote, he turned the TV on. This time, he didn't stop me when I began to walk away. Even with my throbbing cheek and aching scalp, my steps felt lighter, my father's declaration of pride echoing in my head.

"Hey, Mama," I greeted when I entered the kitchen, smiling at Stella and Noelle, who were coloring at the dining table.

They spared me little waves, then went back to drawing, too busy chattering amongst themselves to speak to their big sister.

"Denali," Mama replied, peeking over her shoulder, before going back to stirring some sauce, her auburn coils piled on top of her head.

Mama said nothing else when she saw the bruise blooming on my face. The disapproving look in her eyes—eyes so like my own—cut through me. No doubt, she'd heard and was angrier with me than she was with my father. She'd wanted me and my sisters to be better than her, and that meant being a model student who didn't get into altercations.

"Daddy wanted me to help you cook, so what do you need done?"

"Food's almost done, so I don't need your help."

She was upset with me. If her tone wasn't enough evidence, then the glares she kept throwing over her shoulder were.

"Mama—"

"Don't, Denali. The only thing I ask of you when it comes to school is that you get passing grades and that you stay out of trouble. You do the former just fine, but every damn week you do some shit to land you in the principal's office. You're lucky that you've only faced disciplinary action twice."

"You know it isn't every week—"

"It's still too damn often!" she yelled, slamming the spoon down on the counter to face me, her seven-month pregnant belly protruding. Noelle and Stella gathered their things and padded out of the kitchen, retreating to their rooms as they so often did when things got heated between me and our parents. Mama didn't notice their departure, too busy reaming my ass. "Why can't you just keep your hands to yourself?"

"He grabbed my ass! If Daddy doesn't care, why do you?"

When it came to me, she let him be the disciplinarian and silently stewed over my behavior. I didn't know what changed today.

"Because I want a good future for you, Denali, and that won't happen if you get expelled."

"Mama—"

"I don't want to hear it," she said, turning back to the sauce. "You're such a disappointment sometimes, girl. Go take a walk until food's ready. I don't want you here right now."

Her words stung just as much as Daddy's hands. Clenching my jaw, I stormed out of the kitchen, fighting another batch of tears.

"Come back before the street lights come on, girl," Daddy said as I opened the front door, before going back to ignoring me.

That wasn't shocking. He was happiest when I was out of his way.

With no one around to see me cry, I let my tears flow as I walked to the old playground. My neighborhood was in dire need of major renovations, but was insulated from the worst of Washington Park's violence. People weren't stupid enough to leave their doors unlocked 24/7, but children playing outside was a common sight. A few houses had been renovated and flipped and were quickly snatched up by young families looking to lay down roots. Seeing those happy families, full of hope and showering their children with love, always filled me with jealousy. What had I done to be deserving of parents who didn't love me? It wasn't my fault they'd fucked without protection as teenagers.

The playground had a few other occupants, but the swings were free. I hopped on the one nearest to me, lost in thought as I swung. If it'd just been an ass grab, I might've just shoved Jonathan away. But trying to unbutton my jeans and slip his hands into my panties was an offense I couldn't ignore. Daddy agreed with me, but the school and Mama thought I'd overreacted. Self-defense was legal in Illinois, so why did I even get in trouble?

So lost in thought, I didn't notice the flash of red hair running in front of me until my feet connected with a little body, making them squeak.

"Shit!" I yelled as the kid fell to the rubber tile.

I hopped off the swing and hurried to the child, a little white girl with flaming red waves and blue-gray eyes with a gold ring around her pupils. She looked to be around my sisters' age. I glanced at the other people at the park, wondering who she belonged to.

"Are you alright?" I said, holding out my hand to help her up.

"Yep," she chirped, accepting my hand and letting me pull her up. "You just grazed my arm. Which is good, because it would've hurt a lot if you kicked my head."

"Yeah," I agreed, swiping at my puffy eyes to get rid of lingering wetness. "I'm happy I didn't. You need to be more careful, kid."

"I'm not a kid!" she said with a foot stomp, the action only making her look younger. "I'm seven, which is almost ten, which is basically a teenager."

Flawed as it was, her logic made me fight a smile. "No, thirteen is a teenager. Seven is a child. Practically a toddler."

I added the last part to fuck with her. Based on her jaw-dropping and chubby arms crossing over her chest, it worked.

"Nuh-uh!"

"Yuh-huh. Do you still wear diapers?"

"I do not! I've been potty-trained for five years, thank you."

"Alright, kid," I said, allowing myself to smile at her, her big personality lifting my mood. "Go back to your mama, and don't run in front of swings anymore."

"I don't wanna go back," she said with a pout. "It's boring."

I cocked a brow, then looked at the other people milling about. A teenage couple was cuddling on the bench, and an older couple was helping their toddlers on the jungle gym. One glance let me know she wasn't with either of them. Everyone else was Black, which she clearly wasn't.

"Can't I stay and talk to you? You're pretty and nice. Well, kind of nice, because you called me a toddler. But you did help me up, so it evens out."

"You speak pretty well for a seven-year-old," I said as I returned to the swings. I wasn't a nanny, so if she wanted to run around, I wouldn't stop her. "I had a nasty lisp at your age."

"I like reading," she said, jumping on the swing next to me. "Plus, I'm smart. I'm skipping second grade and going straight to third."

I gave a round of applause. "Congrats."

"What grade are you in?"

"Eighth grade."

Her striking eyes rounded. "So, you're a teenager?"

"I am."

"Awesome! I can't wait to be a teenager. Mommy says I can get my ears pierced when I turn thirteen. She makes me wear clip-ons right now, which are stupid."

The more she spoke, the more apparent her Southern accent became.

"Where are you from?" I asked, barely swinging to maintain the conversation.

When Mama first got pregnant, I was so excited to have a sibling. I was ecstatic when the twins popped out, but as they grew older, they only interacted with each other and barely gave anyone else the time of day, complete opposites from the little girl next to me.

"Memphis. We're visiting because my new daddy—well, I hope he'll be my new daddy—is from here and came down for his mother's birthday. She's super old, but nice. She made fudge for me and my siblings. Anyway, what's your name?"

"Denali."

"Like the mountain?"

"Correct."

"I wish I had a cool name like that. Estelle was my grandma's name. If she hadn't died when Mommy was pregnant with me, I might have a better name."

I nearly choked on my spit at her callous words. Granted, she didn't know her grandmother, and kids weren't known to mince their words.

"You know, stranger danger is a real thing. You shouldn't reveal so much to someone you don't know."

She scrunched her button nose in distaste at my piece of advice. "Mommy always says never talk to adults I don't know. You're a teenager, so you don't count."

I thought of Jonathan and frowned. He was just a year older than me and already trying to commit felonies. "Age doesn't determine how dangerous someone is, kid. A teenager can still hurt you."

"My name's Estelle, remember?"

"Can't forget it. It's similar to my little sister's name."

"What is her name?"

"Stella."

"I like Stella better than Estelle. It's prettier. Denali is kind of like Dennis, who's my older brother, but his name is stupid." She hopped off the swing, then held her hand out to me. "Wanna walk me back to Mrs. Milton's? I can't talk to strangers if

I'm back with my family, and we know each other now, so you aren't a stranger."

My eyebrows rose. "Mrs. Milton is your stepfather's mother?"

Once or twice, she mentioned that she had a son working in the South doing…something with oil. I couldn't remember what, and she'd never specified the city.

"Uh-huh. You know her?"

I pushed aside my shock, reminding myself that it was the 21st century, and interracial couples were no longer a rarity.

"I do."

The sixty-one-year-old woman was the grandmother I never had. I wouldn't reveal to Estelle that Mrs. Milton sheltered me and my siblings when things got too bad at home. Not only was it a mature subject, but it also wasn't her business.

When seconds of silence passed, she wiggled her fingers. "Are you walking me home or not? Mommy might be looking for me, and I don't want to worry her. I should've told her I was going to the playground before I snuck out, but I forgot."

I accepted her hand, stood from the swing, and began to lead her to Mrs.

Milton's house. "It isn't sneaking if you get permission."

"Oh. True."

Estelle was a little chatterbox, yapping away as we walked to Mrs. Milton's, able to keep the conversation alive no matter how lackluster my reply. When we arrived at the brick duplex I was all too familiar with, the door swung open on the second knock. Relief blanketed Mrs. Milton's tawny face when she saw Estelle, and she smiled at me.

"Thank God you found her, Denali. We were looking everywhere for her," she said, then turned around and yelled, "Sheron! One of my neighbors found her."

"Oh, thank God!" a woman with a thick Southern accent exclaimed.

Footsteps thudded to the door, until a pretty white woman who was about 5'5 came into view, a mass of thick mahogany waves on her head. Estelle released my hand and ran into her mother's outstretched arms.

"Never do that again, Estelle. I was worried sick."

The scene was heartfelt and sent a pang of envy through me. There was no yelling or violence, just relief and motherly love. Never had my parents been so lenient with me. The smallest infraction always earned a punishment.

The woman—Sheron—looked up, smiling at me. "Thank you so much, sweetie. Where'd you find her?"

"At the playground," Estelle chirped before I could, wiggling away. "Denali's pretty nice, even if she did kick me."

"She ran in front of the swing, ma'am," I explained quickly, her wording making me cringe.

Sheron looked back at her daughter. "Now, why would you do that?"

Estelle shrugged. "I dunno. I'm hungry. Is food ready yet?"

"Yes, it is," Mrs. Milton said, smiling as Sheron escorted Estelle away, before turning back to me. She examined me closely, frowning at the mark my father's slap had left. "He hit you again?"

"It's no big deal," I lied, my words reeking of bullshit.

Mrs. Milton wanted to get the cops involved. The one time I'd agreed, Mama had sided with Daddy. It was one of the few times I'd fear he'd actually beat me to death. Because it'd been the summer and school hadn't been in session, he hadn't avoided hitting my face. The black eye had taken three weeks to fade.

She took my hands in hers. "Denali, sweetheart, no man should be putting his hands on a little girl. Why don't you come inside and grab a plate? I made more than enough."

The offer was so tempting, and one I'd accepted before. However, Mama wanted me home for dinner, and Daddy wanted me home for sundown. I'd already pushed my luck enough.

"I can't," I said, pulling my hands away, even though it pained me to do so. "I gotta get back home before it gets dark. I got in trouble at school, so—"

She held up a hand, forcing her smile to return even as sadness shone from her onyx eyes. "Don't worry, baby. Get home and come back if you need to."

I nodded, bending down when she hugged me. At thirteen, I already towered over her 5'2 frame, my summer growth spurt pushing me to 5'7. My chin rested in her graying dreadlocks, the scent of rosemary oil wafting from her hair. It was a smell I enjoyed, and one that always soothed me.

"Things are gonna work out, Denali. God always has a plan, baby, and He'll see you through this."

I wished I believed her words, but I didn't. I'm sure the women my father pimped, or the addicts he dealt drugs to, had been told something similar, yet their lives were bleak, statistics that people looked down upon. But I wasn't one to stomp on another's faith, even if it didn't resonate with me.

"Thank you, Mrs. Milton. I'll come back tomorrow."

She nodded and released me. "I'd like that."

I looked past Mrs. Milton, noting Estelle peeking around the wall that led to a small hallway. When she saw me, she waved before disappearing from view. Mrs. Milton looked with me, huffing out a laugh.

"That little girl has a big personality. I'm happy you came across her, and not someone worse."

"She does," I agreed, the topic of Estelle a far lighter one. "She can talk her ass...I mean, head off."

"I know teenagers cuss, Denali," Mrs. Milton said with another laugh. "But thank you for trying to respect my gray hairs. My boy and his woman are leaving on Monday. Stop by before then. I'm sure Estelle would be happy to see her new friend again."

"I'll try to," I said, hoping that I'd be able to leave the house and not be grounded for a minor offense.

Mrs. Milton was a kind woman, Estelle was an amusing little girl, and her mama didn't seem half-bad, either. Pathetic as it might be, I'd like nothing more than to escape my toxic home and witness healthy family interactions. That, unfortunately, was the closest to a normal home life that I'd ever get.

Chapter One

DENALI

Five years later…

Birthdays were supposed to be a special occasion. For most families, they were a day filled with laughter, well-wishes, gifts, and love. My birthday had never panned out that way. Despite being the eldest child, May 30th was a day with little fanfare. If Mama was in a good mood, she'd bake me a cake and let me pick dinner. If Daddy was feeling kind, he'd toss me a twenty-dollar bill and go about his day. Stella and Noelle always made me something and insisted on spending the day with me. As they grew older, they grew more creative and were the only people in the house who truly cared that I'd made it to another year. Samuel, my five-year-old little brother, was too young to give a damn, and my reputation at school meant I had no friends.

However, today the twins had a dance competition, so they wouldn't be present for my eighteenth birthday. Mama was taking them, so dinner and a cake were out of the question, and Samuel always enjoyed seeing his big sisters light up the stage. I normally went, too, but my busted lip made leaving the house an impossibility. A beating and a grounding were my punishment for kissing a girl at a graduation party three days ago. When I found out who took the picture and sent it to my father, I was beating their ass. I'd never intended for him to find out about Danielle, and I definitely didn't intend to come out as a lesbian to him…well, ever. Progressive was the last word I'd use to describe my father.

A knock on my door interrupted my brooding. I had no phone, no books, no TV, so all I could do was lay in my bed and reflect on how shitty my life was.

"Denali," Daddy said when he opened the door, not bothering to wait for an invitation.

"I could have been getting dressed, you know," I grumbled, not bothering to stand up. I hadn't even changed from my pajamas, because what the hell was the point?

"Yeah, well, you weren't." Walking to my dresser, he pulled out an envelope. "A thousand dollars in there. Take it, pack your shit, and get out."

That had me sitting up. Alarm raced through me. I hadn't intended to leave until the start of college. Foolishly, I hadn't even begun applying for community colleges, because I thought I'd be able to stay in my childhood home through the summer. Wishful thinking, I suppose. My parents had never shown that much care to me, so it was naïve to think they'd do so for anything.

"You're kicking me out," I stated, my voice devoid of emotion, despite the storm that raged on the inside. "Because I'm an adult now."

"Because you're a fucking dyke, Denali," he spat, the word making me flinch.

"Of all the things I thought you'd fucking be, that was never one of them. How the hell can I let you stay here when there are two little girls under my roof?"

The implication that I'd molest my ten-year-old little sisters sickened me for so many different reasons and hurt more than any physical blow my father had ever dealt.

"How can you even say that? I'm not a predator!" I yelled, my cracking voice and teary eyes betraying how hurt I felt. "Let alone an incestuous child predator. I'd never hurt Stella and Noelle, or any child. I've done nothing but protect them."

He snorted. "Like you'd be stupid enough to admit to it. I'm not fucking chancing you hurting or converting them. You have an hour to leave, or I'm dragging your ass out and keeping my money."

The sob that escaped my mouth didn't move him. My hurt quickly turned into fury. "If you want to find a threat to my sisters, look in the fucking mirror, because I'm not the abusive one in the fucking room. You've been beating me since I was a damn child and have the nerve to think I'm the danger."

Retaliation was anticipated, so dodging the blow was easy. I scurried to where I kept a secret baseball bat, a purchase I made after a break-in attempt, and placed it over my shoulder, ready to swing it. My father paused in his advance, though I didn't lower the bat. Rarely did he infringe on my bedroom. It was my sanctuary, largely free of his presence and his violence, so I'd never had the opportunity to use the bat on him.

"You have some fucking nerve, little girl," he snarled, though he had the sense to stay the hell away from me.

"What have I ever done to you, Daddy? What did I ever do to Mama for you two to…to fucking hate me so much?"

"Be born," he said, the insult making me contemplate smashing his head in and claiming self-defense.

Except now, I was eighteen. I'd be tried as an adult, and if I were found guilty, I could spend a lifetime in prison. Regret surged through me that I hadn't bashed his skull in days ago, when I was still a minor.

"Your crazy ass mama wasn't satisfied with me fucking her on the low, so she poked holes in the condom," he revealed, the new information making my eyes widen. Up until now, Mama claimed they were high-school sweethearts, and he'd never challenged the story. "Made me lose a real good girl and fucked up both of our lives. I wouldn't have started slinging if I didn't have to provide for a brat and a bitch I never wanted. We could've had a normal life, if only she'd miscarried your ungrateful ass."

"You two fucked up your own lives," I snapped, lowering the bat, not caring if he swung or not.

Who would care if he beat me again? Who would miss me if I were gone?

Storming to the dresser, I grabbed the envelope of money, then went to my closet for a duffel bag. "I don't need an hour. I'll be gone in twenty minutes."

He shrugged. "The sooner, the better."

Daddy slammed the door as he left, leaving me alone to gather my meager belongings. Tears streamed down my cheeks as I threw shit into my bag. I packed all the gifts the twins had given me, the money Daddy had provided, and the money I'd been saving, totaling around three thousand dollars. A week's worth of clothes was next, as well as the few pieces of jewelry I owned. My school backpack and gym bag had everything else I needed. It took me fifteen

minutes to pack and get dressed, the entire
time spent crying. When I could think of
nothing else to bring, I took my bags and left
the room, knowing it'd be the last time I'd
ever step foot into it.

Mama marrying Harvey Milton, or Mr.
Daddy, as I jokingly called him, was the best
decision she'd ever made. My blood father
died when I was two, and a string of
temporary boyfriends followed. They didn't
work out for a myriad of reasons, but
luckily, things with Mr. Daddy had unfolded
beautifully. Now, they had been married for
four years and shared a three-year-old boy
and a one-year-old girl. As ecstatic as I was
to have an awesome stepfather and a little
sister after years of being the only girl, my
favorite part of her marriage was the yearly
trips to Chicago. Since that first trip, we had
gone one to three times a year. With school
out and Mr. Daddy having been given a

raise, a summer trip to Chicago had been in the cards this year, much to my joy. Beyond how much there was to do, I loved Chicago for two reasons.

One, Mrs. Milton, as she was the grandmother I'd never had, even if it was evident we shared no blood. She made yummy food, and didn't protest when I began calling her Granny.

Two, Denali Bernard, Mrs. Milton's neighbor, and the prettiest girl I'd ever seen.

Unfortunately, I didn't see her every time we visited, but catching a glimpse of her always made my heart flutter, and talking to her always made me feel like I was floating. Mama had noticed how much I loved being around Denali, almost as much as I loved being around my cousin, Michelle. But whereas Michelle and her sisters were the sisters I hadn't had, Mama helped me realize that my feelings for Denali weren't platonic. I had a crush on her, though I knew she'd never look twice at me.

Why would she? Not only did she see me as a little kid, but I was also chubby with frizzy hair, acne, braces, and frumpy clothes that didn't fit my developing body right. I was a year younger than Denali had been when we first met. At thirteen, she'd been model material. At twelve, I looked like a troll. I hated looking in the mirror, and no matter how many meals I skipped, my body remained ugly. It was why I'd stayed home with the babies, while Mama and Mr. Daddy took Edward, my eldest brother, and Dennis, my older brother, swimming. Wearing a bathing suit and letting everyone see my stout frame was a nightmare.

"Essie, read," Harvey Jr. demanded, toddling to me with his favorite picture book, '*The Lorax*' by Dr. Seuss.

"Red!" Kayla screeched, echoing her big brother's demand.

"Read, Kay," I corrected, accepting the book Harvey so kindly threw at my feet. "And I'll read, but you two have to play the quiet game while I do. Deal?"

They both nodded eagerly. Smiling, I helped them onto the couch. The 'quiet game' was the only way to get them to shut up long enough for me to finish the book in a reasonable time. Otherwise, they'd interrupt me every two seconds.

Just as I began to read, the doorbell rang.

"Get the door, Estelle!" Granny called from the kitchen.

She was busy cooking, so I didn't bother telling her I was reading to my little siblings, even though they both began to pout. Instead, I just called back, "Yes, ma'am," and went to see who was at the door.

Peering through the peephole, my heart sped up when I saw Denali on the doorstep, before my brows furrowed when I noticed all the bags she carried, the tears streaking her perfect face, and her swollen lips. My heart dropped. It was no secret that Denali's father was abusive, and everyone in the neighborhood knew he was a criminal. Knowing he was hurting her made me want to cry. Parents were supposed to love and protect their children. It was what Mama always did for me and my siblings, and even our cousins. And though we didn't share blood, Mr. Daddy protected us just as fiercely and spoiled us every chance he got. Everyone deserved parents like that, especially someone like Denali.

"I'll go get Granny," I said as soon as I opened the door, letting her enter as I ran to the kitchen. All I had to say was "Denali's here," and she turned off the stove and rushed into the living room.

"Baby, what happened?" Granny asked, taking Denali into her arms when she dropped her bags.

She immediately hugged her back, and I stood there awkwardly, unsure what to do. I wanted to comfort Denali, too, but I didn't have the words or the wisdom that Granny did, so all I could do was watch.

"He kicked me out," she mumbled into Granny's hair, the way her voice cracked making me clench my fists.

"Asshole," I blurted without thinking, drawing both of their attention.

Denali laughed as she pulled away, swiping at her eyes. "Language, kid."

My cheeks flamed at her dismissive words. When was she going to see that I wasn't a child? I was almost thirteen, after all.

"No, baby, she's right. I know that's your daddy, and Imma need you to excuse my French, but he's a lowdown motherfucker," Granny spat, shocking me. I'd never heard her cuss before. "He ain't ever been a father to you, and I pray your siblings get away from him."

Michelle entered my mind. My big cousin and her sisters had awful parents, leading to Michelle leaving for Kansas with a scary biker man. Maybe if Mama's sister had been more like her, Michelle wouldn't have left Memphis. I tried not to panic at the possibility of Denali leaving Chicago to escape her raggedy family, too. If she left, I might never see her again.

"He doesn't hurt them," she whispered, sniffling, before clearing her throat. "He loves them. I'm glad for that. They deserve to be loved."

"And you do, too, Denali. You've been dealt a bad hand, and that hurts my soul," Granny said, taking her hand and leading her to the living room. I followed behind, trying to brainstorm what to say to make her feel better. "You've met my grandbabies, right?"

"Last year, I think," Denali mumbled, waving as my siblings looked at her curiously.

No doubt, their little baby minds were struck by how beautiful she was. Even crying and bruised, there wasn't anyone alive who could compete with her beauty.

"Harvey and Jayla, right?" she asked as she sat down.

"Kayla," I corrected, sitting next to her and picking up the toddler in question.

She immediately began to squirm, her days of enjoying being held already gone.

"Imma go finish cooking, baby. Read one of those Egypt books I got you, or play with the kids. Either way, we talkin' later," Granny promised, leaving once Denali nodded.

Harvey inched closer to Denali, offering her a gap-tooth grin. Jealousy roared through me. I couldn't compete with his cuteness.

"Hi," he said, inching closer. "You're pretty."

She laughed. "Thank you, sweetie."

I'd never been so jealous of a baby. He got a cute nickname, while she only ever called me 'kid'. Taking a breath, I reminded myself that now wasn't the time, even if I couldn't help but glare at Harvey.

"Essie likes you," he blurted, making my face burn in mortification.

"Shut up!" I screeched, covering my face with my hands.

"Essie?" Denali echoed, thankfully choosing to ignore his revelation. "That's a cute nickname."

"Do you two wanna see YouTube?" I asked, needing to distract the toddlers so they didn't embarrass me further.

"Yes!" they squealed in unison.

I pulled out my iPhone 3, Mama's old phone, and my Christmas present. Opening YouTube, I navigated to *Fred*, their favorite YouTuber, even though I found him annoying. The moment they heard his grating voice, Harvey snatched the phone, and Kayla crawled to him, the screen distracting them enough for me to hold a conversation with Denali without distractions.

"Don't tell Mama that they're watching YouTube, please. They're only supposed to have an hour of screentime, and only when Mama or Mr. Daddy is watching them."

Denali cocked a brow. "Mr. Daddy?"

God, why couldn't I say something normal to her?

"Uhm, my stepfather. It's like an inside joke. I know it's kind of stupid, but—"

"It's adorable, Estelle," she reassured, the way she said my name making me shiver. "I didn't mean to interrupt your time with your siblings. I don't mind chilling in the kitchen or on the porch—"

"No!" I said, before clearing my throat. "No, it's okay. I like talking to you. I barely got to see you last time we were here."

"Yeah, sorry about that. I had a job."

"Had?"

"I got fired in December for throwing a drink on a customer. Make sure to keep your calm when you start working."

I shrugged. "I'm sure they deserved it."

"Tell my manager that."

I giggled, and she smiled, though it didn't erase the sadness in her eyes. The elephant in the room cast a shadow that couldn't be ignored.

"So, uhm…what happened, if you don't mind me asking?" I said slowly, not wanting to upset her further.

"It's…complicated. Not a conversation for children, that's for sure," she replied, swallowing and looking away.

"Good thing I'm not a child."

She looked back at me. "You're twelve. Basically, an elementary school student."

"I'm in middle school, and you know it."

"I do," she conceded. "Eighth grade, right?"

I beamed at her. "You remembered."

"Of course, I did." She ruffled my hair, making me giggle. It was already messy, so I didn't care. "Not every day I meet a baby genius."

"I only skipped one year," I said, her praise making my blush deepen.

All I did around her was blush like an idiot, which didn't help her perception that I was a kid.

"Are you staying here?" I inquired after the conversation lulled, hoping she would say yes.

"Nah," she answered, much to my disappointment. "I just need Mrs. Milton to give me a ride to a motel."

Right on cue, Granny returned from the kitchen, rolling out a waiter's cart full of plates. She'd gotten it soon after Harvey was born, since we typically ate in front of the TV, and the cart made transporting food so much easier.

"Estelle, what did your mama tell you about giving those babies that phone?" Granny said as she handed out the plates, spaghetti and meatballs with garlic bread.

"Sorry," I said, quickly snatching my phone back. A glare from Granny hushed the babies when they began to whine.

Granny flicked on the TV, putting it on a channel that showed reruns of old sitcoms. Artificial laughter and corny jokes filled the room as we ate, some quips pulling a laugh out of me and Granny, though Denali remained painfully silent as she ate.

While everyone else ate freely, I made sure to count my bites, chewing as much as possible before I swallowed. When I realized I was eating too much, I began breaking up the food and shuffling it around, trying to make it look like I ate more than I did. Granny always tried to shove food down my throat, not caring how fat I already was.

A shove on my shoulder got my attention. I looked at the culprit—Denali— who was looking at me with concern.

"What's wrong, kid?" she asked, her eyes darting between me and my plate. "You aren't eating a lot."

"I'm just full," I lied, a part of me giddy that she cared, even if she'd never understand why I'd need to restrict what I ate.

I was sure she could eat anything and still have a perfect body.

She didn't seem like she believed me, but she just nodded and looked at Granny. "Hey…after we eat, can you take me to that motel a few blocks away?"

"Whatever you need, baby," Granny said without hesitation. "But why don't you spend the night? I'll take you in the morning, and you can tell me what happened then. Deal?"

Denali took a few seconds to contemplate the words, then nodded. "Deal."

Silence fell again, but Denali's agreement made my heart beat fast and presented an opportunity I couldn't pass up. With her under the same roof as me, I could finally show her I wasn't a little girl.

Chapter Two

Estelle

"Bathroom's yours," Denali announced as she walked into the room we were sharing, already wearing an AC/DC shirt and red plaid pajama pants, a towel wrapped around her head.

Granny's duplex had four bedrooms, with only the master bedroom being permanently occupied. Mama and Mr. Daddy took the biggest guest room, claiming the only other double bed. The rest had two single beds and enough room for travel cribs to be set up for Kayla and Harvey Jr. Harvey was with our older brothers, while Kayla slept with me. Typically, the other bed in my room was unoccupied, but for one night, Denali would be bunking with me.

I had to make it count.

"Thank you," I said, mentally sorting through my luggage, trying to remember where the cutest pajamas I'd brought were.

Thrifting in Chicago had become a tradition for me and Mama. Mr. Daddy would take Edward, Dennis, and Harvey Jr. to do boy things, while Granny, Mama, and I would go out to eat, get mani-pedis, and go to Granny's favorite thrift store. This time around, Mama had purchased me a pink pajama set with a button-down top and ruffled shorts. I loved them. They were pretty and flattering.

My mind made up, I grabbed the pajamas, my toiletries bag, and headed to the bathroom.

When I returned, my red waves were tamed into a tight braid, my lips shimmered with sparkly lip gloss, my skin was moisturized, and I smelled like a birthday cake. I looked myself over several times, nerves twisting in my gut as I pondered how Denali would react. All for nothing, because when I entered the room, she was already lying down. Frustration washed over me. She couldn't be sleeping, yet, not before I…well, I didn't know. Harvey had already blown my secret, and she barely reacted. I didn't know if that was a good sign or a bad sign. All I knew was that when she left tomorrow, I didn't know when I'd next see her.

"Denali," I whisper-yelled, not wanting to wake Kayla. "You awake?"

"Yeah," she said with a heavy sigh, sitting up and smiling at me. Her curls were in two braids, the style making her look more youthful than normal. "What's up, Essie?"

I scowled at her. "Don't call me that. It's a stupid nickname."

"I think it's adorable. My little sisters call me Denny."

"Denny is cool. It's what we call Dennis. Essie sounds like Nessie, which is a big, ugly monster that looks like a dinosaur."

"You never did like your name," she noted, patting the edge of the bed. "I still think it's pretty."

"It sounds pretty when you say it," I said shyly, looking at her through my lashes as I sat down. "You have a nice voice."

She smiled again, but it wasn't as bright as the previous one. "Thank you, *kid*."

Crap, I'd messed up. I had to dial it back a bit.

"You look younger with your hair braided," I said, deciding a subject change was due. "I forgot you aren't that much older than me."

She pursed her lips. "I disagree. Six years is a lot."

"Mr. Dad…I mean, Daddy is seven years older than my mom," I pointed out.

Denali might've thought that 'Mr. Daddy' was a cute nickname, but it was childish. To look mature, I'd need to modify what I called Harvey Sr.

"It's different. They're grown-grown."

"Grown-grown," I repeated, my brows furrowed. "What's the difference between being grown, and being grown-grown?"

"Technically, I'm grown, even though I just turned eighteen today. Grown-grown is, like, twenty-five and up."

My eyes widened. "Today is your birthday?"

"Yep." She huffed out a humorless laugh. "Not that it matters. Birthdays have never been a big deal in my house."

"Granny didn't tell me," I said with a pout, trying to dampen down my annoyance towards the old woman.

She was nearing seventy, so maybe she forgot.

"Granny doesn't know," Denali corrected. "Not many people do, because it isn't a special day."

"The day you were born is a special day," I insisted, then looked at the digital clock on the nightstand.

10:27 PM. Enough time to still celebrate Denali and show her how much she meant to me.

"C'mon," I said, getting off the bed and tugging at her hand. "I'll make you birthday pancakes."

"You've always been bossy, you know that?" she protested, though she allowed me to pull her out of the room and to the staircase. "Since the day you met me, you've been bossing me around."

"Do you want the pancakes or not?" I asked, looking back at her and noting how much taller she was than me.

Her growling stomach made me smile, though when mine responded with its own rumble, I frowned. How could I be hungry when I had so much spaghetti earlier?

Denali's giggling snapped me out of my contemplation. "Fine, brat. Cook for me."

"You are allowed to call me by my name, y'know," I said as we reached Granny's kitchen, releasing her hand. "I don't mind."

"Where's the fun in that?"

"I can give you a nickname like 'kid' or 'brat', to show you how it feels," I grumbled, going to get some pots and pans as Denali sat at the kitchen table.

"Oh, yeah?" she said with a cocked brow and teasing smile. "Go ahead." When I stammered, she laughed. "Don't say things you don't mean, Essie."

"Uhm, how about, *girl*?" I replied, struggling to come up with anything better.

A mistake, because she froze, her body tensing. Her smile remained, but it became tight, and her fists clenched. I'd messed up again, but this time, I didn't know how.

"I'm sorry," I added quickly, busying myself with getting the ingredients for the pancakes, since I couldn't seem to say anything right.

"It's okay," she said, though her tone told me it wasn't. "Just...don't call me that. Okay? Anything but that."

"Okay," I agreed, deciding not to probe further. "Uhm, Granny has blueberries and chocolate chips. Which do you want in your pancakes?"

"I dunno," she answered, relaxing a fraction. "I've only ever had pancakes plain. Mama doesn't like to cook anything too fancy."

I recoiled. "Those aren't fancy! They're baseline pancakes. Soufflé pancakes are fancy. Pancakes with berries and cream are fancy. Gingerbread pancakes are fancy. Crepes are fancy. Peanut butter chocolate-chip pancakes with cinnamon ice cream are—"

"Okay, I get the point," she said, the tension leaving her body completely. "I'm a peasant who hasn't experienced any culinary joy."

"Your words, not mine," I chirped, grinning when she laughed, proud of myself for undoing my previous damage. "Why don't I make you both, then you decide which you like better?"

"Only if you help me eat them."

"Only if you help me cook them."

"Deal," she agreed without hesitation, standing from the table and joining me by the counter.

Cooking with her was nice. It reminded me of how Mama and Daddy cooked, laughing amongst themselves, stealing kisses as they prepared the food. Unfortunately, the latter part wasn't in the equation. As she followed my instructions, she made sure to keep several inches between us.

"So," I began as I poured the blueberry batter into a pan. "Do you remember what Harvey said earlier?"

Bringing that up scared me, but nothing would ever change if I remained a coward and kept my feelings to myself.

"When he called you Essie?" she said, making me roll my eyes.

"No, when he said I liked you…because I do. A lot. And I really hate that you see me as a kid, because I'm not, and I really like you, so, yeah."

The silence that followed was deafening. My heart thudded in my ears, and immediately, I wished I could take everything I said back. Fear exists for a reason. It's your instincts' way of protecting you from danger, your brain sending out warning signals that something is a bad idea. Clearly, confessing to Denali was a bad idea.

"I'm flattered, Estelle," she began, her words not giving me a bit of comfort. "But not only do I see you as a little sister or cousin or, well, just a younger relative, you're a child. And I know you don't want to hear this, but I'm not a predator—"

"I didn't say you were!" I interjected, blinking back tears.

Why'd I have to open my big, stupid mouth?

"—And you'll thank me when you're older," she continued, grabbing my shoulder. "Now you might want me to feel the same way, but when you're my age, you'll understand why it'd be creepy if I liked you back."

"You aren't that much older than me," I protested, tears streaming down my face.

"Don't cry, Essie," she said, grabbing some paper towels and dabbing at my eyes. "I promise, you can do a lot better than me. You're smart, kid. You'll go big places and meet people who make me look like trash."

"Stop being so mean to yourself," I snapped, snatching the paper towels away from her. "And don't chastise me. You're pretty, and kind, and funny, and easy to be around, and made me realize I like girls. Why wouldn't I like you?"

"You flatter me," she said gently, patting my hair as she so often did. "But I'm still too old for you. So, let's just finish the pancakes and go back to normal."

"Will you feel different when I'm eighteen?" I whispered, finally wiping away the last of my tears.

"Probably not."

Her rejection of my future self made me want to sob again.

"What about when I'm twenty-five, and we're both grown-grown?"

The sadness that I was all too familiar with seeing on her face returned. "I'd be, what, thirty-one? I don't even know if I'd be around then."

"Don't say that!" I cried, the thought of a world without Denali bleak.

"It's true, Estelle. You have a bright future; I don't. And even if things somehow work out for me, that's a long time from now. One of us, or both of us, could be with other people, and you might not even like me then."

"But if I do, and if we're both available, just promise me that you'll at least take me on a date and give me a chance," I said in a rush, holding my breath as I waited for her to answer.

"We might not be in each other's lives—"

"Stop being so negative and just answer me," I ordered.

She was silent for a few moments before she huffed out a breath and nodded. "Fine. When you're twenty-five, if we're both available and in each other's lives, I'll take you on a date. And if it doesn't go well, you have to promise me that you'll accept that we aren't meant for each other."

"I promise," I said, wishing I had a time machine to jump to my twenty-fifth birthday.

The smoke alarm broke the stillness that followed. Gasping, I turned to the first batch of pancakes, now burned on one side and raw on the other. Just one more way that night sucked.

I quickly removed the pancakes from the flame and rushed to the sink, letting water wash over them in case they wanted to burst into flames. Without needing to be told, Denali grabbed a broom and rushed out. A few thwacks later, and the noise was silenced, the smell of burnt pancakes lingering in the air.

Sighing, I dumped the ruined batch out and began to wipe off the pan.

"Thank God it didn't wake anyone up," I said, my back to the entrance way.

"Wrong," Granny replied, making me swallow a groan, because why not? "Your mama and siblings might be asleep, but my room's on the first floor."

Denali stood behind Grandma, towering over the old woman, her hand rubbing her opposite arm awkwardly.

"Sorry for waking you up, Mrs. Milton," she said, her gaze glued to the floor. "I'll clean everything up."

She waved Denali off. "If you're hungry, cook, just watch the damn food, girls, and clean up your mess when you're done."

"Today's Denali's birthday," I revealed. "She's eighteen, and has only had plain pancakes, so my present to her was going to be blueberry and chocolate chip pancakes."

Granny's eyebrows rose. "You never had blueberry pancakes?"

Denali shook her head, still not meeting Granny's eyes. "No, ma'am."

"And you're eighteen today?"

"Yes, ma'am."

"An adult… that's why your Daddy kicked you out."

"Partially," Denali said, finally looking up, glancing at me. "But it's a long story."

Granny looked at me and nodded, seeming to understand what Denali wasn't saying. "Well," she began, looking back at Denali. "Since I'm up now, and your birthday ain't over yet, why don't I fix you those pancakes? Estelle can help, and you just sit at the table, baby."

"Really?" Denali asked, the surprise on her face hilarious and pitiful at the same time.

Didn't she know that people received special treatment on their birthdays?

"Yeah, baby," Granny said, shooing me out of the way to take over the task of cooking. "I think I have some candles in one of those drawers, too, so we can make yours all fancy. Estelle, go look for me."

I hurried to the drawers, rummaging through the knick-knacks and junk until I found a half-opened pack of birthday candles. When I turned back, my gaze met Denali's. Gratitude had replaced her sadness. She returned the smile I gave her, that one expression righting my world, and making all the suckage of the night worth it.

Chapter Three

DENALI

It'd been two weeks since Daddy kicked me out. The three grand I had was quickly dwindling. Lodging, food, and the laundromat near the motel were eating up the money. The night after he'd kicked me out, Mrs. Milton offered to let me stay with her until the end of summer, but I'd declined. Not only didn't I want to take advantage of her goodwill, but Estelle and her family weren't leaving for another three days, and I'd been around enough babies to know that small children and no sleep were a packaged deal. Instead, I'd accepted the three hundred dollars she'd given me as a birthday present and took her up on her offer to put her address down on job applications. Not that it made much of a difference, due to my past mistakes.

The asshole might've deserved to have a drink thrown in his face, but that outburst was making employment difficult. Likewise, fights that'd resulted in many suspensions made all the community college academic advisors politely reject me. I'd been a slightly above-average student, landing As and Bs in all my classes. But that was the only thing in my favor. I was a lackluster candidate at best, without the history of disciplinary action against me factored in. Volunteer hours, extracurricular activities, languages spoken, awards and achievements, scholarships, and so much more were all considered. I'd signed up to volunteer at an animal shelter, but the callback came when I wasn't home, and whatever my parents said had turned them off from even considering me.

So, surprise, surprise, today's meeting with an advisor ended with words I'd become all too familiar with, "Come back next year."

It was a nice way of saying I was unlikely to get in. I didn't know what they'd expected to change. I wouldn't be able to volunteer much or become fluent in another language, as I'd need to work and hunt down a place to live. No money could be spent on activities that'd give me an edge, as I'd have more important things to pay for. It was too late for me to receive any high-school achievement, and it'd be unlikely that I'd earn an award for anything. By next year, I'd be just as unappealing to advisors as I was this year. The only difference was that I'd be a little older.

"So, how'd it go?" Mrs. Milton asked as I slid into the passenger seat of her 1999 Toyota Camry, a hopeful smile on her face.

She'd supported my attempts at higher education, so she'd brought me to the three community college campuses on the Southside without charging me anything. I would've been fine using a bus or even walking, but she'd shut both ideas down, more protective of me than my parents had ever been. Mrs. Milton had an unrealistic amount of faith in me, believing that things would somehow work out. I desperately wished she were right, but it appeared that she'd be very, very wrong. With the way things were going, the best I could hope for was a dead-end job that paid me just enough to avoid being on the streets.

"Awful," I grumbled, looking out the window as she pulled off, trying to distract myself with the cityscape.

Chicago's Southside might've been a scary place to outsiders, but to me, it was home. Washington Park was a neighborhood that captured the city's essence. It was historic with a thriving art scene and a lot of green space, hence the name. But it was also a gangland paradise filled with crime.

"Aww, baby, what happened?"

"Same thing as last time," I said with a sigh, looking away from the window to stare at her. "And the time before that. I was rejected, and this time, I was told that a military career may suit me better than academic pursuits."

My goal had always been to attend a community college to get the required shit out of the way, then enroll in a four-year program. I wasn't entirely sure what degree I'd get, but I knew I wanted it to be something that involved helping children. Maybe I needed to consider a community college outside the Southside. Commute, however, would be a nightmare.

After a heartbeat of silence, Mrs. Milton said, "It's an option to consider, Denali, although you don't need to make a career out of it. Enlist in the army, do a stint or two, then return to civilian life and reap the benefits. It's what my son did, and how he put himself through college."

Her words made me deflate. I wasn't a very patriotic person and didn't support America's constant interference in foreign nations. The politicians who started the wars that risked my countrymen's lives had never done shit for me, so why would I put my life on the line for their endeavors? Put simply, I'd never envisioned a career in the military. Even so, Mrs. Milton's advice wasn't bad, and with the way things were looking, it could end up being my only option.

"I'll think on it," I finally said, albeit with a heavy, soul-weary sigh. "Just…let me apply to a couple of more places."

"It's just a suggestion, baby. As long as you don't end up slinging drugs, or selling or shaking ass, you have my support."

"Thank you," I whispered, her words meaning more to me than she'd ever know.

Over a week after Estelle and her family left, nothing had changed, except that I was a little more broke than before. I was still unemployed with zero prospects. So, after a trip to the library to research what benefits I'd be entitled to, I decided to take Mrs. Milton's advice and head to a recruiter to sign my life away. It was far from an ideal scenario, but once I was out of the military, higher education would be more achievable than it currently was for me.

The recruiting office was stationed between a pawn shop and a loan shop, two other places that preyed on the desperation of the Southside's underprivileged. An American flag flapped in the wind, the colors faded from too many years of sun and weather exposure. My heart was heavy as I opened the glass front door that contained the U.S Army star logo. I'd passed this place dozens of times and never imagined walking through the door. If I had my way, I would've never known what the interior looked like.

But life had different plans for me, so I took a deep breath and entered.

The air inside was cool, reeking of cleaner and coffee. It was too bright, the buzzing fluorescent lights painting the area in a harsh white light. The linoleum floors were scuffed, and the expected propaganda and motivational posters were on the walls, with a flatscreen in the small waiting area.

The bell above the door notified a recruiter of my arrival. His dark hair was short, no doubt meeting regulations. His blue eyes widened as they landed on me, before a smile spread across his face, one that looked too easy-going to be organic. No doubt, he'd practiced it hundreds of times to put poor, unsuspecting fools at ease.

"How's it going?" he said, circling around his desk and walking towards me.

He was tall, uncomfortably so. I was nearly six feet, and he still had several inches on me. The way he looked me over did nothing to put me at ease.

"If things were going good, I wouldn't be here," I said honestly, shoving one hand in the pocket of my hoodie, the other holding the folder Mrs. Milton helped me get together. Ignoring his surprise, I continued. "I graduated high school a few weeks ago. I know that the army can help me pay for college, so here I am."

He gave me another fucking once over. It took everything in me not to snap at him. Instead, I just tightened my lips into a frown.

"You sure the army's a place for a girl like you?" he finally said, making me recoil.

"What the fuck is that supposed to mean?" I snapped.

It was a mistake coming here. Everything I had tried to do for my future had been a failure. I'd throw in the towel at this point if it wouldn't give my parents the satisfaction of seeing me crash and burn. They didn't care what became of me and likely expected me to end up worse than them. I'd thrive just to spite them.

"You're a pretty girl. Surely—"

"I'm gay, so stop flirting with me, and just do your regular spiel," I ordered, glaring at him.

He held his hands up in a gesture of surrender, then motioned to his desk. "Follow me, ma'am."

The walk to his desk was short and tense. By the time I sat in the uncomfortable chair, my mood was no less foul, but he'd seemed to have switched to professional mode.

"So you graduated," he began, his smile still present, though it was tighter. "That's a big deal. Tell me more about yourself…what's your name?"

"Denali Bernard," I said, sliding him the folder filled with all relevant information. "Everything you need to know is in there. Height, weight, medical history, school transcripts, copy of my ID, all that shit. I have no criminal record, no medical conditions, no loan sharks circling."

He let out a low whistle as he flipped through it. "Prepared, I like that."

He looked through the folder for another minute or two before nodding and setting it aside. "Okay, well, I'm Sergeant Andrews. The folder will come in handy, so props for that. The army will help you pay for college without racking up debt, and you'll be entitled to low healthcare costs, vacation time, family benefits, and special home loans, amongst other things."

I nodded, relaxing in my seat. "Sounds good. So do I just sign some shit, or—"

He laughed. "As much as I appreciate an eager woman, you gotta slow your roll,

Denali. You ever took the ASVAB test?" At my blank look, he chuckled again. "I'll take that as a no. So, you've got to take that first. It'll show you what jobs you qualify for, and we'll match you based on your scores and interests. Then you'll head over to the MEPS, Military Entrance Processing Station," he clarified again at my furrowed brows, "where you'll have to pass a physical exam. You're a high school graduate, so you meet the academic requirements. If you meet the physical requirements, you'll work with someone to choose a job within the army, sign the contract, take the Oath of Enlistment, and start preparing for basic training."

"And how long is basic training?"

"Ten weeks, give or take. Most people pass, and once that's out of the way, you'll start training for your specific job."

The influx of information made my head spin. Clearly, my research wasn't as thorough as I thought it'd been. My rapidly decreasing funds flickered across my mind. The process wouldn't be as instantaneous as I thought. Hopefully, Mrs. Milton was still open to letting me stay with her until I'd be shipped away.

"When can I leave for basic training?"

"A few days to a few months, once all the other shit is out of the way."

"I'd want to leave as soon as possible," I said firmly.

If I were eligible, there'd be no reason for me to linger. I'd pack what was needed, say goodbye to Mrs. Milton, then leave.

"Well, then, if you're free this week, I'll schedule you for the ASVAB, and then we'll take it one step at a time. This is a big decision—"

"No need, I already decided that I'm joining," I interrupted. "And yeah, I'm free all week, and the week after that."

He studied me closely. Unlike before, there was no amorousness in his stare, just curiosity.

"Your parents okay with all this?" he finally asked.

"They don't care what I do, and frankly, I don't give a fuck if they aren't. They kicked me out, so they can't dictate my decisions."

My words had more venom than intended. Andrews' raised brows made my jaw clench. I looked away, embarrassed that I'd revealed so much.

"Bad blood there?"

"What do you think?" I grumbled.

"I've been there, you know," he said gently, making me look at him. "Got kicked out for being a troublemaker. Hated them for a while, but we're close now."

"Yeah, well, I think our situation is a little different."

I stomped down my annoyance, reminding myself that he meant no harm. Thankfully, he got back to the topic at hand.

"We'll get you scheduled for the ASVAB and then the medical exam. If everything checks out, we'll get you a ship date."

"Good."

His words were a relief. The aimlessness caused by failure after failure was starting to feel suffocating. The military might not have been my first choice, but at the end of the day, it was better than nothing.

Chapter Four

DENALI

Four months later…

Andrews made good on his promise and got the ball rolling the same week I visited him. Numbers had always been easy for me, so it didn't come as a shock when the ASVAB determined a fitting career would be a financial management technician. Being stuck behind a desk as a glorified accountant might've been awful to most, but it was better than being at risk of stepping on a landmine and getting blown to smithereens, and it would equip me with skills I could use when I exited the military. Of course, I still had to complete the physical—which I passed—and basic training.

Within a month, I was saying my goodbyes to Mrs. Milton and being shipped off to Fort Jackson, South Carolina. It was the largest of all basic training locations, and a significant portion of female recruits were sent there. The Red Phase was hell, but I'd adjusted to the flow of things by the time I entered the White Phase and breezed through the Blue Phase. The army might not have been my original plan, but I still gave it my all. By the time the ten weeks of boot camp were up, I'd passed with flying colors and could move on to AIT, which would take another ten weeks.

However, things had never gone smoothly for me, so why would my new career be any different? It only took one night and one fuckhead for it all to fall apart.

Sergeant Motherfucker—or Drill Sergeant Trevor E. Carson, as he was officially known—was quickly becoming the bane of my existence. Within the first week, I learned why he had a reputation among the women of Fort Jackson, because he flirted with them whenever he could get away with it, despite the ring on his finger. Most women dismissed them as jokes, and some seemed to relish the attention, but I was among the small portion who despised it.

And unfortunately, he seemed to have homed in on me.

When I joined the military, I expected a grueling routine, shitty food, and possibly being shipped to war. A married man's lust was not on my list of possibilities, but there I was. I should've been celebrating moving onto AIT, not trying to dodge a creep. The times he'd cornered me had left me sick, and his 'joking' remarks always made my skin crawl. A part of me longed to report him, but I'd learned not to rely on higher authorities to get shit done. The worst part was that his reputation as a flirt didn't hinder him in the slightest. He was seen as one of the chiller sergeants, which might've been why his words were dismissed as harmless, and his seemingly happy relationship with his wife was used as an excuse for why he couldn't be an actual creep, a sentiment I disagreed with wholeheartedly.

A ring didn't stop a motherfucker from being a motherfucker. Daddy and Mama got married shortly before my birth, and it didn't magically make them better people. Sergeant Motherfucker was in the same boat. Trevor Carson might've had a beautiful wife and a kid on the way, but he was still a creep begging to get a harassment suit against him. Whenever I was in his presence, I felt his eyes on me, his predatory, pervy gaze making my skin crawl. Since he found out that I was technically mixed, he'd become even more aggressive toward me.

In the 21st century, the concept of multiethnic individuals shouldn't be astonishing. Segregation ended decades ago, and even before the law allowed it, love and lust knew no color. Yet, for all the talk of society becoming 'colorblind,' color was very much seen. When someone who didn't properly fit into one color existed, people grew confused. Ironically, those who were 'colorblind' were the worst offenders, wanting to know every branch of my family tree, of just how someone so 'unique' came to be. Saying my mama baby trapped my father in high school wasn't satisfactory.

They were only satisfied when I divulged that both of my parents were biracial, with two Black grandparents and two unknowns. If my mama's claims were true, some Native American blood flowed through my veins.

Then again, she was a foster kid and a fucking deceiving bitch, so chances were she was lying her ass off about that.

I had no dilemma about my ethnic background, no crisis over where I fit in, no whining about never being enough, or anything of the sort. My DNA was the least of my issues, so it was never a focus for me. I was just me and didn't let the little boxes created by dead bigots define my identity. If someone didn't like it, they could go fuck themselves with a dirty dildo.

I did, however, very much so have a problem with the way dumbasses reacted to my heritage. My least favorite? The fetishizers. Whereas I wanted to slap the small-minded folk who were confused, I longed to bash the heads of those who sexualized me just for existing. Sometimes, I gave in to that desire, resulting in more than one fight. Unfortunately, it was impossible to attack my superior officer without severe consequences. Sergeant Motherfucker knew this and took full advantage of his immunity. His latest incident was cornering me yet again and grabbing a fistful of my hair to sniff. He'd laughed when I'd pushed him away, telling me to 'lighten up' as I stormed off.

That night, I stared in the bathroom mirror, wondering what the fuck he saw that made him so obsessed. I was pretty, yes, but other recruits were just as, if not more, attractive, so why me? Why couldn't I get a break for once in my life? Sergeant Motherfucker's attention was more exhausting than the grueling training. It was a constant battle, a war waged that I didn't want to be a part of.

Fuck him, and everyone who protected his ass. He must've had friends in high places, as I saw no other reason for him to be so bold.

What was it about me that made shitty people target me?

I should've continued lying in bed and pondering that question and ignored the knock on my door. I'd intended to, but the pounding grew more insistent, making it clear that I wouldn't know peace until I opened the door. With an annoyed sigh, I yanked it open, regret slamming into me when I was greeted by the sight of Sergeant Motherfucker.

He shoved past me as if I invited him in, then held up a small gift bag. "I got something for you, 'Nali."

"Denali, and you shouldn't have, Sergeant Carson," I said, wanting to scream.

"I told you to call me Trevor, remember?" he replied with grating tsks, strolling to my desk and setting the bag down. "And I wanted to. Moving onto AIT is a big deal."

"Thank you, but you shouldn't be in here—"

He chuckled, then returned to where I was still standing, closing the door that I continued to hold open, dashing my hope that he'd get a clue and leave my room. He tried to ruffle my hair, but I jumped back, scowling at him.

"Lighten up, sweetheart," he chided, the unwanted pet name making my scowl deepen. "You're too young to be such a hard ass."

"I'm tired, Trevor, so—"

"C'mon. You can stay up a little longer, for me." He nodded to the desk, his green eyes holding a gleam I didn't like. "Open it."

"I just said I was tired," I snapped, crossing my arms over my chest as I remained rooted in place. "In case you didn't catch my hint, I want you to leave so I can sleep."

My mounting anger didn't faze him. He just cocked a brow, an infuriating smirk on his face. "And I want you to see what I got for you. I'll leave after, promise."

His constant assholery was exhausting, adding to my fatigue. I wasn't lying about being tired, though it wasn't only a physical need to sleep. Always being on edge was mentally straining, though relaxing for long wasn't possible when someone always wanted to try me. Sergeant Motherfucker was the latest reason I was constantly tense, and unlike most assholes who'd stressed me out in the past, I couldn't deal with him with my fists. I'd had more than one fantasy about pounding his stupid face into the floor, but alas, acting on them would be ill-advised. I couldn't wait to finish AIT and be stationed somewhere far, far away from him.

"It'll only take a second," he coaxed when I didn't move.

"This is unprofessional—"

"Nothing is wrong with a man getting his friend a gift," he said, interrupting me for the umpteenth time.

"Except, we aren't friends," I replied flatly. "You're my *married* drill sergeant."

He shrugged, returning to my desk and lifting the bag. "I could be both. And don't worry about Shelia. She and I both like to have fun, so we have an…understanding." As I recoiled, he shook the bag, rattling the contents. "Now, enough stalling, 'Nali. The sooner you comply, the sooner you can get back to bed."

It was clear the motherfucker wouldn't leave until I did what he wanted. I didn't trust him one bit, so I wanted him out of my sleeping quarters as soon as possible. His presence had me uneasy. The sooner he left, the better, so I swallowed my pride and crept to him, snatching the bag away and walking to my bed. I set it on the edge, tensing as I felt him looming over me.

"Go ahead," he urged. "Open it up."

"I'll open it when you take some steps back."

"Feisty," he said with another stupid chuckle, though he did oblige with my request. "I like it."

I ignored the remark, dumping whatever he got me onto the bed. A bottle of scotch, a generic congratulations card, and a jewelry box tumbled out. I blinked, then picked up the alcohol to examine the bottle. It was a 750ml bottle of *Johnnie Walker Black Label,* aged twelve years. Pursing my lips, I looked back at Sergeant Motherfucker's grinning face.

"I'm eighteen. I can't drink this," I said flatly, holding out the bottle for him to take.

He waved me off. "Everyone has their first drink before twenty-one, and no one has to know."

"If they find this in my room during an inspection, I'm fucked."

"Hide it in the vent. No one checks there, trust me. That's what I did when I was your age."

"Sergeant—"

"Trevor," he corrected.

"Trevor," I bit out, walking to him and shoving the bottle against his chest. "Let me be blunt. I don't want it, because I don't like scotch."

Or any hard liquor, for that matter. I understood the appeal of getting fucked up, but I also had functioning taste buds that didn't enjoy drinkable rubbing alcohol going down my gullet.

He grinned victoriously. "So, you have drank before."

"I only like beer and wine, so—"

"So, you should expand your tastes, 'Nali." He took the bottle, then set it on my desk. "Open the box, then you can get your beauty rest. Maybe it'll make you less cranky."

Swallowing back a retort, I picked up the jewelry box and opened it. In it was a simple pearl choker and matching earrings.

"They're real," he said proudly. "Noticed you didn't have any jewelry, so I thought I would remedy that."

"Thank you, but I can't accept this."

He cocked a brow. "Why not?"

"Because how the hell would it look for me to wear pearls given to me by my married drill sergeant?"

Most people would assume I was his side bitch, which I couldn't blame them for, as I'd think the same thing.

"Like you have a very kind drill sergeant," he said, frowning when I tossed the jewelry back into the bag. "Those aren't against regulation, you know."

"I'm aware, but I'm not keeping it. Give it to your wife or something."

"She has enough shit, Denali, and no one would know that I gifted them to you unless *you* said something."

I looked away, jaw clenched. He was right, but he should've been able to understand that I didn't *want* to accept them. I didn't want anything from him, unless it was peace and silence. That would be the best gift he'd give me, leaving me the fuck alone.

"I insist you accept it," he continued, making me look back at him.

"I opened your gifts like you wanted. You didn't say I had to keep them. Now get out."

Unsurprisingly, he didn't obey. Instead, he took the Johnnie Walker and plopped down on my bed uninvited. "Have a drink with me, then I'll leave."

He was frustrating me to no end, wearing my thin patience. I'd grown to 5'10, making him an inch shorter than me. But he was still a muscular male soldier. Dragging him out wasn't a viable option.

"That wasn't the original deal," I said through gritted teeth.

"Shit changes, 'Nali. And a part of being a good soldier is adapting to that change."

"I'm not drinking with you. Get out."

His careless demeanor began to slip, annoyance flashing across his face. "Stop being such a bitch—"

"Only when you stop being such a motherfucker," I yelled, at my wits end. "I've made it very clear that I'm not interested. You want a side bitch, cool, but I won't occupy that role. Get that through your stupid fucking skull and leave me alone."

Even with anger darkening his freckled face, the words were cathartic to say. Being civil wasn't working, so perhaps harsh words were what he needed to get my disinterest through his head.

Letting the bottle fall to my bed, he stood, running a hand through his brunette strands. "Is it so bad that I want you, Denali? You're gorgeous, and—"

"And gay, so you're wasting your fucking breath."

Surprise flickered across his face, replacing his anger. "Oh."

"Yep."

For a brief, blissful moment, I thought I'd finally gotten through to him. That was, until the cocky grin I'd gotten dreadfully used to spread across his face.

"So that's your issue. You haven't been with the right man yet. Don't worry, I'll fix you."

Before I could formulate a reply to his fucked-up words, he was grabbing me with too much strength and shoving me onto my bed. My heart dropped as he draped his body over mine. When he tried to kiss me, I turned my head, his lips meeting my cheek instead.

"Stop being difficult," he purred, gripping my chin.

When he tried to kiss me again, I spat in his face. He recoiled, and I used the opportunity to shove him away, panting as my head pounded. "Get out, or I'll report you—"

A bark of laughter cut me off. "Go ahead and see how much good that does. My brother has my back."

Ah, so that was his problem. Nepotism struck again and was making my life hell once more. I thought of Jonathan George and how he continuously got away with bullshit because he was the son of a school board member.

A cry left me as he pulled me to the edge of the bed. Panic set in as he started to tug at my pajama bottoms, my flailing not deterring him. He dodged my attempts to strike him. When he tried to grab my wrists, I finally managed to kick him, though it didn't make him stop.

"Get the fuck off me!" I screeched as my cunt became exposed.

I never wore panties to bed, a habit I was now regretting.

He forgot about restraining my wrists to drag a finger along my slit. Nausea assaulted me as he shoved two fingers inside me, the rough intrusion making me scream. It didn't deter him, nor did my attempts to punch the fuck out of him. He just kept thrusting and curling his fingers, my screaming protests and struggles doing little. My hips twitched, making bile rise in the back of my throat.

"That's it," he whispered, his thumb finding my clit, trying to force my body to betray me. "Just let it happen."

I took some deep breaths, forcing myself to calm down so I could think. The addition of a third finger made that impossible and made me scream again. The glint of the liquor bottle caught my eye. Without thinking, I grabbed the Johnnie Walker and slammed it against his skull.

"Fuck," he screamed as he dropped to the ground, his hand flying to his bleeding head. "You fucking—"

His words were cut off when I struck him again. Straddling him, I brought the bottle down again, wanting—*no, needing*—to make him pay for what he'd done.

And again.

And again.

And again…

My fear and rage put me in a violent frenzy. Weeks of being harassed just to be nearly assaulted made me ignore his pained yelps and pathetic attempts to apologize. Only when the bottle broke and the pungent scent of scotch filled my nose did some semblance of sanity return to me, making me aware of two things.

One, Trevor E. Carson's head had been reduced to a bloody, mushy mess, bits of glass sticking out of his skin, his body twitching and breathing nonexistent.

Two, my door was opened again, and a horrified soldier stood frozen, taking in the scene with wide eyes. Taylor, if I remembered correctly.

"What the fuck?" Taylor breathed, eyes darting between me and the body.

Before I could open my mouth to explain, Taylor was dashing away. I heard the thudding footsteps and knew that this news would spread like fire, ending my military career before it had properly begun.

Fuck, ending my future, as I didn't have the money to afford a good lawyer. I was absolutely, positively, fucked, and that realization made the tears I'd been holding back finally fall.

Chapter Five

DENALI

Ten years later…

Even after all these years, I maintained that Sergeant Motherfucker deserved my reaction, despite the court system disagreeing. It was argued that, though it was self-defense, I'd used excessive force, resulting in my being sentenced to too many goddamn years of military prison. A decade in the Naval Consolidated Brig in Miramar, California, later, and I still felt that I didn't deserve my punishment. Trevor had been a predator, plain and simple. If he'd walked out of that room alive, he would've gone on to victimize more women once I left Fort Jackson. But the argument was moot now, and finally, I'd served my time and had been released.

The elation I'd seen many others experience hadn't yet settled in. I wasn't sure that it would. Prison wasn't ideal, but it wasn't as nightmarish as I first imagined it would be. Military prison was more structured than civilian institutions and enforced the same standards present in the armed forces. The strict schedule meant there was little time for bullshit, the food was edible, the place was hygienic, rehabilitation was an actual focus, and training was offered for different trades. I didn't want to spend the rest of my life locked behind bars, but nothing awaited me in the civilian world. I had no family who would celebrate my return and no friends who might've missed me. I'd been dishonorably discharged, so I wouldn't be entitled to benefits, and work would be damn near impossible to find.

That future looked bleak, and if I didn't hate the thought of giving up so much, I would've thrown in the towel and offed myself years ago. But I hadn't, and I wouldn't. Doing so would give everyone who'd wanted me to fail a win, and I wouldn't let that happen. I'd keep on pushing and piece my life back together as best as I could.

Upon release at 6:15 AM, I'd been given a bus ticket to downtown San Diego. Two hours later, I arrived in the city, numerous stops making a thirty-minute drive take too damn long. The day was spent asking every business I could find if they were hiring. Some gave me paper applications, others told me to apply online, and most just rejected me. All too soon, the sun was setting, and with nothing else to do, I located a cheap bar to fill out the few applications I had. All asked for things I didn't have. A phone number, a home address, and an email address. Some wanted secondaries for everything, and I flinched each time I saw the question 'Have you been convicted of a felony?' By the time I reached my sixth application, I was frustrated and disheartened, and decided just to drink.

Some guy had bought me a whisky sour in hopes of scoring with me, only to be turned away, though I kept the drink to drown my sorrows. Flirting with the bartender had earned me a free beer. She was pretty, and I was heavily debating going home with her for the night to have a place to crash. I had no money, so if I didn't fuck someone for shelter, I'd be on the streets. Doing so would make me a hop, skip, and a jump away from being a prostitute in the strictest sense, but what other choice did I have?

Finishing off my beer, I stood from the secluded table I'd claimed and sauntered to the bar. My ultimate goal was to return to Chicago, maybe to locate my parents or to reconnect with Mrs. Milton. The loneliness facing me was just as bad as the hopelessness I felt.

I pushed my way to the bar counter and held up my empty beer bottle, praying she'd give me a free refill. I had no money on me, so if   I needed to pay for this round, I was fucked. When the bartender came to service me, I offered her my prettiest smile.

"How much for another beer?" I asked, having the sense not to assume she'd give me a free one.

She waved me off, taking the empty bottle and tossing it into a trash can. "It's on the house."

When I received another ice-cold beer, I took a big swig, relishing the buzz that was starting to settle in. "Thank you…?"

I looked at her expectantly. She got my clue immediately. "Alina. And you are…?"

"Denali. What time do you get off?"

No point in beating around the bush, and so far, everything was going smoothly.

Her smile disappeared. "Oh, uhm, I'm engaged." She held up her left finger, showing off the glittering band. "You just looked like you could use a pick-me-up, so I thought I'd waive the fee for you tonight."

I stood corrected. Alina taking me home with her would've been too goddamn lucky.

"I appreciate it," I said, my smile subdued as she turned away.

Once she was gone, I let it drop and gulped down the rest of the beer as I made my way back to my table. I stopped in my tracks when somebody slapped my ass. On a good day, that would've pissed me off. Today, I whirled around, glaring at the fucker who thought that was okay, and slammed my beer bottle against his temple.

Not only did it wipe his leer away, but it shattered on impact, and I considered stabbing him with the broken bottle. Ironic, because my last kill was with a bottle of alcohol, as well. If today were a snapshot of what civilian life would be like, I'd rather return to prison.

Instead, I held back, and when he dropped, I just kicked his balls a few times. His buddy was short and pudgy, so when he came at me, it was easy to break his nose and slam him to the ground next to his friend. The violence was cathartic for me, and it was difficult to stop delivering kicks.

That was, until I heard Alina shout, "Get the fuck out or I'm calling the cops!"

Her words cleared my haze. With a frustrated growl, I gathered my useless applications and didn't resist when the bouncer grabbed my arm and dragged me out of the bar. Attacking him would be foolish, and I knew my limits.

"I suggest you don't come back, lady," he said as he tossed me outside, making me scowl. "We don't allow that sorta shit here."

Could've fooled me, considering the looks of the place.

"He was the one who fucking started it," I grumbled, turning on my heel and walking away before he could say anything else.

I walked aimlessly as I pondered where I could go. Maybe another bar to try my luck again.

"Wait up, goddamnit," I heard a woman call, making me halt. Turning around, I saw a woman who appeared to be in her 30s, red waves fluttering in the night wind. "You got some long ass legs, girlie."

I was silent as I examined her features further. Mama had loved Grey's Anatomy, and the woman before me reminded me of the redheaded doctor. Addison…something. There were some differences—her hair was curlier, her eyes more striking, and her statue stouter, but otherwise, the women could be twins. As I glanced at the redhead again, Estelle flickered into my mind, and I wondered how the little girl was. I suppose she'd no longer be a child, but I couldn't help but remember her as a chubby-cheeked brat.

"You ran to me to say that shit?" I finally said, settling on the sidewalk curb.

Uninvited, she sat next to me. "Nah. Came to give you props for how you handled those two assholes. Shame you got kicked out. They should've given you a job application."

I held up the applications. "That would've been real fucking nice."

She snatched them from me, ignoring my scowl. No sensitive information was on them, so I didn't grab them back and ask her if she was out of her goddamn mind. She let out a low whistle as she thumbed through them. Handing them back to me, she tsked.

"You're a felon. Shouldn't have judged a book by its cover."

I cocked a brow. "Meaning?"

"Meaning that I didn't think a pretty bitch like you had been to prison." Her disrespect made my scowl deepen. It didn't seem to faze her. Instead, she stuck out her hand. "Karma."

The word made me notice a Southern accent, one that hadn't been detectable before.

"What?"

"My name, girlie. It's Karma."

I didn't question why her parents would name her that shit. Instead, I just shook her hand. "Den—"

"Denali Bernard, I know. Job applications, remember?"

"Right."

Relinquishing my hand, she leaned back. "When did you get out of the slammer?"

"Today."

She cackled. "And already starting shit, huh? Bold. I like it."

"I didn't start anything. He slapped my ass."

"Po-tay-to, po-tah-to," she said as she waved me off. "Lucky the cops weren't called."

"Didn't care if they were," I replied, leaning forward, placing my elbows on my knees. "Shit doesn't look too good for me."

"I don't like mopey bitches, girlie."

"Good thing I don't care what you like," I retorted, earning more laughter.

Despite myself, I found myself liking the sound of her laugh and enjoying her company. Perhaps loneliness was setting in earlier than I'd anticipated.

Leaning back, she examined my face, her eyes dropping to my lips. "Meant what I said before. You're real pretty. Ever been with a woman before?"

"I'm gay."

She shrugged. "Doesn't mean shit. You could be a virgin."

"I'm not."

I'd lost my virginity to another woman before I'd been thrown in prison. That hookup had led to my father kicking me out, but it meant I had some experience under my belt when I'd been sentenced. Sex wasn't allowed in the Brig, but most turned a blind eye to consensual relationships that had limited PDA. Even with the risk of punishment, natural urges meant sexual activity wasn't unheard of. Some ladies had fucked around with male guards, while others had the sense to limit their interactions with other prisoners, myself included. My sexual encounters behind bars had been few and far between, but ten years was a long time for no relief.

"That's a relief." Standing, she held out her hand to me, the streetlights revealing a wedding band. "Come back to my motel room, and we can party."

"You're married," I noted, even as I took her hand.

She was offering me somewhere to go for the night, so how she fucked over her spouse wasn't my business.

"Greg and I have a deal. We don't talk about what happens on runs."

Just as I was about to ask what the hell she meant, she walked ahead of me, still grasping my hand. My eyebrows rose when I took in the back of the leather vest. A woman in skull make-up wore a crown, with yellow roses and two actual skulls surrounding her. Above the design were the words 'Royal Harlots', to the side were the words 'MC', and at the bottom was 'Memphis, TN'.

I knew I'd detected a Southern accent.

"You're a biker," I observed as she led me to her motorcycle. A Harley, if I wasn't mistaken.

"Correct," she said, picking up her helmet.

"And from Memphis."

Same as Estelle. I wondered if her mother and Mrs. Milton's son were still together. I hoped they were. Mrs. Milton had been so happy with her expanded family.

"Born and raised," she confirmed as she put her helmet on. "Where you from, girlie?"

"Southside Chicago."

She snickered. "No wonder you're a tough bitch. Don't have a spare helmet, so hang on tight."

She revved the engine, the roaring vibration of the bike electrifying me in a way I hadn't expected. As she sped away, I wrapped my arms around her waist. I let my job applications go, allowing the useless papers to flutter away in the wind. Though she was shorter by a few inches, I managed to rest my head on her back. The chilled air of the night whipped against my exposed skin, the scenery of Downtown San Diego blurring as we sped through the city. It was invigorating, and I wondered how hard it would be to learn to ride a motorcycle.

By the time we arrived at her hotel, my attraction to Karma had strengthened. Inside the room was dim, lit only by a lamp on the dresser, the light of the television, and the glow of the city outside. I watched as she removed her vest and carefully draped it over a lounge chair, before going to a duffel bag and pulling out a small baggie containing white pills.

"Ever done E before?" she asked, setting the pills on the dresser as she went to the minifridge, getting out two beers.

"No."

"Do you want to?"

I shrugged. Quite frankly, I didn't give a damn at the moment, nor did I feel like being sober and hyperaware of my situation.

"Yeah," I said, accepting the beer she handed to me.

Mixing drugs and alcohol with a woman I just met wasn't the smartest idea, but no one would ever describe me as a genius.

"Then let's have some fun, girlie."

I popped the top off my beer and took a long swig, doing my best to ignore the nagging voice in the back of my head. It was screaming at me, telling me not to be a dumb bitch and leave. I tried to drown it out with more beer. Karma's eyes glimmered with mischief as she drank deeply from her bottle, her bright green gaze holding mine. When half of her bottle was gone, she set her beer down and picked up the baggie. Retrieving a pill, she swallowed one and finished off her beer, then walked to me with another.

"Open your mouth," she ordered.

I obeyed, flinching ever so slightly as she set the pill on my tongue. I washed it down with my beer, swallowing the drug easier than expected. Within minutes, the anxiety coiled deep in my gut started to disappear. The late-night talk show on TV became a buzzing noise as I focused on Karma. The way she moved, the planes of her face, the curve of her lips as she smiled. She leaned against the dresser, watching me with just as much intensity.

"You feeling it?" she asked as I tossed my empty beer bottle in the trash can.

"I am," I confirmed, my body feeling warmer.

I took a step toward her, feeling as if I was floating. She picked up her phone, music blaring from it seconds later. I didn't know what was playing, but the beats pulsed through me, and I couldn't help but move along to the song.

"Have a special playlist just for E," Karma said, stepping to me and wrapping her arms around my waist. "Music always hits better when you're on it."

We danced together for one song, the subpar surroundings of the motel room fading away as the music and her closeness filled my senses. She smelled like smoke and lavender, a combination I found myself inhaling deeply as our bodies moved together.

When the song ended, she began undressing us both. Goosebumps formed as the cool air from the air conditioner hit my skin, my shirt joining the growing pile on the floor. Her hands moved swiftly as she pulled her shirt over her head, revealing a black lace bra that was surprisingly delicate. They pushed up her tits nicely and made my mouth water. I reached for the button of her jeans, and she laughed as my fingers fumbled with them. The sound was low and melodic, vibrating through me. When I finished the task, her lips met mine, and the taste of beer still lingered. She gripped my hips and pulled me closer, her touch igniting my nerves.

When we pulled away, she guided me back to the queen-sized mattress, pushing me down when my legs hit the edge of the bed. I watched through hooded eyes as she stood over me, taking in my almost nude body. When she was done looking, she draped her body over mine, taking my mouth once again. The kiss wasn't soft, but I didn't care. My hands tangled in her hair, pulling her closer, the synthetic bliss of the drug amplifying every touch. Each scrape of her teeth on my lip, the way our tongues slid together, how her thick thighs caged me in, all of it heightened the euphoria I felt at that moment.

She broke the kiss to trail a path of wet kisses down my body. I parted my thighs, giving her access to my core when she hooked her fingers in the waistband of my underwear and drew them down my legs. I was bare and spread open for her, my pussy already wet and needy.

"Fuck," she moaned, burying her head in my mound and licking along my slit.

My entire body jolted, a cry leaving me when she wrapped her lips around my clit. The world narrowed to her mouth on my bud, and the pleasure it was bringing me. She sucked harder, laving her tongue over the bundle of nerves, holding down my hips when they began to buck. My breathing became ragged, punctuated by moans.

I gripped her hair, holding her in place as I did my best to grind against her mouth. When she slipped two fingers inside me and curled them, stars exploded in my vision, my orgasm slamming into me. Senseless babbling escaped as my body shook, my thighs trembling around her head as she continued lapping at me. I released her hair, but she didn't stop eating me out. Her moans were muffled by my cunt as she continued her relentless oral attack, leaving me weak and panting.

"You taste delicious, girlie," she said in between licks along my slit and kisses to my clit. "Never tire of the taste of pussy. The one thing Greg can't give me…"

I barely registered her words as I drifted deeper into the drug's embrace, a dizzying sensation of weightlessness. She stopped talking and focused on tasting me. When I came a second time, she lifted her head, her pale skin flushed, and her mouth glistening with my juices.

"Your turn," Karma said, shimmying out of her underwear and tossing them aside.

She crawled over my body, not stopping until she was positioned over my face, her knees digging into the mattress on either side of my head. Heat radiated from her core, her arousal dripping as she gripped the headboard and lowered onto my mouth. I didn't have to be told twice, plunging my tongue inside her. Her fingers wove through my curls, holding my head against her slick heat as she rode my mouth.

I gripped her thighs, my fingers digging into her flesh. She slapped my hand away.

"No touching," she ordered. "Just take it."

I could only moan against her as I obeyed, grasping the sheets as I sucked her clit into my mouth. The sounds echoing through the room were obscene, the sounds of her wetness mingling with my muffled whimpers and her breathy moans. Karma's pace quickened as she chased her pleasure, my tongue working tirelessly to help her reach her peak, swirling around her entrance before finding her clit. Her thighs began quivering around my ears, and I knew she was close.

"Fuck, just like that," she hissed, her grip in my hair tightening, bordering on painful. "Don't you dare stop."

Her entire body seized as she found release, her slick juices flooding my mouth.

I gulped down as much as I could, gently lapping at her wet folds until her tremors subsided. When she lifted herself off, a string of her juices connected us before snapping.

Rolling next to me, she laughed. "Bet you were popular in prison, huh?"

"I rarely fucked anyone," I said honestly, inspiring more laughter.

I didn't see the humor, but I laughed along with her, the ecstasy keeping my spirits high.

Leaning down, she cupped my chin, inspecting the mess she made of my face. Nodding in satisfaction, she leaned in and captured my mouth for another brief kiss. When she pulled away, she reached into the nightstand, pulling out a pre-rolled blunt and a lighter. Sparking it up, she took a hit, then handed it to me.

"Makes the crash easier," she explained as I inhaled the bud, the weed relaxing me further. "Still feel like shit the next day, but it's way fucking worse without it."

I handed it back to her, trying and failing to absorb the information. My head felt fuzzy in the best way possible, and the colors around me seemed more vibrant.

She snapped her fingers in front of my face. "Didn't take you for a lightweight, Denali."

"Never done this before," I said, still sounding normal to my ears. "Normally just stuck to alcohol."

Not to mention, for the last decade, I'd been fully sober, just to have an influx of shit enter my system upon release day.

Sighing, she handed me the blunt and stood from the bed and walked to her mini fridge, taking out a bottle of water. Somehow, I managed to catch it when she tossed it to me. When my stomach loudly growled, she rolled her eyes.

"Drink that while I order pizza," she ordered.

My body was sluggish, but I sat up and obeyed, feeling unusually docile. However, it felt nice to shut my mind off and let somebody else take the reins.

When she was done ordering the food, Karma returned to the bed. "When I first did E, I fell in love, just to have my heart broken the next day. The worst hangover of my life. Couldn't leave the bed for two days."

I scowled at her. "Now, you tell me this."

She snatched the blunt from the bed, where I hadn't even realized it had fallen, and took a hit. Blowing out the smoke, she finally shrugged. "Told you, bud helps. You can crash here tomorrow, though. Not leaving for another three days."

"How much would I have to fuck you to stay here for those three days?" I asked without thinking, inspiring another round of laughter.

It seemed Karma took me for a comedian because everything I said amused her.

"You make me sound like an old pervert, girlie."

"You can't be that much older than me."

She snorted as she handed me the blunt. "You're, what, 22 or 23?"

Her estimation made me grin. "As of May, I'm 28 years old."

"Shit, you look better than I did at 28. I'm 36, for reference, girlie. Eight years your senior."

"Stop avoiding my question and answer me."

"Eat me out like that again, and I might have to take you back to Memphis with me."

Maybe it was the high I was riding, but I wasn't opposed to the idea. In fact, it was a welcome prospect. There was nothing for me in San Diego, and being Karma's personal eater could be a temporary solution until I figured out my next move.

"I'm not against it," I said honestly. She eyed me, and I shrugged, continuing. "Nothing for me here. Nothing for me back in Chicago, and even if there was, I have no way of getting back there. I'm fucking broke. Eating pussy for a place to stay isn't the worst deal."

She considered my words, then shook my head. "Nah. Greg would kill us both if I moved a sidepiece he couldn't fuck into our place."

I deflated, but she prattled on.

"But...I've been to prison before, when I was in my early twenties. Five years for drug charges. Shit was rough, and I had people waiting for me. You sound like you don't have anyone."

"Keen observation."

She ignored me as she kept talking. "I have a big heart, you know, girlie. Plucked a lot of my chapter's girls from the streets and whipped them into damn fine Harlots."

"So this is your M.O.?" I asked. "Find a desperate bitch, fuck her, and indoctrinate her into your club?"

"You make me sound like a cult leader, when, for the record, this'll only be the third time a one-night stand joined my club. The first got knocked up by a Bastard and patched out two years down the line, the second got killed by a Bloody Femme, so hopefully, girlie, you're the lucky third that sticks around for a long time."

I didn't know if she was joking or not, so I said nothing.

"Have you ever considered being a biker?" she asked after a heartbeat of silence.

"As of tonight, I've considered learning to ride a motorcycle."

"Good enough. Be my pussy eater until I go back to Memphis, ride back with me, and prospect into my club. But no hanky panky when we get back to Tennessee. Won't fuck with my marriage like that."

"Where will I stay when I get there?"

"We have housing on premises. An entire dormitory."

My eyebrows rose. "How fucking big is your clubhouse?"

"Me and my bestie bought an abandoned factory to start our own MC, before Duchess patched us over and made us Harlots. Used the loan she gave us to renovate it and the smaller buildings and turned them into the United Nations."

I didn't know who the fuck Duchess was, but she sounded important. More pressingly, I had no idea what the goddamn United Nations had to do with a motorcycle club.

"The...fucking what?" I stammered, wondering if I was higher than I thought.

Surprise, surprise, my confusion made Karma laugh. "Love telling newbies that shit. The name of our clubhouse is the U.N. Diverse membership. Comes with the territory of living in a diverse city. But enough explanation. You'll learn this shit soon enough. You down, or nah?"

"I am," I said, chasing my surprise away with another hit to the blunt. "Real fucking down."

"Great." She held out her hand. "Nothing is official yet, but welcome aboard, girlie." Before I could shake her hand, she pulled it away. "Just so you know,

Denali, you're gonna play by my rules. Fuck over me, and I'll fucking gut you."

"Your name's fitting."

"That's why I'm called Karma."

"It isn't your real name?"

"Nope, and don't ask what my real name is, because it isn't your business," she said, holding out her hand again.

This time, she didn't pull away. With a handshake, I sealed my fate, a pesky spark of hope blossoming within me.

Chapter Six

Estelle

Four years later...

Girls' night was a sacred event. Following our graduation from Rhodes College, Tess, Lauren, Danielle, and I spread out across the greater Memphis area, but we vowed to maintain our closeness, which meant setting aside a night just for us. Once a month, I ventured from the relative safety of Bartlett and headed into the heart of Memphis to meet with my best friends. Beale Street might've come with dangers, but a great time was guaranteed. It was one of the most renowned entertainment districts in America for a reason. After weeks of being consumed by my upcoming nuptials to Aydin, my fiancé, unwinding with my girls was much needed.

"Stay home with me tonight," Aydin said, wrapping his arms around my waist as I put my earrings on. "You spend enough time with your *friends*."

I decided not to nitpick on the emphasis he put on the word. Aydin could be clingy, and I'd learned long ago to choose my battles when it came to him. We'd been arguing enough, and I wouldn't call him out on his behavior and spark another disagreement. It'd put a damper on girls' night, and I knew he was only acting like this because he was guilty. He always wanted me close after an argument.

"I see them once a month," I reminded him, shrugging him off to get my perfume.

"You text them all the time," he protested, trailing behind me as I moved around the room, gathering my things. "Missing one night won't hurt."

"You know I can't bail on girls' night without a good reason."

"Keeping your man happy is a good reason."

"And missing my friends is a fantastic reason for me to go out tonight."

My words came out snappier than intended, but I'd been so frustrated with him lately. Our engagement was dragging on, with no wedding date set, no location agreed upon, and zero concessions on his end. That was the cause of today's argument, as simply asking what date he had in mind set him off.

His parents were from Ankara, Turkey, immigrated to New York City in the 1990s, and moved to Memphis for…some fucking reason a few years after he was born. Despite being born in America, he was a proud Turkish man and wanted our wedding not only to have several Turkish customs but to take place in Ankara. I wanted to honeymoon in Turkey and get married at Memphis Botanic Gardens. It was my dream venue, though I wasn't opposed to a second ceremony in Ankara. Aydin was, however, and didn't care that most of my family couldn't attend a wedding in Turkey.

All the drama had made the excitement over our engagement fizzle out. Relationships were about compromise, yet he refused to budge on anything, leading to more than one argument. I refused to have zero say on my big day and wished he would stop making things so difficult. I naively thought the wedding planning process would be a smooth one, and the fact that he was making it anything but was causing boatloads of tension in what used to be a happy home.

As a teenager, Mama told me that abusers don't show their true colors until it's too late. Aydin hadn't put his hands on me, but what if this behavior was the beginning of the end, a sample of the husband he'd be?

Blinking, I stomped my thoughts down and resumed finishing up my look. "It's just a few hours, Aydin. You're a big boy, so you'll be alright."

"Hours of other men looking at you." He looked me up and down, his lip curling up in disgust. "You look too good to be alone. What if some asshole hits on you?"

"I won't be alone. I'll be with my friends, and you don't have to worry about another man, Aydin." I held out my left hand, the lab-grown diamond twinkling under the light of the room. "All I'd have to do is show them this, and they'd know I was taken, and out of their price range."

Lab-grown didn't mean cheap, as Aydin had shared that he paid well over five thousand dollars for my ring. When he broke down the details, it was understandable why. The three-carat round diamond was flanked by smaller marquise-cut floral diamonds and encased by a 14k white gold band. I would've loved it if it cost only five hundred dollars, but knowing he paid so much for it made it even more special and made the cloud hanging over us all the sadder.

He put his hands up in a gesture of surrender, though I saw the displeasure swirling in his light brown eyes. "Alright, my love, you win. But just know that I'll be very, very sad until you get back."

Instead of answering, I planted a quick kiss on his lips, which seemed to placate him. When I tried to pull away, he pulled me back, initiating another, more heated kiss. Despite how upset I was with him, my body responded, melting against his. It wasn't until he began tugging at the straps of my lace mini dress that I pulled away, fixing the garment and stepping back.

"Distracting me won't work," I teased, my lipstick smeared over his mouth. I'd have to reapply the red hue before I left.

He clicked his tongue. "It was worth a try, my love."

"I'll be back before you know it."

The smile he gave me was strained, but instead of arguing anymore, he retreated to the en-suite bathroom. While he did his business, I reapplied my lipstick, then went to where my phone was charging to let my girls know I was on the way.

Too bad I picked up the wrong phone.

Aydin and I both had Samsung Galaxies, and before I could remedy my mistake and pick up the proper phone, I noticed a text that read 'I miss you' from someone named Alex. I racked my brain for everyone in Aydin's life that I knew, but blanked on anyone with that name. Curiosity getting the better of me, I typed in the passcode— my birthday—and opened up the text. Immediately, I wished I hadn't.

A minute of scrolling revealed flirtatious exchanges that burned me up with jealousy, and nude photos that angered me beyond belief. She had sharp, ambiguous features with bleached blonde hair that contrasted against her tanned skin. Her almond-shaped eyes, though, stuck with me. They were a piercing, icy blue. They were so striking, I wondered if they were fake.

But real or fake, it didn't matter because she was my fiancé's side bitch. When Aydin walked out of the bathroom, I pitched the phone at his head. He looked at me with wide, bewildered eyes, which morphed into anger when he realized it was his phone that I threw.

"What the fuck—"

"Who the hell is Alex?" I yelled, interrupting whatever he was about to say.

Shock and guilt stole away his fury, confirming that he was a lowdown, cheating motherfucker.

"You went through my texts," he stated, his tone emotionless as he schooled his features. "Violated my privacy—"

"Cut the shit," I snapped, refusing to give in to my urge to cry and ruin my makeup. "I picked up your phone by accident and saw a text from her."

At the end of the day, Alex's identity didn't matter because it wouldn't take away the fact that he was a cheater. The ring on my finger suddenly felt too heavy, and yet, the thought of taking it off filled me with grief.

"It doesn't matter," I said flatly, grabbing my purse and storming to the bedroom door. "Don't wait up."

"Estelle, wait!" he called, his footsteps thudding behind me as I entered the living room.

Before I could leave the house, he was in front of me. "I swear, Estelle, Alex is nothing to me. I met her a few months ago when you went to that book convention, and I was so lonely without you—"

"So, it's my fault you cheated?"

"Cheating implies I slept with her. A kiss and pictures aren't the same thing."

What stupid logic.

A humorless laugh left me. "So, I can send nudes to the guys in my DMs now? Fucking kiss a random at bars for funsies?" Based on his anger swiftly returning, he didn't like that idea too much. "Because with your logic, that's perfectly fine—"

"For me," he interrupted, adding fuel to my fire. "It's different with you. You're my woman, and—"

I wasn't a violent person, but his hypocrisy made me do something I vowed I'd never do: raise my hand to a significant other. He hadn't expected the blow, so my punch to his nose sent him careening into a wall.

"You crazy bitch!" he howled, clutching his bloodied nose.

I ignored him. Out of the corner of my eye, I saw Crush retreat into his shell. The wooden top of the box turtle's 90-gallon terrarium doubled as our entryway sideboard. Shoving past Aydin, who was glaring daggers at me, I grabbed my keys and left our apartment, already mourning the relationship I gave four years of my life to.

After discovering Aydin's correspondence with another woman, dancing with my friends was unappealing. I'd hoped the rounds of shots would make the cloud hanging over my head disappear, but downing the tequila only made me tipsy *and* sad. To their credit, when cheering me up failed, my friends volunteered to linger nearby and listen to my venting. But I'd said everything that could be said to Aydin, and recounting the events once was more than enough for me. So, instead of dragging them down with my sadness, I shooed them onto the dance floor when a song they all liked came on. Typically, I enjoyed it, too, but tonight wasn't a typical night.

I felt like such an idiot. I'd defended Aydin to anyone who criticized him and tried to ignore his imperfections by focusing on all the ways he *was* perfect. Yes, he could be demanding, controlling, secretive, and stubborn, all traits that led to our fair share of arguments. But he was also handsome, attentive, a good lover, a provider, funny, and until tonight, I thought him to be loyal.

My mind drifted to my cousins, the daughters of my late Aunt Maeve. The woman had countless demons, all of which drove a wedge between her and my mother, and resulted in my cousins living in Kansas City, Kansas. All three women had joined the KC chapter of the Royal Harlots, with the eldest, Michelle, becoming the chapter's president. Following a failed attempt on her life, I'd visited my cousins, and Michelle, Lake, and Juno all had something to say about Aydin. Like usual, I'd shut them down, unable to see the red flags that they could. The failures of their parents meant they didn't have an easy life, their rough upbringing leading to an astuteness I lacked.

My stupidity drove me to order another shot. It was downed within seconds, the burn only a temporary distraction. My phone vibrated for the umpteenth time. I knew it was Aydin. He was always like that when I went out, blowing up my notifications until I answered. He said it was because he worried about me, seeing as Memphis wasn't the safest city. I lived in a decent area, and being a native to the city, knew what neighborhoods to avoid, but I still found his concern sweet. At least, I had found it sweet when I thought it was genuine concern. That illusion had been destroyed, and now I saw his demands that I give him regular updates as a ploy to prevent me from giving him a taste of his own medicine by cheating.

I stared at the engagement ring I loved so much, twisting it around my finger. I hadn't taken it off, though I knew I'd never look at Aydin the same again. Removing it felt too permanent, and as much as he hurt me, leaving the man I'd shared years of happiness with was a crushing thought. Yet, if I stayed, he'd think he'd be able to do what he wanted with no consequences. The more I considered what to do, the worse my headache became. I looked at the dance floor, smiling when Tess blew a kiss at me. Stewing in misery was only bringing down the mood, so I stood from the bar and made my way to the dance floor. For a night, I'd try my best to put Aydin out of my head and dance the night away with my friends.

"Finally," Tess squealed, grabbing my hand to pull me in between her and Lauren. "I thought you'd be moping at the bar all night."

"It was tempting," I admitted, starting to move to the beat as my mind registered the song. "But it'd be a waste of a night."

"Period," Lauren said, while Tess whooped.

"Where's Danielle?" I questioned, not seeing my third friend anywhere.

"She zeroed in on a fine-ass dude and bounced," Lauren answered, grabbing my hips, while Tess threw her arms on my shoulders.

"Figures," I grumbled, shaking my head.

Dani was a free spirit, and while I respected and sometimes envied that, I often feared she'd go home with the wrong person. One-night stands were fine, but the girl barely gave notice before she left with her fuck of the evening. Being a pretty blonde bombshell meant she could pull whoever she wanted, but being short and petite made her an easy target. At the very least, she could tell us the name of the dude, where she intended to go, and let us take a picture of the fucker. The handful of times we pressured her into agreeing, she threw a hissy fit, leading to us just giving up and hoping for the best.

I closed my eyes, trying to block out my thoughts as I danced with my friends. The song was one Tess would describe as 'slutty pop-rock,' and we moved to the beat accordingly, shaking our assess and winding our hips whilst we ground on one another. While Dani and I identified as bisexual, Tess and Lauren were strictly dickly, so our suggestive dancing was just harmless fun. Yet, it drew plenty of attention, which I realized when I opened my eyes and found a stunning woman staring back at me from a table near the bar.

My mouth went dry, the intensity of her gaze making it impossible for me to look away. I didn't know her ethnic background, but the woman reminded me of my animated childhood crush, Princess Jasmine. Both shared deeply tanned skin, big brown eyes, and a wealth of thick black curls. She was near six feet, with a slim, athletic figure. I used to starve myself in hopes of achieving a body like hers, but years of therapy allowed me to admire her toned physique with zero envy.

As she did so often, Denali crossed my mind. Her sudden disappearance haunted me and my grandmother, and I'd never forgotten her beauty. She was just as stunning as the stranger. The two women could be sisters.

The longer I stared, the less gracefully I moved, catching the attention of Lauren and Tess. They followed my line of sight.

"Dude, she's eyeing you heavily," Tess said, nudging me with her elbow, making me lose even more rhythm.

"And she's just your type," Lauren said in a singsong voice.

Tall, toned, and not white. Beauty was present in every ethnicity, but most of my past partners were people of color, not pasty white-Americans with distant Scottish heritage like me.

"I'm engaged," I reminded them, my voice sounding weak to my own ears.

They snorted in unison.

"So? Aydin was engaged when he was texting that bitch," Lauren shot back. She stopped dancing, placing her hand on my shoulders and guiding me off the dance floor. Tess followed behind us. "It's only right that you flirt with somebody else, and she looks like she'd happily help you with that."

"And if you end up fucking her, promise we won't tell," Tess added, making Lauren hum in agreement.

"That'd be—"

"Consequences," Lauren interrupted. "You've been good to that man, and he fucked over you. If you don't want to end things, that's your choice, but having a little fun with somebody else would just make things even."

She released her hold on me, gave me a pointed look, and returned to the dancefloor, her box braids swishing behind her. Tess shrugged, nodded to the mystery woman, and walked away. Their orders were clear: give Aydin a taste of his medicine. It was a tempting thought, even as my stomach twisted in guilt. I didn't want a tit-for-tat relationship, nor was I poly. I'd tried that shit in college and nearly had a mental breakdown. Yet, denying myself a conversation on the grounds of loyalty felt silly after seeing Aydin's sexts.

Taking a deep breath, I steeled my nerves and approached the woman. As I drew closer, I noticed two things. One, her resemblance to Denali was uncanny. Two, her leather vest, and I realized all her friends wore one, too. It dawned on me that they weren't typical leather vests, but motorcycle cuts. The excitement I felt was illogical, but that lifestyle had fascinated me since Michelle had become Athena, even with the dangers I knew were present.

When I got to her table, she just leaned back and cocked a brow. No doubt, she'd witnessed the entire exchange, as her eyes never left me. The snickers of the other women made my cheeks flame. Clearing my throat, I said the first thing that came to mind.

"Are you a biker?" I blurted, immediately wanting to take the words back when her gaze sharpened. "I-I noticed your cut, and—"

"The fuck you know about cuts?" one of the other women at the table interrupted, worsening my embarrassment.

God, but this was a mistake.

"My...my cousin is a biker, too," I explained, wondering if I should just cut my losses and walk away.

Interest lit the mystery woman's eyes, and she cocked her head to the side. "What's her club, babe?"

My Spidey senses tingled. Her voice was deeper and huskier than Denali's had been, but it'd been so damn long since I spoke to her, and the similarities were present. As Mama and Grandma loved to say, if it walked like a duck, quacked like a duck, and looked like a duck, it was a no-brainer what the fuck it was.

Then again, I was half-drunk, the strobe lighting of the place contorted people's features, and the music was blaring, so it could be wishful thinking.

"What's yours?" I asked, thinking back to Michelle's attack. If they were the enemy, giving myself away would put a target on my back.

Thankfully, the women gathered at the table found me amusing, as instead of blasting my ass for the question, more laughter ensued. My nervousness might've been a blessing in disguise, as it made me too pathetic to be threatening. The woman who captured my attention smirked, then stood and turned around. My eyes widened when I took in the club's rockers. I'd been correct, the women were bikers.

Not just any bikers, however, but Royal Harlots, one of the most notorious female MCs around. Their escapades—and those of their twin club, The Royal Bastards—made national news often. The unfolding Kansas City saga had escalated to violence across the city, making me fear for Michelle. The Royal Bastards and Harlots seemed to be the ones coming out on top, but people associated with both clubs had turned up dead in Kansas and all over the country following the destruction of the KC Bloody Scorpions.

"That's my cousins' club," I said when she sat back down, feeling more at ease. "She's with the KC chapter. Mic....Athena."

Denali's Doppelgänger cocked a brow. "Your cousin is the Prez of her chapter, no?"

"She is," I confirmed. I looked pointedly at the empty seat. "Can I sit?"

"Nah," Denali 2.0 said, standing up as disappointment washed over me. "You don't want to be around these fools, babe."

Laughs and groans met her words.

"I fucking resent that, Everest!" one of the women said, though humor laced her tone.

Everest. The similarities continued.

"Fucking choke on it, Val," she replied, taking my hand and guiding me away. "Let me buy you a drink...what's your name?"

"Estelle. You?"

She froze. I wondered if I said something to offend her. Everest studied me closely, her gaze darting between my eyes and hair.

"No fucking way," she breathed. "Estelle...Pratt-Milton, right? Your Mama and Daddy hyphenated their names when they got married, and they did the same for you and your brothers when he adopted y'all."

My jaw dropped. The fact that she knew that information meant one thing. I wrote under Estelle Pratt to maintain privacy and never disclosed what she just told me to the public. Much to the joy of my childhood self, the woman who was flirting with me and *holding my hand* wasn't a Denali Doppelgänger, but Denali Bernard herself.

Before my mind fully processed the revelation, I was throwing myself into her arms, enveloping her taller frame in a tight embrace. She froze for a moment before she returned the hug, a breathy laugh leaving her. Neither of us said anything as we held one another. We let our bodies do the talking. Her arms felt so right around me, and I never wanted her to let me go. But all too soon, we were pulling away from one another, and she resumed guiding me to a bar.

"What happened to you?" I blurted once we scored two barstools. "I…you dropped off the face of the Earth. Grandma thought you'd been stationed overseas. Were you?"

My words came out in a rush. An array of emotions flickered across her face before she schooled her expression. She shook her head. "I was in prison, Estelle. But that's a long-ass story."

My eyes widened. A billion questions ran through my head—mainly what the hell had she done—but it was evident she didn't want to talk about it. Denali was never a cruel person, so I knew whatever her crime, it was out of necessity, driven out of survival instead of selfishness. With that in mind, I held my tongue, watching as she ordered beer for us. A grapefruit beer for me, and a Bohemia beer for her. The drink tasted nothing like the fruit but did have a sweeter aftertaste than most brews. However, within a few sips of beer, I was tired of the silence.

"So…you're a Harlot now," I stated, noting the obvious, unsure what else to say. "And when did you move to Memphis?"

"Moved to Memphis about four years ago. Prospected for a year, became the treasurer last year," she said proudly. "But I'm tired of talking about my ass. Let me take you on a ride so we can catch up. Shit's too loud here."

"I'm engaged now," I said, holding out my ring.

Knowing what Aydin did, the words felt hollow.

She cocked a brow, a piercing present that hadn't been when she was eighteen. "The fuck does that gotta do with me?"

As a teenager, she seemed reserved. As a grown-ass woman, that was gone. When I spoke again, my voice was breathier, showing how positively my body responded to her new demeanor.

"What do you have in mind?"

She shrugged, finishing her beer in one gulp. "Dunno. We'll ride and see where we end up."

I was silent as I considered Denali's offer. Aydin's face flashed through my mind, making me feel guilty about considering leaving with the sexy biker chick before me, one I'd desired since before I knew the meaning of the word. That was the root of my guilt, as her offer wasn't a salacious one. But, Lord, did I want it to be, and that filled me with conflicted feelings. Despite his mistake, I was still Aydin's fiancée. And yet, that hadn't stopped him from texting other women, so why should it stop me from going on a spin with Denali?

"Well?" she prompted, her brow cocked once more, a smirk playing at her full lips as if she sensed my weakening resolve. She stood and held out a hand. "You leaving with me or what, babe?"

A thrill shot through me, her raspy voice as enticing as the excitement she promised. Words failed me, so I simply nodded and placed my hand in hers.

"Good girl," she purred, making me shudder as an ache formed between my thighs.

This would be an exciting evening indeed, and if I played my cards right, things would get salacious. It'd be exactly what Aydin deserved.

Payback was a bitch, after all.

Chapter Seven

Estelle

Thirty minutes later, Denali and I were sitting in a mom-and-pop diner. Riding on her red Harley motorcycle, which she'd named Lobster, had been thrilling, and being able to cling to her only made the ride more enjoyable. I'd been slightly disappointed when we ended up at a restaurant instead of a motel, but munching on pancakes and drinking coffee made it fade. Seeing her order blueberry pancakes took me back to her eighteenth birthday, where we so drastically failed at making the sweet breakfast treat to celebrate her milestone. Little was said as we ate, but when Denali finished off her final pancake, she rekindled the conversation.

"How are you and the family, kid?"

It took everything in me not to scowl at her. At twenty-six, I was far from a kid, closer to thirty than twenty-one. As Denali had put it all those years ago, I was grown-grown. The promise she made to me entered my mind. I wondered whether she remembered her vow to take me on a date when I hit twenty-five.

"Kayla and Harvey Jr. are in high school," I said around a mouthful of pancake, pulling out my phone to show her pictures. "Harvey is starting his senior year, and Kayla is starting her sophomore year."

I turned my phone to her. On the screen, Harvey Jr. and Kayla stood side-by-side, her four-inch heels making her the same height as our brother. Her hair was in Fulani braids with red beads at the end, matching her red flare dress. Harvey's locs were finally beginning to drop and were long enough to be put into a small ponytail. He'd always adored Grandma's dreadlocks, so when Mama and Daddy gave the okay for him to start his loc journey, he was ecstatic. The picture was from Mama's birthday two months ago. For every special event, my mother required several family photos.

"Holy shit," Denali breathed as she saw my younger siblings, a smile gracing her face. "Last time I saw them, they were babies. So were you."

"I was twelve," I reminded her. "A kid, not a baby."

"Same difference."

I rolled my eyes, then scrolled to another picture, this one of Mama and Daddy on their twentieth anniversary together, and their eighteenth wedding anniversary. They married on the same date they made their relationship official, which I always found so sweet. Every year, they wore white on that special day, had a big brunch in the afternoon with family, and a private date during the evening. The white of their outfits made Daddy's caramel skin pop, and contrasted with Mama's deep auburn curls.

"Your parents are still together," Denali noted, her smile growing. "Any more siblings came into the picture?"

"Nah, after Kayla, Mama was done," I said, scrolling to the next photo, of my older brothers and their spouses. "Dennis and Edward are both married now. Eddie adopted a child with his husband, and Denny is having his first baby with his wife."

Edward came out shortly after I did, and he often credited me with giving him the courage. I never stopped teasing him that he copied me.

"They're older than you, right?"

"Yep. Eddie is thirty-one, and Dennis is twenty-eight."

Now for the picture I knew she was waiting for: Grandma April. After a fall that nearly left her paralyzed five years ago, she chose to move to Memphis, so her son and my mother could more easily care for her. Ignoring the cane she now relied on, she'd made a full recovery.

"Mrs. Milton?" Denali breathed, her eyes wide as she examined the picture of Grandma holding up a painting she drew during an art class at her senior-care community.

I was fortunate not only to make a living off my writing, but to be very well-off from it. When I got my first big payday, instead of letting me pay for her apartment, she requested that I foot the bill for luxury assisted living in East Memphis. It was what she wanted, so I did it.

"She just turned 81," I said, scrolling through more photos of Grandma. "She's living her best life in a senior living community. They have all kinds of amenities. Chauffeurs, housekeeping, chefs, exercise programs, a walking trail and garden, courtyards, a library…well, you get the point."

"She's living it up," Denali said with a chuckle. "I'm glad. She deserves it."

"I wish we knew you moved down here," I sighed, putting my phone away. "She'll be ecstatic when I tell her. She still talks about you, you know."

Denali's eyes widened. "She does?"

"Why wouldn't she? You were like another grandchild to her, and you just disappeared one day."

She winced. "Yeah…maybe don't tell her I was in prison. I, uh, don't want to disappoint her more than I already have."

Reaching out, I laced my fingers with hers, happy that she didn't pull away. "You didn't disappoint her. You worried her," I corrected, squeezing her hand. "But don't worry, your secret's safe with me."

"Thank you, kid," she said, pulling her hand away all too soon. "You still haven't told me about yourself, excluding your engagement. Congrats, by the way."

"Thank you. And I also have tattoos now," I began, hoping that pointing out my ink would remind her that I was a grown-ass woman. "And I'm an author. A bestselling one, if you can believe it."

"I can. You've always been smart."

Her compliment made my heart flutter. It seemed that nearly fifteen years of no contact didn't dull my crush. Then again, childhood crushes always hold a special place in someone's heart.

"I was actually aiming to be an English teacher, and ultimately, a college professor," I said, longing for the darkness of the club we left, which would've hidden my blush. "Then I submitted a short story to a contest, won 1st place, and things took off from there."

Nodding, she took her phone out of her cut's pocket, clicked around, and slid it to me. My heart sped up when I saw the words 'New Contact' on her screen.

"Put your info in, kid, and send me the link and shit to your book."

"Books, actually," I said, picking up the phone to oblige her request. "I have thirteen published."

My first book was released in my senior year of college, with mediocre results. It didn't deter me, though, and when I released my third book months after graduation, it earned thousands of dollars in the first three months. Investing that money in my fourth book expanded my fanbase, and by the fifth book, a year and a half after I earned my bachelor's degree, I had a few bestsellers under my belt.

She let out a low whistle. "Goddamn, girl. You've been busy."

"I've been writing professionally for five years," I pointed out, sending a quick text to myself, then sliding her phone back to her. "That's less than three books a year."

Three books a year was a fluke. Most years, I only managed to get two novels out. I was proud of my writing career and all that

I accomplished with it, and adored my fans. They got me to where I was, and I lived for book signings and meet-and-greets.

However, there was no denying that many of my peers could produce twice what I did in the same time frame, if not more, and such a phenomenon was only becoming more common with the rise of AI. As a little girl, I never imagined that machines would threaten creative jobs, but life was strange, and people were greedy.

"Be so fucking for real, girl," Denali said with a snort. "You know damn well that's impressive, so don't try the humble act with me."

"It's impressive for non-authors, but rookie numbers in the indie publishing industry," I explained as I added Denali's number to my contacts, the sight of her name in my phone making me giddy.

I tried to remind myself that it meant nothing, just two old friends catching up. Yet, I knew the vibes she'd been giving off at the club. Before she realized who I was, she was attracted to me. I was twenty-six now, so knowing my identity shouldn't have changed a thing.

"You make a living off it, don't you?"

I nodded. "I do."

A damn good one, as I raked in six figures a year. More than Dennis, a dental hygienist, and Edward, an electrician. As the best-paid child, it made sense that I was my mother's favorite, though she claimed to favor us all the same.

"You're killing this shit, so the output doesn't matter," she said, returning her phone to her pocket and exchanging it for her wallet.

When I took my last bite, she dug out enough cash to cover our tab and tip the waiter, then threw it on the table. Standing, she held out a hand to me. Excitement filled me, just for it to crash and burn when she opened her beautiful mouth.

"C'mon, kid, let's get you back to your friends."

Even if I wanted to—which I didn't—I couldn't stop the scowl that spread across my face. "I'm twenty-six, Denali. A grown ass woman, not a child."

"Okay then," she said, her voice tinged with mild amusement. "*Essie*, let's get you back to your friends. Better?"

Her use of my nickname would've pacified me if she weren't trying to get rid of me.

"No, it isn't," I snapped, crossing my arms over my chest and glaring up at her. Even in my three-inch heels, she still had an inch or two on me. "You were feeling me back at the club. What happened?"

"Didn't know who you were then."

"What difference does it make? We're both grown-grown, remember?"

Her lips quirked into a smile. "Can't forget it, babe."

Babe. Much better than 'kid', and oh so sexy coming from her.

"So, what's the problem?"

"Aren't you engaged?"

A twinge of guilt flickered through me, but I stomped it down. Even if I hadn't discovered those texts, my attraction to her wouldn't have magically evaporated. But I would've ignored her when she was eye-fucking me across the club, because I did love Aydin. He'd forgotten our commitment to one another, and in doing so, he reignited a childhood quest to capture Denali's attention.

I dropped my arms to my side and looked away, thankful that the diner was practically deserted. "It's complicated right now." Taking in a breath, I met her gaze once more. "But Aydin isn't here. If you don't want me, just say that, and I'll stop making a fool of myself."

It'd be easy to blame the alcohol coursing through my veins for my behavior, but it'd also be an untruthful cop-out. I wanted Denali, and if playing coy wasn't working, then I'd have to be blunt.

"We just reunited," she pointed out, her voice steady and expression unreadable. "You wanna complicate shit already?"

"It's only a complication if someone finds out."

"You've always been sneaky, you know that?" she said with a sigh. "First time I met you, you'd snuck your little ass out of Mrs. Milton's home."

I smiled at the memory, one I was happy that Denali hadn't forgotten. It was one of the few times Mama had ever spanked me. The cardinal rule for my siblings and me was that anything that endangered ourselves or others earned ten strikes to the rear. However, it'd been worth it, as that bratty act had introduced me to Denali. Even after all these years apart, I still considered her among the prettiest women I'd ever encountered.

"You aren't really in a position to judge," I shot back.

As a Harlot, sneakiness and secretiveness were a requirement to stay alive.

"Guess you're right."

She considered me, her eyes roaming over my figure. When her gaze settled on my tits, she licked her lips. Emboldened, I thrust my breasts out further. I used to starve myself for a model-like figure that I never achieved, but I'd learned to appreciate my curves. Based on Denali's appraisal of my body, she did, too.

Finally, she sighed and grabbed my arm, tugging me out of the diner.

"You win," she grumbled at my questioning look, pulling me towards Lobster.

The victory was heightened with anticipation, though her tone of voice cut both short.

"Don't sound so enthused."

She shot me a look, one that had guilt unrelated to Aydin rising in me.

"If you don't want to," I began as she helped me onto her bike, just to be cut off by her snort.

"If I didn't want to, I wouldn't be taking your ass to a motel. You'd be walking back to wherever the fuck." A pause. Then… "Or dead, depending how well you took no for an answer."

A chill ran down my spine as I was shocked into silence. She looked at my face and snickered, though I doubted she was joking. The Royal Harlots could be just as brutal as the Bastards, and even as a teenager, Denali had a violent streak that'd resulted in her fair share of fights. Denali's earlier comment about going to prison crossed my mind, but I had enough sense not to ask her about it. Instead, I just wrapped my arms around her waist as she revved her engine, happy that she wanted me, too, for more reasons than one.

When I left my apartment, sex hadn't been on my mind. I just wanted to hang out with my friends and forget about Aydin's betrayal. Then, Denali had entered the picture, and my thoughts took a lewd turn. Thankfully, my persistence paid off, and she was now laid bare beneath me, gripping my hair as I ate her out. Little was said when we reached the motel. Instead of making idle chitchat, we got right down to business. I'd pulled one orgasm from her, but it wasn't enough. She tasted like heaven and sounded like sin, and I wanted more.

"Fuck, Essie," she moaned as I sucked her swollen clit back into my mouth.

Her voice was breathy and hoarse, a consequence of her first orgasm. It was so fucking hot, and I wished I could record how ruined she sounded. So soon, too, as I didn't intend to stop until she'd come on my tongue at least three times to make up for lost time. Besides, after tonight, I doubt I'd be able to sample her again, so I had to make the most of it.

Denali's pussy was as pretty as the rest of her. Covered in a neatly trimmed layer of hair, her lower lips were plush and even, with a sensitive clit that was easy to find. Her feminine scent was addictive, and I found myself licking lower again, burying my face in her mound as my tongue swept through her folds. My hands kneaded her ass cheeks as I feasted, my thighs squeezed together as the flavor of her arousal heightened my own. Despite how delicious she was, I paused tongue-fucking her to suck her clit back into my mouth, making her hips buck.

I took several seconds to lavish her clit with attention before I dipped my tongue back into her hole to sample more of her juices. I repeated the process multiple times, the sound of me dining on her wet pussy mingling with the moans and whimpers I pulled from her. My own arousal mounted, my slick dribbling down my thighs as I pleasured Denali. The sting of her pulling my hair only made me more excited, doubling my determination to make her come again.

Releasing her clit from my mouth, I flicked it gently with the tip of my tongue. In lieu of massaging her perky ass, I buried one hand between my legs, and the other between Denali's. It was easy to slide two fingers inside of her, and I tried to finger our pussies at the same pace. She squealed when I hit that spongy spot that always made me come hard and fast, her walls fluttering around my digits.

Heat radiated from her, her slick dripping down my hand as my fingers pumped in and out of her. All it took was one hard suck on her clit to make her come undone a second time.

"Oh, shit," she cried, her body convulsing as her cunt clamped down.

Her nectar flowed from her, staining my fingers, dribbling down her ass crack, and making a mess of the motel sheets. It was a beautiful sight, one that'd be forever ingrained in my memory. My fingers slipped from her, but I wasted no time working on orgasm number three. This time, instead of pulling at my hair, she gripped the sheets, her body limp and pliant as I continued lapping at her core.

"Fuck," she whimpered, her voice cracking as her body jerked with each glide of my tongue.

She was overstimulated; that much was easy to see. But she wasn't pushing me away, so I continued. I tongue-fucked her with abandon, my nose pressed firmly against her clit, my fingers pumping in and out of my aching pussy. My first orgasm washed over me seconds before her third slammed into her. My moans were muffled by Denali's cunt, while a wordless scream left her, echoing off the walls of the motel and no doubt disturbing any neighbors. Not that I gave a damn. In fact, they should be thankful they were able to hear the beautiful sounds of Denali's pleasure.

My hunger for her finally satiated, I pulled away, admiring the mess I made of her. "You made such a mess," I cooed, dragging two fingers along her slit to collect her juices, before straddling her hips and slipping my digits past her lips. "Suck."

She obeyed my order without question, her eyes glazed over with pleasure as she sampled herself. When I was confident that she'd thoroughly tasted her slick, I pulled my fingers away and pressed a quick kiss to her lips.

"Good girl," I praised, peppering kisses along her sweaty face. "You're doing so good for me."

She gave me a dazed smile but said nothing. Not that she needed to say a thing, as her body had already spoken a thousand times. I wanted to make it sing at least once more before the night was over.

"You ever tribbed before?" I asked, thumbing at a nipple until it pebbled under my touch.

It was an act I thoroughly enjoyed, though it was dismissed as a pornographic myth created for the pleasure of perverts by others. I believed the same thing, too, until a college situationship showed me the light. The pornified version wasn't very practical or enjoyable. However, with some modifications, it felt heavenly.

"Hasn't everyone?" At Denali's question, I cocked a brow. At my look, she rolled her eyes and amended her words. "Hasn't every queer woman, I mean? Doesn't do shit for me, but—"

"Then you aren't doing it right," I interrupted with a tsk. "I promise you, it can feel real good."

She shrugged, her gaze lidded and deeply tanned cheeks slightly flushed. "Go on, then. Show me how it's done."

Up until now, I'd been the dominant one. Hearing her commanding tone, though, sent pleasure through me. Her permission granted, I wasted no time getting to work. Denali was pliant as I positioned us. As always, it took some trial and error, but soon, my right thigh was over her left, and her left was over my right. I shifted until our cunts were touching, the feeling of her soaked pussy against mine letting me know that we were in the right position. Satisfied, I began to grind against her.

"Fuck," I breathed when our clits connected, making both of our bodies jolt.

As I ground against her, Denali's hips bucked upwards to meet mine, making the mild discomfort that always came with this position worth it.

"Okay," she murmured, continuing to cant her hips to meet my thrusts. "Not bad…"

Her mutterings made me giggle and made me even more determined to make her come like this.

"Stop overthinking it," I ordered, one of my hands finding her throat, while the other returned between her legs to aid her along by rubbing her clit. "Just feel."

It took a few seconds, but soon, she was melting against the sheets, her eyes fluttering shut as I found my rhythm. The sensation of her warm flesh sliding against mine was better than I could've imagined. My body was still buzzing from my first orgasm, so it wasn't long until my second began to build. I held back, though, wanting Denali to get off before I did. My hips sped up as I ground harder against her, my hand squeezing the sides of her neck while the other rapidly flicked her bundle of nerves.

"Fuck," she panted as she surrendered to the sensation. "This is…wow…"

"Just feel, remember?" I said, holding back my release starting to become difficult.

Her breathing grew ragged, my thighs clenching with each pass of my pussy. With a sharp cry, she came for a fourth time. Her sticky juices mingled with my arousal, her slick folds fluttering as her back arched, thrusting her tits upwards. Being on top of her allowed me to witness how beautiful she looked when she came. Her lips were parted as she moaned, eyes screwed shut, skin glistening with sweat.

"That's it," I praised, allowing the hand on her throat to fall away, opting to play with her tits instead. "Doing so well for me, pretty girl."

I continued to grind against her. All it took was a few passes of my clit over hers to find my own release. Throwing my head back, I cried out as my body shook. My juices coated her lower half, returning the favor she dealt me and marking her pussy with my essence. It added onto the mess of the motel bed, but that wasn't our problem.

My orgasm subsiding, I collapsed forward, my large, sweaty tits pressing against Denali's smaller ones. Panting and trembling, I captured her lips in a messy kiss. The resulting moan I pulled from her was muffled by our joined mouths. I clung to her as our tongues met, the anchor of her body much needed.

"Told you it could feel good," I mumbled against her mouth.

"Shut up," she grumbled, making me giggle. She chuckled as I rolled off her, the sound raspier than normal. "You surprised the hell out of me, you know that?"

I propped myself up on an elbow to look at her. "How so?"

"Didn't take you for a dom, is all."

"Didn't take you for sub," I fired back, a smile playing at my lips.

More than one of my lovers had echoed the same sentiment. Apparently, something about me screamed submissive when in reality, I favored dominant roles when fucking. Especially with other women, as with men, I was more of a switch.

"Guess we both surprised the fuck out of each other," she said, returning my smile.

"Yeah," I agreed, not resisting when she pulled me into her arms.

As we lay there, Aydin crossed my mind, but I quickly pushed him away. What he didn't know wouldn't hurt him, and he brought this upon himself. Besides, I'd have all the time in the world to deal with him, but only a night with Denali. My fiancé could wait, but for now, I'd enjoy the stolen time with the sexy biker I'd wanted for years.

Chapter Eight

DENALI

Three days after my one-night stand with Estelle, the girl had yet to leave my mind. When she'd fallen asleep, I'd slipped out of the motel. It was a coward's move, having her wake up to a cold spot next to her, but it was an easy one. As fun as the night had been, the chapter of my life in which Estelle and her family played an active role was closed. They were all doing well, and I'd found a family—albeit an unconventional one—among the Royal Harlots. They accepted me, quirks and all.

Perfection wasn't expected, only loyalty, which was easy to give. Karma had saved me. Florence 'Big Mama' Thorton, the VP of the Memphis chapter and Karma's best friend, had become a surrogate mother to me. Valentina, the dumbass who'd accidentally given me my road name by not knowing fucking geography, was the closest thing to a best friend I had. And the other women—my sisters—made me feel like I belonged.

The Denali I'd been back in Chicago was long gone, replaced by a version of myself that was content with her lot in life. Estelle had seemed genuine about us reconnecting, but my presence would only bring chaos, disrupting the happiness the Pratt-Milton clan had found. If nothing else, I owed the family—especially Mrs. Milton—peace. Maybe I'd send Mrs. Milton an anonymous present as a 'thank you' for all she did for me, but that would be it.

Val snapped her fingers in front of my face, snickering when I slapped her hand away. "Focus, Evy. Minutes are over."

I'd done the quarterly financial report last month, giving me two more months before I had to get my ass up in front of the membership to break down every expense again.

"Everest," I corrected with a scowl. "Stop calling me that stupid ass nickname."

She laughed again, always getting a kick out of fucking with me, while I rolled my eyes and looked to where Karma stood on a platform that'd been present when the old factory had been purchased. Two stripper poles had been added, with a podium placed in the middle of them, which Prez leaned against, ready to conduct our monthly Church session. Nina 'Siren' Escobar, our Sergeant-at-Arms, lingered by her side, ready to defend our Prez if shit popped off. Siren was a knockout beauty with a surprisingly good voice. Hence, her road name. She was just three years older than me, but she'd been in the club much longer. Due to the nature of her role, she was the only armed member in attendance.

After Glory, our Chaplain, offered the non-denominational invocation, the Secretary, Geri, came to the podium and droned on about what was discussed last time, prospects passed out beers, and whatever the hell else the membership wanted. A perk of being an officer was getting served first, and likewise, we had our pick of seats. Val always sat with me, and I always sat at a two-seater near the bar. She'd joined a year before I did, and for some odd reason, decided that we would be the best of friends. Unfortunately, she'd gotten her wish.

"Alright, ladies, let's get down to business," Karma said, banging her gavel on the podium. "First off, a reminder to everyone that our back-to-school drive is on September 1st, so you all have another two weeks to gather supplies for the kiddos."

The Harlots hosted various charitable ventures throughout the year, garnering donations and local goodwill. The creation of social media accounts the year before I joined the club helped highlight these events. In my estimation, they were part of the reason why the club had gone from twenty members when I joined to forty-one four years later. Double, and that's not including the ten prospectors.

"Our monthly birthday BBQ is next week…"

As Karma went over the general announcements, my mind began to drift. Prez was a pro at Church, and normally, I locked in doing the monthly meetings. But Estelle refused to leave my fucking mind. Just thinking about how she handled me made heat rush through me. She'd been determined to show me how much she'd grown up, a task she more than succeeded in. When I'd first seen her at the club, I was feeling her. I'd always been a sucker for a pretty face and a curvy body, and Estelle had both.

Then, I'd learned who she was, and all the bigoted accusations my father made all those years ago flooded back to me.

It was illogical, but my memory didn't care. A beer had silenced those ugly words, and pancakes and conversation had made me reconsider my stance, leading to a mind-blowing experience. Some guilt still lingered, but Estelle was grown-grown, and what was done was done. I didn't regret it one bit, and she was among the best lays I'd had in years. She was talented in bed, and my body craved her again. However, I was nothing if not willful, and I wouldn't fold so quickly just because she fucked good.

"Who got you so distracted?" Val teased, drawing me back to the present.

"None of your business," I snapped, happy my deep skin tone hid my flush.

Her eyes widened. "So, it is someone? Was it that redhead from the other night?"

She wiggled her eyebrows, making me scowl.

"Refer to my previous answer, Valentina."

"Touched a nerve if you're using my full road name."

"Fucking focus on Karma," I hissed, knowing this back and forth would go on as long as I engaged with Val. The woman never ran out of words.

The position of the stage meant we weren't in Karma's line of sight, and our hushed tones prevented anyone else from hearing us, so we wouldn't get chewed out for not focusing on our Prez. However, out of respect for her, I forced myself to pay attention as she closed out the general announcements.

"Anyone want to add anything?" she asked as usual, falling silent for a handful of seconds to give others a chance to speak. "Nothing? Going once, going twice."

A few snickers rose, but tension hung in the air. Or maybe it was my imagination because I was still so hung up on Estelle and our night together. Perhaps the tension emanated from me.

Karma glanced at her phone to check her agenda. When she set the phone aside and glanced at us, the seriousness on her pretty face alarmed me. "We have a problem, ladies. No, we have several problems. Last year, it was big news when our brothers in the Kansas City, KS chapter of the Bastards teamed with a Bloody Scorpion."

"Roman Mac," Siren reminded us as if we could forget. "Known amongst the ladies as a beautiful savage."

I'd call the nickname corny if it wasn't so accurate, because he was notoriously brutal *and* one fine motherfucker. I wasn't into men, and even my tongue dropped when I saw him. Pretty women were a dime a dozen, leading to me having a body count that'd make many consider me a thot. Yet, handsome men were rare, making me do a double-take whenever I encountered one.

Karma scowled. "I didn't fucking hear that. He shouldn't be known to my girlies as nothing but the fucking enemy."

"Fuck, we will go on forever about Roman," Val griped, low enough so only I heard, in a tone I recognized.

Bitterness, hinting at a fling going sour. I lifted a brow. "You did him?"

She sniffed and lifted her chin. "Papi wouldn't even look twice at me. He saw Siren, and his dick homed in."

"Wait, wait, wait. They were an item?"

"Oh, please. No one will ever lock Roman Mac down."

"Are you two finished whispering among yourselves?" Karma demanded, glaring at Val and me, and reminding me that all it took was a twist of her neck for us to be in her line of sight.

"Sorry, Prez," Val said with a grin. "Zipping my lip right now."

"Dream on, baby," Big Mama called. Born to Jamaican immigrants, she'd been close to Karma since high school.

When Prez met Duchess and ended up with the Harlots, Big Mama was eager to aid her in any way she could, patching in alongside her. She was a huge presence, with towering height and a curvy, plus-sized frame. The pictures I'd seen of her when she was younger let me know she used to be a knock-out, pretty enough to have been a plus-sized model if the industry existed two decades ago. Rough living had taken its toll, though, and while ugly couldn't be used to describe her, she wasn't what she once was.

"The day you stop talking is the day we're pulling out our leathers and white gloves in a going-home celebration," she continued, inspiring more snickers.

"I don't talk that much," Val complained, making me raise a brow at the blatant lie.

"You should say nothing with your zipped lip, mate," Kiwi chastised with a snort. Natalie Young—*Kiwi*—was born in New Zealand and came to America for college. For whatever reason, crime and motorcycles called to her. "Remember—"

Karma whistled, drawing everyone's attention back to her. "Continue this discussion *after*," she chastised, giving all offenders except Big Mama a hard look. "Roman, along with Reese Sinclair—"

I liked Reese, the SAA for the KCK chapter of the Royal Bastards. Apparently, so did a couple of other chicks since more murmurs arose.

"And the rest of our Kansas City brothers," Karma powered on, because opinions were flying around about which Bastard was the best looking and the best to fuck, "destroyed the Bloody Scorpions in their territory."

"Legend," Chains called in her throaty voice. Our Enforcer was fond of chains when dealing with problems. Her grandmother had been born in Berlin and was lucky enough to flee when a very bad mustachioed man got into power. "A Bloody Scorpion coming to our side."

"Because of his sister," Karma supplied. "She's the legend, Roman Mac's sister and Reese Sinclair's person. Things escalated from that situation," she continued, because more comments were flying about. Some were admiration, others were disdain, fueled by jealousy and mistrust.

Mainly, *yes*, Roman Mac's sister was the legend. She must've been as insane as that motherfucker to fuck with a Bastard, despite who her brother was.

"The Scorpions' sister chapter wanted to avenge what happened to their brothers and shot up our sister."

That was some fucking bullshit, especially since one of ours aligned with those Bloody Femme bitches mainly over dick and jealousy. Fendi's pussy was bent out of shape because she wanted a Bastard who'd kicked her ass to the curb years before. Nor did she appreciate losing her position as Kansas City Prez to a much more likable chick.

Fucking bitch. Fendi had almost gotten Athena killed over fucking foolishness. She should've turned in her fucking patch.

"We have reason to believe the local Scorpions are aligning with the Turkish Mafia. They've been spotted at some Scorpion hangouts, specifically one man who I'm guessing is a broker for those fuckers," Karma spat, nodding to Geri.

On cue, Geri stood with the folder she'd brought in and opened it up, pulling out a stack of papers that she began handing out to us before returning to her seat. Those papers turned out to be grainy photos of a suited man with sharp features and styled curls. I filed his face in my memory, then set the photo on the table.

"Hear me out," Val whispered, raising her hands at my sharp looks. "I'll kill the fucker if needed, but he's fine."

"I'm not dignifying that with a response," I said with a sniff.

"You just did."

Not wanting Karma to chew us out for continuing to whisper, I didn't reply to Val this time. After giving us all some time to take in the man, Karma began to speak again.

"We don't know his name, and we got lucky that we managed to get that photo. If word on the street is to be believed, he's fucking around with Luce."

That got everyone's attention. Luce was the president of the Memphis Bloody Femmes, and a crazy bitch. If the broker was her boy toy, he had to go, point-blank period.

"After he started popping up around Scorpion dens, some of our hang arounds and associates have gone missing. Several Harlots from the KC Chapter have been picked off. Athena and I had a conference call with Duchess earlier today. She wants us to monitor the situation here. If the Turkish Mafia and the Scorpions are in bed together, that's very bad for us. Obviously, we don't want any of our people fucked up. It's only a matter of time before they move on from those associated with the club to our members."

Geri lifted her head from her notebook. "Why target us?" she asked, an OG in Memphis' underworld, who kept her real name under wraps. Some smart ass took a piss at her age and joked she was bordering on too geriatric to ride, when she was only fifty-eight. "We didn't send Athena and our KC chapter backup."

"Athena might have ties to the Turkish Mafia because of a family member. They were both born in Memphis."

Fuck. Estelle came to mind. She'd been open about her relation to Athena, and I prayed it was one of her brothers who had ties to the Turkish Mob instead of *her*. Based on the look Val threw my way, she was thinking the same thing I was.

"Get rid of the family member, get rid of the threat," Eli, a new member who had yet to be given a road name and who worshiped Chains, inserted, sparking some murmurs of agreement.

"Did you miss the part of that being Athena's relative?" I drawled, trying to hide how much I hated the thought.

Eli rolled her eyes. "She's in KC. The fuck can she do?"

"Blaze down here and fucking fuck us up," I barked, my eyes narrowing.

Val gave me a questioning look. Eli backed down, so I dropped the subject, though my jaw couldn't seem to unclench.

"Duchess and Athena are looking into the situation, so we aren't doing something so drastic," Karma continued, not addressing the mini-spat that just took place. "We have to stay vigilant for the time being. We don't want shit with the fucking Turkish Mafia. As long as they stay in their lane, we stay in ours. But those Bloody motherfuckers— Scorpions *or* Femmes? On fucking sight. You see one of those fuckheads? Don't ask questions. Shoot the fuck out of them. They mean us no good."

"What if the Mafia starts targeting us?" Kiwi asked. "If we defend ourselves and take one of those fuckers out, we'll start a war."

"We'll have to risk that, Kiwi," Karma said briskly. "Better them than us."

"I move to allow me to hunt them down so I can chain all those motherfuckers to guardrails and blow them up," Chains said.

"Denied," Karma replied, and turned to Geri. "Strike that shit from the minutes."

"You got it, Prez," Geri responded, scrubbing her pen across the page.

"It's not a bad idea," Eli chimed in. "Take them out before they get us. Like you said, better us than them."

Chains grinned at the agreement, while Karma scowled. "No. And if anyone suggests that dumb shit again, I'm pistol-whipping them." Prez looked at Geri. "Strike that from the minutes, too."

"We can keep a tail on the Turkish Mafia," Siren suggested.

"Yeah, Prez," I added, taking everything in even as my time with Estelle haunted me. "We can tap Ryder." She'd gone Nomad a year ago because, within months of earning her patch, she realized she didn't like to be tied down. Now, she bounced from chapter to chapter, completing whatever jobs were needed wherever she happened to be. "She's less recognizable than any of us."

Karma nodded. "Make the motion."

"I motion to get Ryder back to Memphis and keep an eye on the Turkish Mafia," I said.

"Second," Val said.

More murmurs of agreement rose, much to my satisfaction.

"Motion passes," Karma said. "Keep your eyes and ears open, ladies, and don't let this shit leave the clubhouse. We want the element of surprise on our side. That's an order."

There were two more items on the agenda before the meeting closed out. Both were less important than the brewing war. Once Karma dismissed us, I was free to go to my room in the neighboring building on club grounds.

"Everest," Val called as she hurried after me, grabbing my arm to make me halt. "Let's play cards in the courtyard. Weather's nice."

The courtyard was just an extra outdoor space that had a bunch of shit cluttering it. With the overgrown patches of flora, old furniture, and chain-link fence, it was far from glamorous.

I tugged my arm away, shaking my head. "I'm tired, Val. I'm going to rest."

"No, we're going play cards, because we need to fucking talk about that girl you fucked," she hissed, making me freeze.

"Don't—"

"Either we talk here, or at the card table."

I searched her face. Realizing she was serious, I huffed and nodded.

"Fuck, fine."

I was silent as I trailed behind her to the courtyard. Other Harlots had begun filing out of the main building and into the outdoor space, and Val quickly snagged us a table farther away from the rest.

"Speed good with you?" she asked as she started to shuffle the cards.

"I don't want to play shit. Say what you have to say," I demanded, my leg beginning to bounce with my nerves.

If Estelle was the one tied to the Turkish mafia, she was in danger. Plain and simple. The Turks getting involved with the Scorpions and Femmes would make them our enemy, which would make anyone associated with them fair game. The thought of Estelle getting hurt made my blood run cold.

"That girl you fucked…she said Athena was her cousin," Val stated, still shuffling those damn cards, her voice too casual. "Don't know how many relatives Athena has, but if the redhead is the culprit—"

"Don't refer to her like that," I snapped. "Like she's guilty. We don't know who the fuck has ties to the mob, so shut the fuck up."

"You care about her," she noted, hands stilling as she looked at me with wide eyes. "Y'all been talking since you two fucked?"

"No."

"Then why—"

"It's complicated," I interrupted, unwilling to share my history with Estelle with any of my sisters, even Val.

"If she has ties to the Turks, you have to tell Karma. She's leverage over them," Val said as she resumed shuffling. "Whatever you two have going on, you can't let that cloud your judgment."

Since I didn't want to play anything, she seemed content to shuffle those fucking cards endlessly.

"She's just an author, and I resent the implication that I wouldn't tell Karma something so important."

She shrugged. "Don't give a shit. Feelings make people do stupid things. Don't let yours make you a traitor."

Her words pissed me off beyond belief, and I considered breaking her nose for that fucking insult. I barely managed to hold myself back; the importance of my friendship with Val was the only thing preventing me from lashing out. Instead, I stood from the table, not caring when the white plastic chair fell over. Val had the sense to let me storm off to the dormitory, where I could think about the revelations of the day in peace.

Chapter Nine

Estelle

Cheating on Aydin should've made me feel guilty, but instead, I felt nothing over my transgression. I wasn't opposed to tit-for-tat, nor was I against striking back ten times harder when someone wronged you. Not only had he been making our engagement more difficult than it had to be, but he'd been entertaining another woman, and even fucking got physical with her.

Fucking Denali just made things even. However, our one-night stand had also complicated things. Aydin didn't know about her, but I did, and I longed to see her again. That desire seemed futile, as her only reply to the three texts I'd sent was a thumbs-up emoji.

It'd been a week since that mind-blowing night, and I was still thinking about it. The way Denali had submitted to me, the sounds she made, how she tasted, how pretty she sounded, all of it was on repeat in my head. That, more than anything, made me regret sleeping with her. I should've chosen a random person in my quest for revenge, not the woman I'd been sweet on for nearly twenty years.

Huffing, I tried to push her out of my head as I continued bagging swag on the living room floor. My newest release, Thricebound, was an MMF romantasy that'd already earned me a pretty penny. A month after it dropped, I was preparing to host a book signing and a meet and greet at a local bookstore. It'd take place tomorrow, and I still had more to do before I'd be ready.

"Still going at it, babe?" Aydin said as he entered our apartment.

When I'd returned the morning after fucking Denali, he'd literally dropped to his knees and apologized, swearing he'd never make such a mistake again. Since I'd already gotten my revenge, I told him it was water under the bridge, as long as he kept to his promise. The last few days had been great, and reminded me of how things were before our engagement complicated our relationship.

"Unfortunately," I said with a sigh, looking at him to offer a weak smile. "This shit is endless."

"Take a break," he suggested, stepping over shit to plop down on the couch behind me. "I'll order us some food, we can watch one of those cooking competitions you like until it gets here, and you can finish up after."

"Tempting idea, but if I stop, I might not want to start again tonight."

The consequences of putting off creating the swag bags were spending hours shoving shit in a bag and still having too much left to do. My only assistant oversaw my social media accounts and was in Colorado, so having Avery aid me in the dreaded task wasn't possible. Dani suggested I hire a second, local assistant, an idea I brushed off, but one that became so very tempting whenever I had to prep for a signing.

Aydin chuckled and slid off the couch, sitting crisscross next to me. "Well, in that case, tell me what to do, my love."

I paused, looking at him with a cocked brow. Never before had he offered to help me with swag. The few times he did, it was only because of much begging on my part.

"You...want to help?"

"Duh?"

His sassiness made me roll my eyes, though I couldn't help but smile. "I won't turn down that offer. Just watch what I do and join me when you get the hang of things."

He nodded, watching intently as I placed swag into bags thrice, before he finally prepared a bag of his own. I hummed in approval, his movements efficient. He was going faster than me, solely focused on the task at hand, with light chitchat made as we worked. It was nice, and yet, his willingness to help after his transgressions and last week's fight felt...suspect, to say the least. Ninety-five percent of me believed that he was just trying to earn back my favor, while a small voice in the back of my head wondered if he'd already gone back on his promise. It would crush me if the latter were the case, because despite sleeping with and longing to hear from Denali, I did love Aydin. Love cultivated over years didn't evaporate just because someone fucked up, and humans were complicated beings with complicated feelings.

However, despite my love for him, I'd crash out if he stepped out again, so soon after I'd forgiven him. As such, if he cheated on me again, instead of fucking someone else, I'd cut his dick off then leave, plain and simple.

With Aydin's help, the swag I'd been putting off for weeks was done within the hour. While he put everything in the boxes I'd use to transport it to the bookstore, I ordered us some Chinese takeout. My family was never in poverty, unlike my aunt and cousins. We'd been lower-middle class, but that still meant eating out was a luxury. In my opinion, one of the best parts of disposable income was that you didn't have to cook if you didn't want to. Now, eating out was common for Aydin and me, and a home-cooked meal was reserved for weekends or special occasions. We both had careers, I as an author, and he as…whatever the fuck he did at his family's business. Cooking daily was something we just didn't have time for.

"That's bullshit," Aydin complained as I slurped Lo Mein noodles into my mouth. "The judges don't know what the hell they're doing."

With the entire evening to kill, we decided to pig out and watch *The Great British Bake Off.* Aydin tried to act like he didn't enjoy the food competition shows I adored, but his reaction to his favorite being eliminated said otherwise. I found his denial amusing and completely understood his investment in which baker would win. When my mom discovered my ED at sixteen, she did everything in her power to repair my relationship with food, including finding the best therapist she and Daddy could afford, and making me watch the food competition shows she enjoyed so I could see food and eating being appreciated instead of discouraged. It wasn't until I was eighteen that I truly overcame my ED, and it wasn't until I began dating Aydin during my junior year of college at twenty-one that I started to appreciate my body, because he appreciated my body.

"Nah, they deserved to go," I said, happy my favorite was still in the competition. "They're cool and all, but they aren't the most talented. The judges made the right choice."

He looked at me incredulously. "How could you say that? They had the most unique cakes!"

"Unique doesn't equal good," I shot back, setting my now-empty noodle container on the coffee table.

Crush peered his head up at the noise before deciding it wasn't worth his attention and retreating into his shell.

"Whatever," Aydin grumbled, taking a cue from me and finishing off his food, instead of defending his incorrect opinion.

The rest of the episode was spent in silence, minus our chewing and the occasional grumbled comments. By the time it was done, I was full and reeked of onions, garlic, and soy sauce, because I was incapable of eating Chinese without getting some stains on my clothing. By the time my drink was finished, the flavors lingering on my tongue were starting to mutate into something that required a tooth brushing. With nothing else on the agenda and a big day tomorrow, there was no harm in getting ready for bed early.

"Babe?" I began, continuing when Aydin hummed in acknowledgement. "Can you clear the takeout containers away while I shower?"

"Or…" he said, placing a hand on my thigh. "We can do it together, and I can join you."

"Join me after," I replied with a smile, leaning over to kiss him.

His stubble scraped against my cheek, his thinner lips slightly chapped, a contrast to Denali's smooth skin and moisturized lips. Unlike normal, I didn't feel a pang of disappointment when he pulled away.

"We're doing lip scrubs tonight," I announced, pecking him one last time out of guilt before I stood.

He laughed, the throaty sound amused enough to make me giggle. "You calling my lips chapped, love?"

I shrugged. "Your words, not mine."

His snickers followed me as I breezed into our bedroom, then into our en suite bathroom. Brushing my teeth could wait until after my shower, but I rinsed my mouth out with mouthwash and water to get the pungent aftertaste to disappear. When my breath was minty enough, I turned the water on, stripped down, and hopped into the shower. My 2B waves were able to go 2-4 days without a wash. Since I'd washed my hair yesterday, I skipped that step tonight.

By the time I'd cleansed my face, Aydin entered the bathroom. He, too, washed his mouth out before stripping down and joining me in the shower. Aydin took his fitness seriously, creating a hard body that I loved to look at. A layer of chest hair tapered into a happy trail, leading into neatly trimmed pubes at the base of his cock. He was of average length, but his thickness was perfect, creating a dick I loved to ride.

Grabbing my hips, he pulled me against him. I didn't resist, tilting my head up so our mouths met. Shower sex in my old apartment had been awful, attempted once, then never again. The same couldn't be said about shower sex in a large walk-in shower with a steam generator and a built-in shower bench.

Wealth truly came with an array of benefits.

I trailed my hand along the hard planes of his body until I found his half-hard cock. Wrapping it around his shaft, I maintained a firm grip as I jerked him off, his flesh thickening under my touch as the water rained down on us.

"Fuck, love," he mumbled against my lips, making me smile against his lips.

I stroked slowly, the water acting as a lubricant as I brushed my thumb over his slit, before sliding it back around his shaft. I repeated the movement over and over again, his cock pulsing in my grasp as he grew fully erect, pulsing in my grasp. His hips began to buck forward, pumping into my hand.

"Does that feel good?" I cooed, kissing down to his neck, nibbling and sucking until I was sure a hickey would form.

Let him explain that away to a side-bitch.

"You know it does," he gasped, his breathy tone making my grin widen.

Precum mixed with the water, making the slide of my hand easier. My free hand continued to roam his body until it found his nipples. His pecs were so big, I often joked he could wear a B-cup bra just fine. And regardless of gender, nipples were a sensitive area, proven by the moan I pulled from Aydin when I pinched them.

The steam of the shower rose around us, the heat of the water amplifying the moment. He was just as reactive as Denali had been, and like her, he had no problem taking a more submissive role from time to time. A threesome with them would be a dream, and perhaps abolish the guilt I continued to feel.

"Don't stop," Aydin ordered, his voice rough.

I sped my hand up, squeezing just enough to make him gasp. His heavy balls tightened under the occasional touch of my fingers. His breathing grew more ragged, his body tensing as he neared his peak.

"C'mon, baby," I urged, sucking another hickey into his skin, this time on his shoulder. "Come for me."

With a deep moan, Aydin's cock jerked as spurts of cum shot up, splattering against the tiles before the hot water washed it away. I kept jerking him, milking every last drop of his cum until he was trembling. With a growl, he grabbed my wrist and recaptured my lips, his tongue delving into my mouth as water pounded our bodies.

He walked me back until my back was pressed against the wet tiles. Pulling away, he rested his forehead against mine as his hand dipped between my thighs.

"My turn?" I asked jokingly.

"Duh," he said with a breathy chuckle, trailing his thumb along my slit. "Fucking dripping for me, huh?"

It was true. I was soaked, and not because of the shower. Pleasing my partner always turned me on. Aydin's fingers parted my folds, finding my swollen clit and rubbing it slowly, nearly making my knees buckle as moans escaped me. Years together meant he knew just how to touch me, knowledge he took full advantage of.

As he played with my pussy, his mouth trailed down to my neck, then to my collarbones, where he kissed and sucked, before he went lower. Capturing a nipple between his teeth, he tugged slightly, making me whine as I arched into him, my hands tangling in his wet curls. Encouraged, he switched to the other tit, before dropping to his knees, water flowing over his face as he hooked one of my legs over his shoulder. I gripped his hair, aching with anticipation as his breath washed over my core.

"Shit!" I cried as he sucked on my clit, my moans echoing off the bathroom walls.

Smirking against me, he lapped at my cunt, his tongue plunging inside me to taste me completely, the sensation of his stubble scraping against the sensitive flesh adding to my pleasure. My fingers tightened in his hair, holding him in place as I humped his face. His tongue thrust in and out of me, before flattening to lick a broad stroke to my clit, which he sucked on like it was a lollipop. He repeated those addictive actions a few times, before he focused on my clit and slipped two fingers inside my leaking entrance.

"Right there," I panted as he hit a spot that made my vision blur.

My body trembled, his entire being enveloping my senses as I ascended to my peak. The pressure built, and soon, I was falling apart. My pussy clenched as I came hard, waves of pleasure crashing over me as

I screamed his name. Slick flowed into his mouth, my body shaking.

When Aydin rose from his knees, my breath was still coming into ragged gasps. Within seconds, the shower water washed away the pussy juice clinging to his mouth. His eyes were dark with desire, his dick hard and throbbing. Strong hands gripped my thighs and lifted me off the damp floor as if I weighed nothing. He was only two or so inches taller than Denali, so I bet she could handle me so effortlessly, too.

Then again, I'd enjoyed subbing her out. There was something addictive about making such a dominant woman submit to me as I made her all apart. Thinking about her during such an intimate moment made me feel guilty, but as much as I enjoyed Aydin's sex skills, I wanted another round with Denali. Preferably, one that followed a proper date.

I shook my head, trying to force Denali out of it, so I could focus on my sexy fiancé, who was right there and attainable. I saw the question burning in Aydin's gaze, so I quickly wrapped my legs around his waist, my arms looping around his neck for extra support. His features relaxed, and he pressed my back against the tiled wall. The surface bit into my skin, but the water and heated steam had warmed them

"Fuck me, Aydin," I begged, wanting to come again and forget about Denali.

Fucking her had been a mistake, for so many reasons.

"I plan to," he growled, shifting his hips so the head of his cock nudged against my entrance.

My pussy was drenched and relaxed from my climax, easily welcoming him when he slid into me in one thrust, burying himself to the hilt.

"Yes," I moaned, my nails digging into his shoulders as he stretched me out.

He was deliciously thick, and his cock was long enough to hit my G-spot, a benefit of the position we'd found ourselves in. With each thrust of his hips, my vision whited. The pleasure I felt was intense, and made my head go empty.

"Always so good for me," he groaned, his forehead resting against mine as he fucked me hard, moving in deep strokes that left me aching for more.

My hips rocked with his, and I grinded down to take his as deep as possible. I leaned forward to capture his mouth in a kiss, wanting us to be as connected as possible. Our tongues tangled as muffled moans left us both. When he broke the kiss, he nipped at my jaw and earlobe, one hand releasing a hip to brace against the wall. His cock plunged in and out of my slick core, the sounds of our coupling filling the space and mixing with the rush of shower water and our sounds of pleasure.

"Come with me," he rasped, my walls fluttering and gripping his shaft like a vice.

The coil in my body built fast, eager to obey his request. I was the first to shatter, my second orgasm ripping through me. It pushed him over the edge, and with one more hard thrust, his semen flooded me, the little implant in my arm allowing for worry-free creampies. He kept a tight hold on me, grinding slowly until we were both overstimulated.

Slowly, I lowered my legs, but stayed against him, my knees feeling weak. The water washed away evidence of what just transpired, and my pussy was pleasantly sore.

"I love fucking you," he praised, grabbing my washcloth and lathering it with soap.

"I love how you fuck me," I replied hoarsely, sighing as he began to gently scrub me.

We basked in each other's presence as he washed me. When it was time for him to wash himself, I took the washcloth from him and returned the favor. It was a quiet intimacy I missed, and it was just as enjoyable as sex itself. Somewhere along the way, we'd drifted apart, but right now, it felt as if we'd found our way back to one another.

Chapter Ten

DENALI

Despite my vow to distance myself from Estelle, I found myself unable to get her out of my head, leading me to purchase one of her books to distract myself. As a teenager, I'd adored books, but after my brief stint in the military and subsequent prison sentence, reading became a rarity. Even after I was released and joined the Harlots, I never reclaimed my title as an avid reader. However, I made an exception for Estelle, purchasing her newest release, Thricebound, the day after my confrontation with Val.

Within three days, I'd finished it.

I hadn't been expecting a high-fantasy world heavily inspired by ancient Egypt, a period I always found fascinating, so that came as a pleasant surprise. The magic and political drama enthralled me, even if I couldn't stand one of the male leads. The author's note revealed she'd based the heroine on the final Pharaoh of Egypt, Cleopatra the 7th, and what would've happened if she and Mark Antony won their disastrous campaign against Octavian, just for the leading lady to fall in love with the enemy.

I enjoyed the book so fucking much that I was dragging my ass to a book signing she was hosting at a local bookstore. I tried telling myself that I just wanted to snag a physical, signed copy, which wasn't a lie, but it wasn't the complete truth. Catching a glimpse of Estelle would be nice, as she still hadn't left my mind. No matter how I tried, no matter how much I reminded myself that she was fucking engaged, I couldn't banish her from my thoughts.

"Where are you going?" Seline 'Kinder' Martin, our youngest probate, asked as I passed where she was lounging on the couch.

She was a pretty girl, with light caramel skin, deep brown eyes, and kinky hair she kept in Senegalese twists. At eighteen, she was too young for me, but she was an undeniable looker. She was also a snarky little bitch who knew how to get under people's skin. Her ties to Geri meant she got some special treatment, causing feuds with some of the other prospects and probates that only made her more of a bitch. Like her mentor's moniker, her road name was a jab at her age, because she was far from kind. Karma found it amusing to call her a kindergartener when she started hanging around at sixteen. That name stuck and was shortened to Kinder.

"Book signing," I answered, making her perk up.

"Can I come?" she asked, lowering her phone to give me her best puppy-dog eyes. "I don't have shit to do today."

I shrugged. "I don't care. It's at The Book Haven in downtown."

At my flippant reply, her shoulders slumped, and her lips pursed. "Just fucking say you don't want me to go."

"I just said I didn't care," I said flatly, trying and failing to hide my annoyance.

"It's public property, so you're free to fucking go if you want to, Kinder."

"My bike's with Rainbow right now," she said, referring to Karma's 22-year-old daughter, who was eccentric as hell and adored fixing up bikes and vehicles. Looking at me through her lashes, she continued. "So, I'll have to ride with you."

I pretended not to notice how sultry her tone became. What was it with young bitches and me?

"Fine," I said, sitting on an armchair. "You have ten minutes to get ready before I ride out."

The smile she gave me made her look deceptively sweet. As she walked away, I noticed an extra sway in her hips that wasn't present when others were around. I quickly averted my gaze, not wanting to give her the wrong idea. My attempts to show kindness to her over the years had already been taken the wrong way. She may have been a tough little bitch, but she was young, and it took a village to tend to the young. It was why, despite my disinterest in her obvious flirting attempts, I continued to engage with her.

Maybe one day, she'd get a fucking clue and leave me alone.

The bookstore was already packed when we arrived. Following the sound of music made Estelle's table easy to find, though the long as shit line meant we had to wait until we got to see her. Based on the fuckton of posts she made, each attendee was entitled to a swag bag, a picture, and a signed book. Her fans loved her dedication to them, but I wasn't interested in anything but my book and seeing Estelle.

"All this for one fucking book?" Kinder grumbled as she looked around, her twists pulled back in a ponytail, showing off her giant hoop earrings. "You could just get it off Amazon, y'know, and skip this shit."

Irritation flared in me. "I don't fucking want an Amazon copy, Kinder. I want a signed copy."

"Whatever," she said with a huff. "I'm going to look around while you stand here, doing jackshit because you're picky."

Before I could reply and tell her to watch her fucking mouth—I was still an officer, after all—she was leaving the line and disappearing behind a wall of bookcases. Shaking my head, I looked forward. I was in a good mood, so I'd let her disrespect slide with just a warning.

My annoyance towards Kinder was replaced with anticipation when I saw there were only two more people ahead of me. Estelle still hadn't noticed me, so I quickly ran a hand over my hair to tame any strays, patted any wrinkles out of my plain black T-shirt, and smoothed out my black jeans and leather jacket. Taking out my phone, I opened the front camera and bared my teeth, ensuring that none of my tinted lip balm had stained my pearly whites, and that my nose was booger-free.

One person ahead of me.

Putting my phone back in my pocket, I fished out a piece of gum, storing the wrapper in the compartment of my jeans and popping the minty stick in my mouth. Call me extra, but I wanted to look presentable. After this, I didn't know when—or if—I'd seek Estelle out again, and I wanted her to have a good parting memory of me. Despite staying away from her being the best choice, the way I left things off was shitty, and Estelle deserved better than that.

I nearly skipped to the table when it was my turn. She still hadn't noticed me, not looking up as she signed a book.

"And who should I make this out to?" she asked in friendly tones, pausing to look up at me.

When she did, her eyes widened, her smile being wiped away as her mouth became an 'O'.

"Denali," I said simply, grinning at her surprise. "Put whatever message you want, babe."

"Babe?" a man echoed, drawing my attention to the figure behind her that I hadn't been paying much attention to. "Do you know my fiancée, or are you just friendly with strangers, Denali?"

Irritation slid into me at the casual use of my name. Before I could tell him to mind his fucking business, Estelle spoke.

"Aydin, be nice," she chastised, frowning at him. "Denali and I are old friends. I've known her since I was seven."

I smirked at him, her defense of me making me stand taller. Examining him, I decided he was handsome by most standards, obviously taller than me with a decent physique. Something about him was familiar, but I couldn't put my finger on what.

"Funny," he said, a phony smile on his face. "I've never heard you mention her before."

"It's complicated," she replied, before refocusing on me, her pretty smile making a grand return. "It's nice seeing you, Denali. I wished I'd known you were coming. I would've given you a VIP pass."

I waved her off. "I was just stopping by. I read Thricebound. Shit was good, so I wanted a real copy of it."

Pride gleamed in her eyes. "Thank you. I watched a Netflix documentary on Cleopatra and got inspired. Her life was so interesting. You used to like Ancient Egypt, right? I remember Grandma had a stack of books on Ancient Egypt in her old home, reserved for you."

Knowing she remembered such a mundane fact made butterflies spawn in my stomach.

"Sure did," I confirmed, the warmth I felt being destroyed when fuckface— Aydin—cleared his throat.

"Why don't you introduce us, babe? Then I can take y'all's picture, and you can move on to the next fan, yeah?"

My lips thinned at his bossy ass tone. Yes, other fans were behind me, but it hadn't even been five minutes since I walked up to the table. Her posts made it clear long wait times may be present, and people still showed up, so they knew what they were getting themselves into.

"No need to rush us," I said, fantasies of punching him running through my mind. "We're just catching up."

"If you two are friends, you can catch up after."

"Aydin, please, not now," Estelle pleaded, heightening my dislike of that bastard. "And not with someone who came to support me. If you're getting tired, go sit down instead of lashing out."

"I'm not a goddamn toddler—"

"Then stop acting like one," I snapped, making both of them look at me.

I met Aydin's glare with one of my own. I was never one to back down from an altercation, and if he kept trying me, he'd learn I wasn't one to play with.

"Both of you, get your asses off your shoulders," Estelle ordered, drawing my attention back to her. "Aydin, this is Denali Bernard, an old friend. Denali, this is Aydin Osman, my fiancé. You two know each other now, so be nice."

The use of my full name wasn't appreciated, but staying mad at Estelle was something I was never capable of.

"Yes, ma'am," I teased, ignoring Aydin's grumbling.

The fucker looked so familiar, but I'm sure I'd remember meeting such an asshole.

Nodding, Estelle grabbed one of the swag bags from under the table and placed the book in it. "Good. Ready for your picture now?"

"Sure am."

Aydin raised the Polaroid camera around his neck as I made my way behind the table. I crouched down so our heads were side by side, smirking at the camera, the tightening of Aydin's jaw amusing the fuck out of me. When the photo was printed, he shook it out, and I returned to my spot.

"It was nice seeing you, Denali," Estelle said, looking at me through her lashes. "We have to get together again sometime."

I licked my lips. It didn't take a genius to realize she wasn't talking about meeting in a stuffy bookstore, but fucking in secret again. The offer was tempting, though I knew declining would be the best option. Today was supposed to be a goodbye, not something to add fuel to the sparks flying between us.

"We'll see," I said simply, deciding that it was best not to promise anything.

"Here," Aydin snapped, handing me the picture.

I took it from him, scowling as he ran his hands through his hair, pushing it out of his eyes...fuck.

Oh, fuck.

Fuckity fuck fuck.

Either Aydin had a twin, or the Turks' broker was Estelle's fiancé.

Chapter Eleven

DENALI

"Everything okay, Denali?" Estelle asked, as I stood there like a dumbass, shocked out of my fucking mind.

More than shocked, I was scared. Not of Aydin, I'd blow that fucker away without a second thought. No, I was scared *for* Estelle. Withholding this information from Prez wasn't an option, but it pained me to know that Essie would become a target. I'd bet money she didn't know, but ignorance or not, it wouldn't prevent her life from being in danger.

Clearing my throat, I nodded. "Fucking perfect, babe. I'll be seeing you—"

"Denali!" Kinder called, interrupting my exit. "Finally made it to the finish line, huh?"

She walked to me, and despite being shorter, she reached up and rested her elbow on my shoulder when she was at my side.

"Got your book?" she continued, not noticing the accusation burning in Estelle's eyes.

Her smile had disappeared, replaced by narrowed eyes, her gaze flickering between me and Kinder.

"Yeah, *kid*, I did," I said, shrugging her off.

The use of 'kid'—code for untouchable, for obvious reasons—got Estelle to relax, though it made Kinder scowl.

"I'm not a—"

"Hello," Estelle said, interrupting Kinder's coming complaint. "Would you like a book and picture, too?"

"Nope, just here with her. She fucking insisted on coming here for a signed copy," Kinder said, her tone shockingly polite.

Her eyes flicked to Aydin. They widened, and she looked back at me. Before she said shit she shouldn't, we had to leave, pronto.

"Nice seeing you, Estelle," I said, grabbing Kinder's elbow. "Take care, okay?"

"Same to you, Denali," she replied, looking at where I touched Kinder.

Nodding, I pulled Kinder away, not releasing her until we were out of the bookstore.

"That's him," she said, putting the pieces together far quicker than I had. "The author bitch is engaged to a Turk."

"Don't call her that," I said sharply, storming to my bike. "She doesn't know he's mafia. I'm sure of it."

"You know her," she stated, her displeasure clear from her tone.

"We're friends. I've known that woman since she was seven years old. She doesn't know," I repeated, praying to a God I stopped believing in long ago that my words were true.

Either way, she'd become a target, but knowing meant certain death. Worst of all, because of my affiliation and history with Estelle, Karma might make me kill her instead of Chains, so I could prove my loyalty.

This was so fucking bad.

Of all the men, why'd she have to choose him? Of all the millions of Turkish people in the world, how come fate made her end up with one in the fucking Turkish Mafia?

"We have to tell Karma," Kinder said, stating the obvious as we hopped onto Lobster.

"No shit," I grumbled, before starting Lobster up, the roar killing the conversation.

Riding was always therapeutic to me, but today, not even that could ease my mind.

Estelle

Typically, following a book-signing, I popped open a bottle of champagne to celebrate a job well done. But this time, as soon as I got home, I went straight for the tequila. I didn't even bother with a glass, instead taking a deep swig from the bottle.

"Why the hell are you drinking so early, Estelle?" Aydin asked sharply as he emptied the contents of his pockets onto the marble countertop.

He was still riding the asshole train, it seemed.

"Because you were a prick," I snapped, taking another swig, because fuck him.

Aydin normally accompanied me to my book signings, and he was usually an awesome assistant, helping me set up and taking pictures with me and my fans. Once or twice, he'd even served as my model. This book signing, though? He ruined it, plain and simple. He threw shade to everyone who stepped to the table, rushed them, and was an all-around asshole. His interaction with Denali took the cake, and while neither of them noticed, the way my beloved fans had been looking at us mortified me.

Never before had he shown his ass in such a massive manner, and certainly never at a career event.

"Your behavior reflects on me, and being an asshole to my fans isn't acceptable," I continued, considering issuing an apology online to my fans for Aydin's shitty behavior. "I mean seriously, Aydin, what were you—"

"Did you fuck Denali?" he blurted, interrupting my berating.

Yes, a fact that left me conflicted.

"What the fuck?" I exploded, because he'd been acting a fool before Denali even entered the building. "Why the hell would you think that? I told you, she's an old friend, and you have no room to judge how I interact with my friends, especially after you cheated."

"That isn't a denial."

"I'm not denying what doesn't need to be stated!" I yelled, at my wits' end.

Everything had been going so well between me and Aydin. It pained me that today, of all the days, was the one he chose to be a possessive, jealous asshole. Most of all, it hurt to realize that the man I'd fallen in love with might not have ever existed. I was seeing aspects of his personality I never had before, ones I desperately wished would go away. It made the ring on my finger feel like a ton of lead.

"And Denali had nothing to do with your behavior, Aydin, because you were rude to almost everyone from the start. If you woke up on the wrong side of the bed, you should've stayed the fuck home."

"Then you would've been bitching about me not helping, because I can never fucking win with you."

I recoiled as if slapped. "Okay, whatever the hell has gotten into you, get it out and talk to me like a mature adult. What you're not gonna do is walk around here like a moody menstruating teen, because you won't open your fucking mouth and talk to me!"

"It's my apartment," he said, continuing to be a rancid dick instead of heeding my advice. "I pay the rent, so I'll walk around however the fuck I please, woman."

"Both of our names are on the lease, so suck a fucking dick, Aydin," I shot back, going for a third swig of alcohol, this one to stop me from killing my fiancé.

His smile was vicious. "You'd like that, huh, with all the weird gay shit you write. I mean—"

"Finish that sentence at your own peril," I said in low tones, wondering why he was so determined to hurt me today. Yesterday had been a dream, whereas today was a massive headache. "I told you already, if something's bothering you, talk to me instead of lashing out blindly. Your behavior right now is unacceptable."

He took a step forward. I cocked a brow, daring him to continue this fuckery. Instead of saying or doing anything, he grumbled something under his breath in Turkish and stalked to our bedroom, slamming the door behind him. Alone, I sat at the island, my head pounding, a combination of drinking on an empty stomach and arguing with my fiancé.

Since the beginning of our relationship, Aydin had shown instances of intense jealousy. At the start, I stupidly found it endearing and loved the possessive sex it led to. Likewise, Aydin hadn't hidden that the books I wrote weren't his cup of tea, but he'd been respectful about it, so I hadn't cared. We even joked about it at times. But as I sat there, half-drunk and devastated, moments that I once brushed off replayed in my head, red flags I hadn't seen now obvious. Why hadn't I seen them before? Was it youth, or willful ignorance?

Planting my face in my hands, I allowed my tears to flow. This engagement had been a nightmare, and it was only getting worse.

How would he be when—if—we married? Would his behavior escalate further, or would he finally mellow out? On the off chance that the latter occurred, I wasn't sure I'd be able to tough it out and find out. We'd been arguing constantly, he refused to compromise over anything about our wedding, he'd cheated first, and he was awful at today's signing. The warning signs were piling up, and I'd be a dumb bitch to ignore them.

I'd give him until the morning to apologize. If he did, I'd suggest couples therapy and warn him he had one more time to fuck up before I walked away. If he didn't, this would be my final straw, and I'd call off our engagement. Even with him becoming a massive asshole, even with our infidelity, the thought pained me.

On the bright side, being single meant I could pursue Denali without guilt.

As soon as the thought came, I pushed it away, guilt hitting me. How could I hold cheating against him, when I'd done the same thing? Perhaps it was a sign that our relationship was beyond saving.

When my tears dried, I stood, remembering that I needed to feed Crush.

Fuck, if we broke up, who'd get Crush? We both loved the turtle. Maybe we'd need a custody arrangement.

The absurd thought made me laugh, the sound devolving into a sob as I fixed Crush's food. Greens, a handful of berries, and a chopped sardine made up the main components of his meal. Freeze-dried treats that were comprised of shrimp, mealworms, and crickets went on the side, reptile calcium dust with vitamin D3 poured over them before the critters joined the bowl. Preparing Crush's dinner was nice, a dose of normalcy when things felt so very upturned.

"Here you go, boy," I whispered as I placed the bowl in his terrarium. "Eat up. It might be your last meal with mommy and daddy together. You'd choose me if I leave, right, boy?"

Crush didn't look up once as I quietly rambled to him, his food more important than his mother's drunk devastation. Aydin's phone began to buzz, but I ignored it, staying by Crush's terrarium until he was done. When he was, I took the bowl from him and returned to the kitchen.

Aydin's phone was still buzzing with text messages.

Swallowing, I grabbed the tequila and took another swig, then grabbed his phone. In the back of my mind, I knew what I would find, but seeing that he was still sexting Alex pissed me off, especially after his show today. And seeing that she referenced them sleeping together last week—presumably the night I went out with my friends—made the room spin.

How dare he ruin my event, because he was paranoid I'd fuck over him as he'd done me?

Perhaps, if today had gone well, I would laugh at the irony of us cheating on each other on the same night, and calmly ponder if the marriage would go forward. But the day had been shit, so I stormed into the room and threw the phone at Aydin's stupid face.

"Fuck!" he screamed when the device hit his forehead, before bouncing onto the mattress. He shot up, swaying on his feet. "What the fuck is wrong with you, Estelle?"

"You fucked Alex, you rancid motherfucker," I growled, twisting off my engagement ring and throwing it at his feet. "That was why you acted like such an asshole today, because you knew you were dead fucking wrong. And, *fucking and*, you're still texting her! You sent her a dick pic this morning!"

"Put the ring back on, Estelle," he ordered, as if he had the right.

"Fuck you," I yelled, kicking the ring under the bed to accentuate my point. "We're over. I forgave you once for cheating, but I won't let that shit slide again. I'm getting a fucking hotel tonight, and coming for my shit tomorrow, you miserable dickbag."

I started towards the dresser. With a growl, Aydin grabbed my shoulders, his fingers digging into my skin as he forced me to sit on the bed. He ignored my yelp, glaring down at me. His eyes, those warm, beautiful amber eyes, had iced over. I had so many more words for him, but something told me silence was the best option.

"You aren't doing shit, because you aren't leaving me. Go fuck someone else if you want to get even, but you're staying here, putting my ring back on, and becoming my wife."

"Or else what?" I whispered, resisting the urge to tell him I had already fucked someone else. I had survival instincts, after all.

All aggression suddenly left him, his shoulders slumping as his gaze grew misty. "I'd fall apart without you, Estelle. I need you, love. We can work through this, just don't leave me."

It was so tempting to give in, but I had self-respect. Clearly, the more I let him get away with, the more he'd do.

"No, Aydin—"

"I'll stop using," he blurted, taking me aback. "I've done coke on and off since last year, Estelle, and you didn't even notice because you were too consumed with your fucking books, but I'll stop, I swear."

His revelations shocked me, before outrage and anger set in.

"You're fucking lying," I hissed, unable to believe he'd craft such a lie. "I've been around addicts, Aydin, and you don't show any goddamn signs—"

"I'll show you the texts between my dealer and me. It's how I met Alex. She gets me free coke—"

"Just stop!" I exclaimed, stumbling to my feet, my intense headache making standing steadily hard. "Stop, Aydin. We're over, okay? I love you, I do, but we clearly don't work together."

"Just look, Estelle, please," he said, grabbing his phone, showing me the screen as he went to his contacts.

Clicking on someone named Mr. Gardener, he handed me the phone, allowing me to scroll through dozens of text messages related to drugs. More specifically, Aydin's drug use. My heart dropped. I didn't know how to respond, but suddenly, his behavior made more sense. After three months sober, he was craving a hit, and the absence of a high was bringing out his worst self. Aunt Mauve was like that. A sweetheart when her need for drugs was satisfied, but hell on wheels when she was sober, lashing out at anyone and willing to do anything for a hit.

"How come you never told me?" I whispered, handing him the phone.

He shrugged, pocketing his phone. "I wanted to see if you noticed. You didn't, and I didn't have to hide it when you traveled without me."

I was silent as I processed his words. They still felt like a manipulative lie, but the texts dated back to eighteen months ago, three months before he proposed to me.

However, his reason for keeping his drug use from me only reinforced my theory that I didn't truly know Aydin.

"Why?"

"Stress from the new role my parents gave me," he whispered, shame twisting his features. "I couldn't deal, but I didn't want to fucking disappoint them, love. Since the engagement, you haven't been going on fucking trips as much, so I haven't been getting my hits, and it's driving me crazy. I'm sorry for lashing out, baby, because I love you so much…"

He was manipulating me. Even if his words were true, his reveal was tactical. But even knowing this, I couldn't bring myself to continue to fight with him. He needed help, not scorn.

"I love you too," I said honestly, sitting on the edge of the bed. "But this has been unacceptable. The cheating, the arguments, your behavior today. If you want us to work, you're going to rehab, and you're cutting contact with your dealer, and that bitch *Alex*."

The words felt so hollow because he'd promised before to stop fucking with her, yet he continued sexting her. As a child, I swore to myself I'd never end up like my aunt, with a man who took her for granted, and was obviously toxic. As a grown woman, leaving Aydin now made me feel like a monster. I'd let him heal, then break things off.

"Okay," he agreed, nodding furiously. "Okay, Estelle, whatever you want."

He retrieved his phone again, ensuring I could see the screen as he deleted both offending contacts. Looking at me for approval, he tossed his phone on the bed when I nodded.

"You're going to put my ring back on," he began, bending down and quickly retrieving it. "We'll pretend today never happened and move on from today, okay?"

"Okay," I parroted, holding my hand out so he could slide the ring back on.

Satisfied, he kissed my forehead, ignoring my slight wince.

"I'm going to take a bath," I said when he pulled back, hoping soaking in hot bubbles calmed me down.

My legs felt like steel as I walked to the bathroom. When I reached it, the door slammed behind me, the wood a barrier from the stranger who'd invaded my Aydin.

Part Three

Switchin' Up

Chapter Twelve

Estelle

Nothing seemed the same since Aydin revealed his drug use. I analyzed every interaction between the two of us, scouring my mind for signs that my put-together fiancé had an addiction. Every instance of increasingly erratic behavior and outbursts had me cringing. I'd chalked it up to stress from our engagement, which occurred soon after I moved in with him. Once he adjusted,

I thought he'd go back to normal. Never did I think drugs were the source of his behavior.

I didn't know how to feel. My emotions were haywire, and the guilt I felt over my one-night stand with Denali had morphed into guilt that I was still thinking about leaving Aydin. I'd seen how drugs had ravaged someone's life, and his recent behavior had me reconsidering everything. Mama shared how she footed the bill for Aunt Mauve to go to rehab after Michelle was born, just for her to relapse months later, and never kick her addiction. Would Aydin be the same way, in and out of rehab, as he battled his demons? If that was the case, I wasn't sure I could do it.

Call me a selfish bitch, but Michelle and her sisters had suffered due to their parents' addictions. Everything else took a backseat to their vices, hardening all three girls before they'd reached the age of eighteen, and Michelle had the toughest life of all her siblings. Warrior had saved her from becoming like her mother, and in turn, she'd saved her siblings from going through what she had.

Sighing, I continued scrolling on my phone, trying to silence my thoughts. Aydin was on a business trip to New York. His aunt and uncle ran the NYC branch of their business, while his parents managed all dealings in The Delta. Why'd they'd gone so far away instead of settling in Boston or Philadelphia, I didn't know, and never cared. In fact, I used to be grateful that they'd chosen Memphis as their base of operation. Without that choice, I never would've met Aydin. I was still grateful and still loved their son. I just wasn't sure if I was still *in* love with him.

Looking at brain-rot TikToks wasn't clearing my mind, nor were posts from my fans or looking at IG baddies doing various things. Now that I was secure in my size 12/14 body, I took inspiration from women who looked different than me, admiring their clothes, hair, makeup, posing, etc., and simping for a select few. But absolutely nothing, not even pretty women, put my mind at ease.

Not only was I guilty regarding my changing feelings toward Aydin, but I was so fucking worried about him.

In NYC, he'd have access to God knows what and might come back more addicted than he'd been before. No matter how things turned out between us, I didn't want that for him. With or without me, I wanted him to thrive and make good choices that would lead to a long life, not a short and turbulent one.

Social media was taking my mind off diddly shit, but I was still scrolling, scrolling, scrolling. The hum and drum of it was hard to kick, especially when life seemed extra bleak. If only my brain would shut the fuck up, so I could enjoy cute animal videos that may or may not be AI, outfit inspirations, and people doing dumb shit.

After another fifteen minutes of scrolling, I came across a post that caught my eye. Pausing, I reread the flyer on my screen multiple times, gnawing on my bottom lip as I looked over the details of the Royal Harlots back-to-school drive. Their charity work was as well-known as their criminal deeds. All the good things they did for the people of Memphis made law-abiding citizens tolerate their presence, despite the havoc that often came along with the leather-clad ladies.

I checked my calendar, seeing that it was, in fact, September 1st. The event started an hour ago, and I had more than enough unopened office supplies to gather up and bring. Pencils and pens, loose-leaf paper, unused notebooks. If I hurried, I could be ready with things to offer the kiddos within an hour.

And, more importantly, catch a glimpse of Denali.

She might've changed a lot, but I knew she'd still jump at the opportunity to help underprivileged kids. Or, she should, seeing as she was in that position once, too.

My mind decided, I finally tossed my phone aside and stood, feeling eager for the first time since Aydin put everything into doubt.

The drive was being held at a local church, who were partners at the event. Something was amusing about holy folk and outlaw bikers working together, but I had the sense to keep that to myself. Only Denali would protect me if I pissed them off, and she'd be vastly outnumbered.

"Welcome to the drive!" a short brunette greeted, easily identified as a part of the church-goers with a single look. "Donating or picking up?"

"Donating," I said, holding up the bags I threw all the shit in. "Just wanted to give back to my community."

"Aww, that's great. You can set the stuff over there. Those lovely ladies will sort it out," she said, pointing to a table brimming with supplies.

I licked my lips when I saw Denali. She wore her cut, but her curls were in a ponytail, and her shorts revealed her endless legs. The memory of the heaven between her thighs had my mouth watering, and as I approached her, I couldn't help but fantasize about those legs being wrapped around my waist as I introduced her to my double-ended strap-on.

I recognized some of the women who'd been sitting with Denali at the bar. One in particular, a looker with tanned skin, hazel eyes, and a wealth of rich brown hair, was right by her side, nudging and laughing with her. Jealousy rose up in me, but I swallowed it down, reminding myself that these women were a sisterhood. Camaraderie was to be expected, and I still had a fiancé.

The laughter stopped when the woman saw me, her expression going neutral as she looked me up and down. She nudged Denali with her elbow, pointing with her chin when she looked at her.

"Your girl is here, Everest," she said, her words teasing, but her tone anything but.

Denali made a face at her. The two exchanged a glance, one that held many unspoken words and had me shifting uncomfortably.

"Go see if Siren needs help, Val," Denali finally said, turning to me, her features relaxing when her friend walked away. "Didn't know you were coming."

"Neither did I," I said honestly, holding up the bags. "But I have so much extra shit, and nothing else to do, so here I am."

The corners of her lips quirked up as she took my stuff. "Happy you did. Always nice to see you, Essie."

Her words pleased me to no end. Twisting my engagement ring, I returned her smile. "I feel the same way about you."

"What'd you bring?" she asked, eyes flickering between my face and my ring.

"Notebooks, paper, pens, pencils. Basic shit."

She hummed, holding out her hand. Sparks flew when our hands brushed, and I swallowed, chanting Aydin's name in my head. He was my fiancé. My future, whereas she was my past, no matter how blurred the lines were getting.

I watched as Denali quickly sorted through everything, nodding in approval. "Good shit, Essie."

"You know you can call me Estelle."

"You used to hate your name," she reminded me. "You outgrew that shit?"

"I'd be miserable if I hadn't," I said, too overjoyed that she remembered such a basic fact about me.

Just as I was about to say my goodbyes, Denali's friend, Val, made her return, grinning widely.

"Talked to Prez for you," she announced, barely sparing me a glance. "She said you're free to take off with the redhead, if you want."

"Estelle," Denali said, her tone sharp. She looked at me. "It's up to you, *Essie*."

I shrugged, trying to play nonchalant, when my heart was pounding out of control. "As long as you call me Estelle, we can go wherever you want."

Her laugh made me giggle. Val looked between us, and when Denali started toward me, Val grabbed her wrist.

"Just remember what we talked about. 'Kay, Everest?"

Denali snatched her hand away from her. "Can't forget it, Valentina."

Without another look at her friend, she placed a hand on my lower back and guided me toward the parking lot.

"So, where do you wanna go?" she asked when we were out of earshot of Valentina.

"On a date," I said without hesitation. "You owe me one, remember?"

She paused, looking down at me with a cocked brow. "I remember the terms being that we both had to be single."

"He's out of town."

"Trouble in paradise?"

Fucking understatement of the century.

"You can say that," I said breezily, trying to pretend it didn't hurt me. "And besides, what does it matter to you?"

"It doesn't."

"So, then, what do you say?"

She considered me, huffed out a laugh, then nodded. "C'mon, brat. I have a place in mind."

DENALI

I couldn't fucking believe Estelle turned up at the school drive. The book signing was supposed to be my goodbye to her, even if her asshole of a fiancé tainted the moment. But there she was, looking so goddamn pretty in her floral sundress, red hair cascading around her shoulders. She was a vision, a beauty that the ancients would've made statues of. It was part of the reason I was happy to see her. She was easy on the eyes, and most of all, I wanted a do-over of my botched goodbye, even if Val had pissed me the fuck off and nearly ruined this one. I'd put a bug in her ear to not fuck with Estelle.

Scowling, I started toward my bike but halted when I realized Essie wasn't by me.

Estelle, who was halfway to her fucking car, had the same realization. We looked over our shoulders and met each other's gazes.

"My car is over there."

"Fucking 'A'," I responded, wondering what the fuck *her* car had to do with *my* ass. I nodded toward where my baby chilled under a tree. "My bike's over there. That's what we're using to get to the restaurant."

Estelle glanced around. We weren't in the best neighborhood, so I knew before she told me that she was concerned about her car.

"Let's grab a bite, then I will bring you back for your car before we do anything else."

She smirked at me. "You're getting ahead of yourself. I might have plans later."

I pretended the prospect didn't annoy me. She'd been the one who wanted me to leave the drive to entertain her. Her time was mine. "Then we'll decide if we extend our date in a bit. Right now, get on my bike, or it will end now."

"Fine," she huffed, and sashayed toward me, her hair and tits bouncing.

As we rode to the restaurant and she held onto me, I realized how much I enjoyed her company. How much I'd missed having someone familiar, someone who knew me before I became Everest. However, the type of vulnerability I risked sent my guard up. Suddenly, I wasn't in the fucking mood to talk. I didn't know inane bullshit to talk about that wouldn't delve underneath everything else. I could use the time to question her about her motherfucker.

Or I could double down and stay broody and silent, while swearing we didn't have shit to talk about. The date would end, she would leave, and I could go back to the clubhouse. She and I could return to our separate lives.

I pretended the thought wasn't a crushing one. Her fiancé was on our shitlist, some members were already campaigning for her downfall, and Karma had ordered silence. Distancing myself from her was the best thing I could do to protect her. And maybe advise her to leave that man, since I couldn't outright tell her that he was a dangerous motherfucker to be attached to. As much as I cared about Estelle, I refused to disobey my Prez.

"You're silent," she noted, after we were seated at the restaurant I took her to.

Real Souf Meats was a grilling restaurant that specialized in different meat cooking techniques found across the Southern United States. Karma took me there when I first came to Memphis, and I've loved the place ever since.

"What's on your mind?" Estelle continued.

"You," I said honestly, giving my attention to the décor.

The checkered tablecloths were a charming touch, the lighting was warm, and the wooden interior gave a rustic vibe. In the back, there was a small stage, where live music was performed on weekends.

She blinked. "Me?"

"Did I stutter? You have a man, Estelle, and a great life. You shouldn't be slumming it with me."

She lifted her chin in defiance, forever a hard-headed brat. "You didn't feel that way when we fucked."

"Sex is different from an affair."

Call me a homewrecker, but I didn't care if I slept with a taken woman. A relationship with one, though, was out of the question. It came with too much drama, and if Estelle were anyone else, I would've told her to kick rocks.

"It isn't an affair. Aydin said I could sleep with other people."

Further proof he was a trifling motherfucker. Estelle was a catch, and if he wasn't cheating himself, he wouldn't want to risk someone sweeping his woman off her feet.

"Why have a roster when I could just have you?" she continued, replacing my outrage with offense.

"Wow, being your side chick. I'm honored," I said, sarcasm dripping from every word. Sighing, I started to stand. The impromptu date was already a bust. "C'mon. I'll take you back to your car."

"Don't do that," she snapped, glaring up at me. She took a deep breath, sounding calmer when she spoke again. "At least let's eat our food before we go."

I considered her for a moment, then nodded, plopping back down. "Fine."

We were silent until the waiter brought the appetizers out. He made googly eyes at us both, and we each ignored him. When his eyes dipped too low, I cleared my throat and lifted a brow, which got him to fuck off.

"Things aren't going well with Aydin," Estelle said when we were halfway through our onion rings. "I love him, but he isn't who I thought he was."

Fuck. Did she know? Had he told her he was mafia?

"What does that mean?"

"Promise you won't tell anyone if I vent?"

"My lips are sealed, Essie," I said gently, as if my heart wasn't racing.

Ignorance was the only thing that would save her. If she knew, all bets were off.

"Aydin…does drugs. I just found out. We've been fighting so much lately. I don't know if I even want to marry him."

Relief flooded me, before worry swept back through me. Druggies were motherfuckers.

"Is he hurting you. Physically?" I clarified, because his actions were clearly hurting her.

"Not yet?"

She didn't fucking know? "What the fuck—"

"We both know what drug use does to a person, Denali," she interrupted. "I saw it with my aunt. You saw it with your father.

I'm already seeing it with him. He cheated first. Sexted a woman named Alex, and slept with her the same night you and I reunited. It's why I'm doubting everything."

Anger swept through me at the pain on her beautiful face. The motherfucker should've worshipped Estelle, not fuck over her. That alone was enough to get him fucked up.

"Why are you staying with him, babe?" I asked as gently as I could. "You deserve better, and you have a thriving fucking career to think of."

"I know that, but up until recently, he's helped me with my career, and I love him."

"Pay someone to help you, and love isn't always enough," I pointed out, thinking of my mother.

She claimed to love my father, but it hadn't stopped their relationship from being the definition of toxic, resulting in ample abuse.

"I'm starting to realize that now," she whispered, looking so fucking pitiful. "He says he'll get into rehab, but he hasn't even started looking, and brushes me off whenever I come to him with programs I found. It's like he doesn't want to get help. I love him, I do, but I'm not sure if I'm still in love with him, and that makes me feel so low. I just...I just wish he'd never changed. I'd wish he never started using, and that I never learned everything I did about him."

"Is that why you're here?" I asked, hurt at the prospect of being used to relieve her tension. "To distract yourself?"

Even if forever wasn't in the cards, I didn't like being used.

"It's why I came to the drive," she confessed. "But it isn't the only reason. I've liked you since I was a little girl," she whispered, pink rising in her cheeks. "This," she continued, gesturing between us. "Is a dream come true. And maybe, you're why I'm doubting everything. My crush hasn't gone away, even after all these years. What kind of wife would I be, wanting someone other than who I was married to?"

"A shitty one," I said without thinking, clearing my throat when her shoulders slumped. "But you aren't his wife now, babe, so that gives you time to consider everything. I want you, too. I shouldn't, but I do. But if you belong to someone else, dead whatever the hell we have going on."

"We're friends. Aren't we?"

I gave her an incredulous look. "I've never fucked my friends. I never wanted to take my friend to a bathroom to eat her out. I never wanted to—"

"I get the picture," she breathed, her face reddening, but her light eyes gleaming with desire. She licked her lips. "Give me time to decide, Denali. But while I do, don't shut me out. You just reentered my life. I don't want to lose you again."

"I don't want to lose you, either," I said, her words meaning more than she knew. Few people outside the Harlots cared to keep me in their lives long-term. "But I also want you to be happy. And if your happiness means a life without me in it, I understand."

She huffed a laugh, though it was sad. "You've always been a sweetheart."

I snorted at her joke. "I'm a bitch that's done fucked up shit, Estelle. The opposite of sweet."

"Life dealt you a bad hand. That doesn't mean that at your core, you aren't sweet. You were just standing in the fucking heat to pass out school supplies for children. Many people wouldn't do that. You may have done bad things, but it doesn't make you a bad person."

"You're too sweet."

She rolled her eyes. "I'm cheating on my fiancé, daydreaming about you constantly. That isn't sweet."

"Don't copy me," I teased, tickled over the irony of her words.

She giggled, a charming chime that made me smile. "Anyway…after I get my car, do you want to trail me to my apartment? Aydin is in New York for the week."

"For what?" I asked, trying to ignore the anticipation I felt in my chest and in my pussy.

She looked at me through her lashes. "We can have a couple of drinks. And you can stay the night. It isn't safe to drink and drive, after all."

Who was I to refuse such a kind offer? Besides, if I couldn't tell her about Aydin, luring her away from him was the best option. If I treated her well enough, she'd forget all about her raggedy fiancé, securing her safety, and enabling us to give things a real go.

Chapter Thirteen

DENALI

"Nice place," I said as I strolled past Estelle and into her apartment.

After we ate, I escorted her back to the church so she could get her car. She texted me her address, then sped off. Calling Val out for being a messy bitch while Karma was occupied delayed me. I didn't know what game she was playing, sending me on a date with Estelle while being suspicious of her.

"Don't fucking berate me; thank me," she'd said with a scowl, before storming off.

Instead of grilling my friend, I'd just come to the apartment. The large terrarium table took me aback. The turtle inside stared at me for a moment before going about its business.

"That's Crush," Estelle said as she escorted me to the living area.

It had an open floor plan, with a large island separating the living/dining room from the modern kitchen. Large windows allowed the fading sunlight to stream in, and the décor looked like something out of a home design magazine.

"*Finding Nemo* fan?" I asked, my lips quirking into a smile.

The first movie had been a childhood favorite, and one I hadn't seen in years. The stoner turtle that Estelle had taken inspiration from had been my favorite character, right after little Nemo himself.

She nodded, returning my smile as I sat on her sectional couch. "I love it."

I watched as she went to her kitchen, retrieving a bottle of red wine. She held it up. "Wine good with you?"

"As long as it's sweet. Bitter wine tastes like fucking medicine."

"It's a ruby port."

I stared at her blankly, and she giggled.

"Portuguese wine that's fruity and sweet," she explained as she grabbed two wine glasses.

"Ah."

There was an air of awkwardness as we began to drink. Estelle turned on the TV after gulping down half the contents of her glass, clearly discontented with the silence. I didn't know what to say. I'd said everything on my mind at the restaurant, except the one thing I couldn't say: *leave Aydin, because your safety depends on it*. Karma ordered the Harlots to keep things under wraps, and as my Prez, I had to obey her.

Huffing, I finished my wine in two gulps, then poured myself another glass, ignoring Estelle's questioning look. Irritated, I snatched the remote.

"Why am I here, Estelle?" I finally said once I turned off the TV.

I'd come to fuck, the first stage in my plan to lure her away from Aydin. Over our meal, we'd been keeping a steady conversation going, laughing and flirting. Yet, once the check was brought out, breath mints melting on our tongues, things cooled down.

"To hang out."

"You aren't speaking."

"Neither are you," she shot back, before running her fingers through her red hair. "It just feels different, letting you into the space I share with Aydin."

"You're having cold feet," I observed, trying to ignore the disappointment I felt.

She was a good woman, loyal to a motherfucker who didn't deserve it.

"No," she said, continuing to play with her beautiful waves. "I've been thinking about you since that night. I'm not going to pass up the opportunity now. My emotions are just all over the place." She laughed breezily, but it sounded forced. "I guess you think I'm a hot mess, huh?"

"No, I think you're a woman who's hurt and fed up," I replied gently, placing a hand on her exposed thigh, squeezing to comfort her. "Mrs. Milton told me, years ago, that when you're at a crossroads, trying to decide which path to travel, none will feel right until you reach the final destination."

"She said the same thing to me when I was trying to decide which college to go to. I didn't know if I wanted to go to one in the area or leave Memphis. When I chose

Memphis, it didn't feel right to I was in my sophomore year."

"It's a good piece of advice."

"Grandma always has sage advice."

I nodded, unsure what else to say. We'd lived such different lives that I couldn't give an example akin to the one Estelle had. Silence descended again, bringing back the awkwardness. My secrets were as much of a problem as her hesitation. We were safe for each other, so I couldn't look down on her for choosing me to forget her problems for a couple of hours. But as we struggled to maintain a steady stream of conversation, I wondered if that was the only thing between us. Attraction and comfort that stemmed from history together. Both important components of a relationship, but not enough to sustain it alone.

Moreover, if I pursued things further with her, I'd have to choose between a chick and my club, a position I'd never been in before.

Estelle cleared her throat. "Tell me who your favorite character was from Thricebound?"

My eyebrows twitched, but I didn't snap them together. The fuck was she going way off track for? At the moment, we were the main characters, and I had zero interest in talking about fictional ones, no matter how damn good her writing was.

"Aydin has been the cover model for several of my books."

I squinted. "Is that supposed to impress me?"

She flushed and pursed her tempting lips. "No," she huffed. "I'm just trying to kickstart conversation."

"You never had problems before. You'll do fine without bringing that motherfucker up and killing the fucking vibe. The fuck is wrong with you?"

Estelle sniffed adorably. "You don't have to be fucking rude about it. Just say you don't want to talk."

As the older one, I could guide her, but I wasn't one to drop my guard and talk to fucking talk. It was part of protecting myself. I sipped my wine. It was...
"Decent," I said, realizing I could speak the fucking thought instead of thinking about it and continuing to sit in silence. "The wine is decent."

Estelle smiled, and her shoulders relaxed a fraction. "Probably high praise coming from you," she murmured.

"You bet your ass." The sadness in the depths of her eyes almost made me catch a case. However, killing that motherfucker for personal reasons would get me sanctioned, beaten, and/or out bad for potentially starting a war. "I might pick up a bottle for myself."

"I have an extra bottle. I can give it to you."

"Or we can share it." I patted the spot next to me, a buzz finally setting in. "I'm a little cold, sitting here by myself. Bring your fine ass over here and warm me up."

She blushed but sprang to her feet and brought herself to me. I put my arm around her shoulder the moment she sat next to me. She sank into me. For a moment, we basked in the silence and each other, reveling in our moment of peace. Awkwardness slid away, and it felt right, as if this was where I belonged.

The practical side of me knew this was an illusion. The moment I walked out of her apartment, reality would set in, and I'd wonder if I lost my fucking mind. My feelings left me exposed. To protect myself, I had to protect her, and vice versa.

Sex was easy. Physical expression didn't require any emotion. It was all about pleasure. It was why I had a string of partners, without ever being in a serious relationship. Never before had I trusted anyone enough to dedicate myself to them and claim an ol' lady, even if some club ass had vied for the position since I'd joined. Estelle, however, made me rethink that stance, just because she was her.

I brought my hand to her hair and sank my fingers into the silky strands, stroking her scalp, deciding to answer the question I'd brushed off. "Prince Ahmose was my favorite character from Thricebound. He was a good brother to Taurset, and a great tactician. It broke my heart when he died."

"That was the goal," she said, making me snort. She shrugged. "I had no more use for him, and his death served the plot more. It was why Taurset decided to hold Drusus hostage, instead of allowing Aamon to kill him."

"She should've let Aamon kill that motherfucker. I couldn't stand him."

Her jaw dropped. "He's a tragic hero!"

"He's a miserable fuckface. He should've been tortured more before Taurset allowed him in her bed."

"You know, Aamon wasn't supposed to live, either," she revealed. "It was supposed to only be Taurset and Drusus. Then I changed my mind and made them a throuple."

The revelation made my jaw drop. "Aamon is miles better than Drusus, and you wanted to kill him? Bullshit."

"Hence why I changed my mind."

I rolled my eyes, and she laughed, the happy sound inspiring my own chuckles.

"What else did you like about Thricebound?" she asked when her giggles went away.

"I know it's controversial, but…" I began thinking about the reviews I read, and how fans were torn between loving and hating the scene. "Where Taurset fucked her maid when she was mad at the heroes. Fucking loved reading that gay shit."

"Had to remind my audience that I'm fruity," she said with more giggles.

A content Estelle was a giggly Estelle, and I loved it. Her laughter was a sweet sound that I enjoyed immensely.

"Mission accomplished."

As if I could ever forget her sexual orientation, after our night of passion. It was on my mind constantly, try as I might to think of other things.

"I'm tired of talking," she said suddenly, before lifting herself and sliding onto my lap. "So…let me show you just how fruity I am."

Her line made me grin. I hummed low in my throat, sighing when she pressed her lips against mine. My arms wrapped around her waist, holding her close as we kissed. Remnants of the breath mints she gobbled at the restaurant lingered, but the flavor of the wine was at the forefront as our tongues touched. My mind went delightfully blank as the kiss deepened. Her fingers tangled in my hair, keeping my head still as we locked lips. The slight sting was delicious, and I wanted to do nothing more than to stay in that position.

Estelle, however, was an impatient little thing.

Pulling away from my lips, she began to tug at my tank top. Chuckling, I set her aside and stood, making a show of removing my shorts, my eyes locked with hers as I tossed them aside.

"Fuck, Denali," she breathed, leaning back against the couch cushions and revealing her panties.

As I undressed, she rubbed her pussy over the damp fabric protecting her core. It excited me and made me forget about making a production of undressing. I carefully draped my cut over one of the armchairs, took my top and bra off, and kneeled in front of her.

"Take this shit off," I ordered, tugging her dress as my hands went for her panties.

"Impatient," she cooed, shoving at my head when I tried to bury it between her knees. "You've waited this long. Wait a little longer."

I growled, but obeyed, sitting back as she removed her dress and panties. I groaned when I saw she wore no bra, her heavy tits springing free.

"Lie down on the couch," she ordered, snapping me out of my admiration of her curves.

Instead of obeying, I leaned forward, trying to take a nipple into my mouth. She lightly tapped my cheek. Not enough to even sting, but it got her point across.

"Lie down, Denali," she repeated.

This time, I huffed out a breath, but obeyed, trembling in anticipation.

"Good girl," she cooed, before straddling my face. "God, I've wanted to do this for weeks."

She adjusted until her glistening cunt was snuggly on my mouth. The scent of her musky arousal made my mouth water. I couldn't resist taking a taste. My tongue darted out, gliding through her wet folds, and she gasped.

"Fuck, wait a minute," she breathed, though her hips grinded down when I repeated the action. "Denali."

Her tone held a warning. I didn't tease her again, patiently waiting for further instructions. Excitement rose within me when she draped her body over mine, her face lodged between my legs.

"Now," she said, tongue snaking out to tease my clit, making me shudder. "You can taste me now."

Permission granted, I lapped at her entrance before circling her clit. Estelle's moans were muffled by my flesh. She mirrored my actions, licking and sucking my pussy with fervor. The room quickly filled with the sounds of tongues on flesh, muffled gasps and cries, and the creak of the couch.

"Fuck, you're so wet for me," Estelle breathed, lifting her head long enough just to mutter those filthy words.

Her words sent a thrill through me, my pussy clenching around nothing. I sucked her clit with urgency, making her thighs tighten around my head, the feeling of her weight on my face making me all the more eager. A gorgeous woman on my face was always a treat. Flattening my tongue, I dragged it back to her slit, collecting more of her juices, then plunged it inside her entrance. She cried out as I began tongue fucking her with shallow thrusts, before I licked back to her clit.

"Keep going," she whimpered, her words muffled.

I had no intention of stopping, even if her tongue on my heated flesh made it difficult to focus. She spread my folds with her fingers, giving her unbridled access to my sopping core. Mimicking me, she latched onto my clit, sucking until stars were bursting behind my closed eyelids. The vibration of my cries made her grind fast as her tongue swirled in tight circles, going as low as possible, before returning her attention to my clit.

"Taste so fucking good," she babbled in between licks, a better multitasker than me.

Whereas I was consumed with her taste, wanting nothing more than to make her fall apart on my tongue, her talkative ass managed to mumble out dirty words as she brought me closer to pleasure.

Her taste was tangy and sweet, the delicious juices dripping out of her coating my chin and lips as I worked relentlessly to throw her over the edge. Our bodies became slick with sweat, and her fingers joined her tongue. While her mouth attacked my clit, her fingers slid inside me, curling them in a way that made my toes bend. It made me whimper and fucked up my rhythm for a second before I got used to the sensation. I mirrored her actions in reverse, letting my tongue stay lodged in her pussy as my thumb rubbed her clit.

"Don't stop, I'm close," she panted, our moans blending into a filthy symphony.

She added a third finger. Pressure built fast, coiling low in my belly, and alighting every nerve. Her body tensed.

She cried my name as she came, resting her head against my thigh as she rode out her high.

Her fingers stayed inside my cunt. A few curls, and I was joining her in ecstasy. My pussy spasmed around her fingers as pleasure flowed over me. We lapped down each other's releases, our tongues tracing lazy patterns over flesh, neither content to end up 69ing.

Estelle was the one who put a stop to things. Rolling off me, she wiggled until she was in my arms. As I caught my breath, I held her close, our bodies warm and sticky. When she kissed me deeply, I knew coming over had been the right choice.

Chapter Fourteen

DENALI

Emergency Church was always a tense event. In my years with the club, it had never been called to announce something good, only when shit hit the fan.

"What the fuck do you think this is about?" Val asked as we filed in.

"No fucking clue," I muttered, hiding my nervousness with practiced ease.

We didn't have to wait long to find out. When everyone was seated, alcohol in hand, Karma took the stage.

"I'm not going to beat around the fucking bush," she said, the normally upbeat note to her voice absent. "Eli is dead."

Her announcement made a gasp go through the room. My heart sank to my toes.

"The fucking Femmes got her. I've already spoken to Duchess and Reign," she continued, her voice cracking as she referred to the president of the Memphis Royal Bastards. Clearing her throat, she soldiered on. "I don't think I have to tell any of you what this means."

War.

They took one of ours, so we'd have to retaliate tenfold.

Eli and I hadn't been close, but she was only twenty-four, and more importantly, a fellow Harlot. Her life was valuable to me for that reason alone, and the Femmes would have hell to pay for taking her from us. Unlike the normal rowdiness of Church, everyone was subdued and solemn. Most of all, Chains, who'd been training Eli to be another enforcer.

"Tell me you're fucking joking, Prez," Chains croaked, her devastation clear. "Eli...fuck...I just saw her yesterday."

Karma's smile was sad. "I wish I were, girlie. Eli is flying high now."

Eli's death ended the high I'd been riding since I spent the night at Estelle's two days ago. The night had been great for more reasons than one. Snacks and riveting conversation in between fuck sessions made it one for the books and marked the first time I'd ever stayed the night at someone's place. We'd christened most areas of her apartment, and I'd been in such a chipper mood when I returned that my sisters immediately took note and teased me over it.

Eli had been one of them, and now she was dead.

"I'm going to blow their fucking clubhouse up," Chains said following Karma's shocking announcement and explanation. A sniff punctuated the threat. "We can't let this shit fly."

"And we won't," Karma declared, her expression guarded. "Those bitches will pay for taking one of ours."

Cries of agreement rippled through the room. I clenched my jaw, downing the beer I was nursing, wanting to destroy every Femme and Scorpion who had the misfortune to cross my path.

"Her mother has been notified," Prez continued, swallowing as she said the words. "She knows we'll pay for the cremation. She's…she's opted to have a private ceremony for her daughter for only blood relatives, as is her right."

She raised her voice at the end to be heard across the room. No funeral to honor one of our own was a travesty, but her mother had the right to do what she pleased for her daughter. Being a mother herself, Karma was more sympathetic to the woman than a lot of the other members.

"It's her right, ladies," Karma repeated, sweeping the room with a glare. "We aren't going to add to a mother's grief by disrespecting her wishes."

"You heard the woman, people, so shut the fuck up," Siren yelled, silencing the last murmurs.

Karma nodded at Siren before refocusing on the room. "Eli will be placed on the Free Bird wall, and we'll celebrate her life here at the club the way she deserves. I will extend an invitation to her mother, but I don't expect her to come."

"That woman's talking out of grief, Prez," Kinder said. "If a group of us went to talk to her, she'd see the logic in blending the ceremonies together."

"Shut it, Kinder," Karma ordered. "I've already made my decision. This is a non-issue. We need to figure out what to do with those cunts that took her from us. She was just a kid with her whole fucking life ahead of her."

"What about the Turkish Mafia?" Siren asked. "Did they have a hand in this?"

My guard went up, and I straightened.

Karma shrugged. "I don't—"

"Why don't we ask Everest's little friend, Estelle?" Kinder sniffed, throwing a glare my way. "She's engaged to one of those motherfuckers."

I couldn't fucking believe that little bitch outed Estelle like that. For a moment, I gaped, but the comments flinging about seeped into my brain and I got to my feet, growling, ready to beat the fuck out of Kinder.

"Order!" Karma called, banging the gavel and halting my intentions. "Order this instant, or I'm fining the troublemakers." When the sisters quieted, she laid her gavel down again, drew herself up, and looked at me. "Is this fucking true? You've been hanging around with a woman engaged to one of our known enemies?"

"It isn't what you think, Karma," I gritted, fury pounding through me and a need for vengeance. "I didn't know who the fuck she was engaged to until I went to her book signing, and even then, it took me a moment to recognize him. Estelle has no fucking clue what that motherfucker does."

"Didn't Kinder go with you to that book signing?" Karma asked, searching out that snitch-bitch.

"I did," Kinder said hesitantly, realizing she might've fucked over herself. "But I saw how shocked Everest was. She didn't know, Prez. Once she had that info, I didn't think she'd want to hang out with her again."

Lifting her brow and far from being a stupid woman, Karma's gaze fell on Val. "Explain yourself, Valentina."

Val glanced between me and Karma. "It wasn't a setup," she said, deciding not to address either of us directly. She looked toward our president, not at her.

"So, you knew that Estelle is engaged to a motherfucker in the Turkish Mafia and didn't say anything?" Big Mama asked incredulously. "Then you just fucking decided to be a benevolent bitch and ask Karma to let Everest leave early?"

"That shit could've gone so fucking bad so fucking quick, Val," Geri said with disapproval.

"I wasn't thinking," Val mumbled. "I…yes, I knew who Estelle's fiancé is, and I wanted Everest to tell you."

Karma snorted. "Since she wasn't, you took it upon yourself to force the situation?"

"We didn't know why that woman showed up at the school drive, Chickie," Kiwi said. "Ever thought about that? Suppose she did know we're her old man's enemy and came to lure Everest away to harm her or hand her over? We wouldn't have known until it was too late."

That was a reasonable worry, although I knew I had nothing to fear. "A valid point," I conceded, "but Estelle wouldn't betray me like that." I ignored the grumbles and met Karma's gaze. "I've known her for years, Prez. She isn't that kind of girl."

"When was the last time you saw her before you ran into her at the bar?" Siren asked me.

I swallowed, wanting to wish I'd never seen Estelle or left with her. The worry I felt for her was a new experience. It meant she'd gotten under my skin. My sisters could take care of themselves. I'd defend them to the death, but I was also able to keep a certain distance from them, separate my emotions from my duty and our friendship.

"Answer the question, Everest," Karma ordered.

"Fourteen years," I admitted. "It was fourteen years since I last saw her."

Karma banged the gavel. "Fifteen-minute recess," she declared, laid the gavel on the podium, and crooked her finger at me. "I need to talk to you in my office."

Sighing, I nodded, thinking of all the ways I'd torture Kinder and Val. Bitches.

"What the fuck are you doing, Everest?" Karma demanded as soon as I entered her office. "Fucking around with a Turk's fiancée."

"Prez, I've known her—"

"I don't give a fuck," she hissed, cutting me off. "You haven't seen her in over a decade. A lot of shit can change in that time, girlie, and I'd be damned if I have one of my best members killed because a bitch melted down her walls."

"Aydin is out of town," I revealed, grasping at straws to take the heat off me, and by extension, Estelle. "In New York. She tells me shit she thinks is harmless, because she doesn't know who he is. Like how he's a druggie and fucking a woman named Alex—"

"Alex?" she cut off, eyes widening. "Do you know Luce's real name?"

My brows snapped together. "Isn't that shit short for Lucinda?"

"But it isn't her given name. It's Alexendra Monroe Davis. I should know, since I went to school with that heifer," she grumbled, shocking me to my core.

Fuck me with a rock and call me a whore, but you could've knocked me over with a feather. Shock and fear mingled. If Aydin's Alex and Luce were one and the same, that was just one more threat to Estelle.

Taking a breath, Karma continued. "Find out more about the broker, Everest. He's the key to shutting this shit down."

"Does that mean...?"

"You have my permission to continue entertaining Estelle, but remember that she's just leverage. Us or her, I expect you to choose us, got it?"

"Yes, Prez."

If everything went according to my plan and Estelle left Aydin, I wouldn't have to make that choice. All I had to do was make her see what a motherfucker he was, a feat easier said than done.

I was hoping Denali would contact me, if only to say how amazing our sex was, but she'd gone radio silent, ignoring my one phone call and text message. Each time I saw her, I realized how little Aydin and I had in common anymore. I questioned if we'd ever been compatible. His drug use told me 'no', which he'd begun before I moved in. I couldn't believe how blind I'd been when his erratic behavior should've clued me in. I wasn't sure if it'd been naivety, or plain disinterest that made me brush it off.

How could I notice everything about Denali, whom I didn't live with and hadn't seen in years, yet the man I planned to marry and who slept next to me most nights was like a stranger to me?

"Baby, where's your mind at?" Grandma's voice broke into my wandering thoughts.

The only thing I'd had to look forward to in the two days since I'd last seen Denali was my weekly visit to my grandmother's apartment.

We'd had a delicious meal of BBQ spaghetti. When Grandma cooked, she added pulled pork, which I preferred. But she had become so frail. Cooking was difficult for her nowadays, so she sat on her walker near Vernon, the chef I hired for her, and instructed him on how to cook. When I pointed out he had a degree in culinary arts, she'd harumphed and continued bossing him. Luckily, he took it all in stride. They'd even compromised on some dishes. Such as the spaghetti. He chopped his pork. I'd never insult him and tell him I wished he did it like my grandma.

He created delicious, eye-appealing dishes.

Sighing, I pushed back from my seat, aware I had yet to answer her. Instead, I gathered our dirty dishes and brought them to the sink. Grandma's cottage in the senior living community had two bedrooms, two bathrooms, a built-in kitchen where her dining table was, and a living room. The open floor plan, beechwood floors, and off-white paint gave the illusion of space. It worked for her, and I was happy to foot the bill, despite how much Dad wanted to do it. She'd stepped up as my grandmother when her son married my mother. I adored her, which is why I paid extra for her to have her every need taken care of.

"Fuck those dishes, baby," she said in a steely voice. "Sit down and talk to me."

I shrugged, not knowing what to say, but I returned to my seat. If I told her about Aydin, she'd tell Mama, Dad, and my brothers. They might spare my little sister, but what the fuck did I know at this point?

"Estelle, talk to me."

"Guess who I saw recently," I said, pointedly ignoring her order. "Ran into when I went out with my girls?"

Pursing her lips, Grandma sniffed and threw me a dirty look. "Tell me after—"

"Denali Bernard," I blurted, shutting her up immediately. For years, my grandmother had wondered what happened to her. When she realized that might be a mystery she never solved, she'd let it go, grieving privately. "Do you remember her?"

She scowled. "I'm not crazy, Estelle. Of course, I remember Denali. How is she? What has she been up to?"

"A lot," I said as casually as possible, heat sweeping through my body and warming my face.

The downside of being a redhead is that my pale skin pinkened easily, the bane of many gingers, including myself.

Grandma lifted her brows at my blush. "Exactly how much of her did you see?"

The question embarrassed me further, and I smiled weakly, worried she'd think less of me because of Aydin. I'd never met Mr. Milton, but even after his death, she placed that man on a pedestal and gushed about what a good man he was. If I confessed everything going on in my relationship, I didn't know if she'd understand.

"Estelle," Grandma said, an order in her voice. "Talk to me, baby."

"A lot's going on with Aydin," I confessed, not sure if I'd get more detailed than that. "I care about him so much, but he's showing a side of himself I don't like. I love him, but I don't know if I'm in love with him."

"And…what does Denali have to do with this?" I shut my mouth, opened it, and shut it again, mimicking a stupid fish. She snorted out a laugh, then sighed. "Baby, did I ever tell you that I fucked the mailman?"

I sputtered, nearly choking on my spit at the reveal. She laughed again, heartier this time.

"Andrew wanted to sleep with his co-worker after a fight and tried to throw it back in my face. After I threw hot grits on his ass, I lured the fine mailman in and gave him the ride of his life. Yes indeed, I did," she said, the faraway, nostalgic look in her eyes making me swallow a gag.

"TMI, Grandma," I complained, my face a flaming inferno now.

She waved me off. "My point is, baby, if you slept with Denali, I won't care, and I won't tell anyone. Love is complicated, not black and white. And I know if you stepped out on Aydin, that motherfucker did something to deserve it. If you got your lick back, that means I raised you right. Now, tell me about Denali. How is that child?"

"Hardly a child anymore," I said, Grandma's words soothing something inside me. "She's thirty-two."

She snorted. "A seventy-year-old is a child compared to me, so answer my question, Estelle."

"Denali is still gorgeous. Still strong. Still magnetic. Just...still her."

"Fourteen years apart ain't dulled your crush, huh, chile?"

"Do you ever get over your first crush?"

"Nope," she replied. "I was real sweet on the preacher's son as a little girl. He ended up being the first one I gave it up to when I was—"

"Grandma, do I need to get you a boyfriend?" I blurted, the reminiscing of her sexual past making me shudder.

"I have a hot pink boyfriend in my nightstand, girl," she said.

This time, I didn't hold back my gag. Old age had made her tongue far looser.

She cackled at my embarrassment. "Oh, girl, I'm still a woman with needs, so don't be shocked. And enough about me. Denali still in the military?"

"Er, no. It isn't my story to tell why, but she's a biker now. Same club as Michelle. Just a different branch."

Grandma had only met my cousin a handful of times, but she'd been a fan. Partially, because we all fed her a sanitized version of the kind of club the Harlots were, chalking up their misdeeds to rumors and self-defense.

She considered my words. "They make good money, don't they?"

"If they're an officer and a part of a big club, which Denali is, then yes."

"So, she's doing well for herself?"

"It seems so. She has a Red Harley Davidson. Those aren't cheap."

After seconds of silence, she nodded. "Good. As long as that baby is standing on two solid feet and able to provide for herself, I'm happy for her."

I relaxed in my seat, nodding as a smile played on my lips. "Yeah. I am, too."

"Invite her to the family dinner this week," she ordered, making me tense.

Not because I didn't want Denali there. I'd love to bring her, but I wasn't sure if she'd be down to go. That is, if she even responded to my invitation.

"I want to see her," Grandma continued, unaware of my nervousness.

"I don't know if she'll come."

"Invite her anyway," she said, the hopeful gleam in her eye hard to miss.

"Alright," I whispered, praying Denali didn't disappoint Grandma.

Or me, for that matter, as Denali was hot-and-cold. If she fully ghosted me or declined my invitation, the experiment that was our situationship might have to end. It was an aspect that saddened me, but I couldn't deal with another flaky partner who lacked communication skills. And if Denali was the woman I thought she was, she'd at least have the decency to respond to me.

Only one way to find out.

While Vernon returned and began working on the dishes, he engaged with Grandma. I, meanwhile, got out my phone and texted her, praying that she'd respond this time.

> **My place tonight?**

I gnawed on my bottom lip as I waited for her to respond. When the phone chimed, my heart leapt.

For?

Wanna ask you something and see you again 😊

Things seemed to slow to a crawl as I waited for her to reply. Finally, my phone dinged again, a smile spread across my face as I read her simple reply.

Okay, See u later

Chapter Fifteen

Estelle

I had intended to extend the invitation to Denali as soon as she walked through the door. Instead, she'd taken me into her arms, silencing me with her lips before I could ask why she'd looked so sad. For a moment, I debated pulling away and demanding what was wrong, but I decided against it. When I melted into Denali, she'd walked me to the couch, kissing me with hunger until she shoved me down.

"Had a shitty fucking day," she growled when we separated, both of us panting.

"Do you need to talk about it?" I said, slightly dazed from the intensity in which she'd greeted me.

"No," she replied immediately. "I just need you right now, babe, so I can take my mind off shit."

I didn't question her further. Instead, a twisted sense of pride blossomed within me, knowing that she thought me...something enough to lose herself in.

Standing, I took her hand in mine and guided her to my bedroom. We undressed in silence. When we were nude, she sat on the bed, looking at me with those brown doe eyes as she awaited further instructions.

Already, she'd learned to submit to me.

"Tell me what you need," I said as we stared at one another, deciding to be selfless instead of just sitting on her face and 69ing with her again. I walked to her, plopping myself on her lap and straddling her. Putting my palm on her cheek, I ensured she stayed focused on me as I spoke again. "Tell me what'll make you feel better."

"You," she breathed, nuzzling into my touch. "Just you. Do whatever you want with me, just keep touching me."

"I don't intend to stop," I said, reclaiming her lips.

My hands explored the familiar landscape of her body as we kissed, teasing the curls at the nape of her neck as our tongues slid together in a wet, messy kiss. Her breasts pressed against mine, allowing me to feel her nipples hardening into tight peaks. I began to grind down on her thigh, the world shrinking to just me and her, as it had each time we joined together.

"I wanna fuck you," I breathed when we pulled away, pushing her shoulders until she reclined fully on the bed, her legs instinctively spreading.

She grabbed my hips, holding them as I continued to hump her thigh. "I figured," she said with a small chuckle.

"No, like, strap you," I clarified, my voice growing breathier as I ground my pussy harder against her thigh, feeling the slick heat building between my legs.

She paused, her hands falling away. Hesitation crossed her face, making me freeze, too.

"Never done that before," she said after a second of silence. "Never been that into toys."

My eyebrows rose, her statement shocking me more than it probably should have. "Really?"

"My fingers have always sufficed. I like feeling flesh on flesh."

"Is that a no?"

She shrugged. "I'll try. Tried fisting before, and I lived, so a strap can't be that bad." Jealousy mingled with my surprise. She laughed at my expression. "I was bored and in prison. Nothing to lose at that point."

"I...okay, yeah," I said, deciding it was best to just breeze past that tidbit of information.

Actually, scratch that. As horny as I was, I was curious, too.

"Were you the fisty or the fister?"

"Both," she said, only raising more questions. Before I could ask another, she rolled her eyes. "Do you want to hear about the other bitches I've fucked, or—"

"No," I replied quickly, not wanting to imagine Denali with anyone else.

I knew it wasn't fair. Neither of us had been virgins during our first night together. I had a whole fiancé, and eight previous lovers under my belt before Aydin. Denali was in an MC, likely with an overabundance of ass to tap.

Deciding we'd done enough talking, I pressed another quick kiss to Denali's lips, before breaking it to trail my lips down to her jaw. I sucked at the soft skin there, before kissing her collarbones. I cupped her perky tits, squeezing them as I rolled her nipples between my fingers. She gasped when I pinched them.

"You like that?" I murmured, smiling against her as she arched into me.

"You know I do, you fucking tease," she breathed.

A moan slipped from her when I kissed her breasts. I sucked a nipple while my hand continued to knead the other. My tongue flicked out, licking the sensitive bud. A light nip made her cry out. Switching sides, I repeated the action before continuing my descent. A few pecks down her stomach, and I'd reached the holy land. I drank in the sight of her naked body, skin flushed, and pussy glistening with wetness. My own cunt throbbed, but this wasn't about me. It was about Denali and obliging with her request to make her forget everything else but the way I touched her.

Burying my face between her legs, I gripped her thighs, keeping her spread open. My tongue swept through her folds, collecting her juices.

"So wet already," I cooed, grinning when she whimpered. "Is this all for me?"

Not giving her a chance to respond, I licked her clit, sucking it until her hips bucked.

"Fuck," she whined, gripping my hair as she rode my mouth. "Right there."

I repeated the action multiple times, going from sucking her clit and tongue-fucking her dripping cunt. Her body writhed, and I flicked the tip of her clit with my tongue as I slipped two fingers inside her. How wet Denali was made the task easy, and she'd needed to be stretched to take my dildo.

"I'm close," she announced as I pumped my fingers in and out; her juices dripped down my hand.

"Then come for me," I breathed against her, giving her clit another hard suck.

She squealed as her body obliged, back arching sharply as her walls squeezed my fingers like a vice. Seeing her come was always a beautiful sight, and her body went limp as I continued fingering her and lazily licking her clit.

I pushed my fingers deeper, not stopping until her cunt enveloped my knuckles. Scissoring them, I brought a thumb to her bundle of nerves, rubbing circles over it until her body was writhing again. A third finger was quickly added, and I switched to thrusting and twisting them in and out of her. She fisted the sheets, her eyes screwed shut as I worked her toward a second orgasm. Her thighs began to quiver, but instead of letting her come, I pulled away.

A gasp left her, her eyes flying open. "What the fuck," she snapped, making me grin.

"Patience, pretty girl."

A frustrated whine left her; the sound only heightened my amusement. "Estelle, please."

Shushing her again, I stood and walked to the nightstand. She watched me through hooded eyes as I grabbed my box of toys, all purchased before I got with Aydin. Thanks to him, they were rarely used, though I kept them clean, just in case. The end meant to go inside Denali was raspberry pink, with veins running along the large shaft. Overlocking the color, it mimicked the real thing pretty well. Instead of a harness, the wearer was supposed to rely on the smaller dildo, with 'rabbit ears' to stimulate the clit. However, using a harness kept it from slipping and gave me greater control.

Pressing the remote, the toy buzzed to life, the combination of the pressure and the vibration making me shiver. I was so aroused, it felt as if I was about to come then and there. I held my orgasm back, however, and grabbed lube and applied it to the toy.

Denali watched the process with hungry eyes.

"Hands and knees," I ordered, my breathing growing labored.

She obeyed without hesitation, presenting herself to me. Her pussy was pink, swollen, and dripping. I doubted extra lube was needed, so I placed it on the nightstand and positioned myself behind her.

"Tell me what you need," I said, dragging the tip of the buzzing dildo along her slit, gathering her wetness.

"You know what the fuck I need, Estelle," she snapped, pushing back against me. The slap to her ass made her yelp, but got her to behave. "Fuck me, please."

Nodding in approval, I thrust forward slowly, the dildo sliding into her inch by inch. She was so goddamn wet that it sank in easily. I admired the sight of her pussy swallowing the dildo, moans flowing from Denali. Her head dropped to the mattress when I bottomed out, my hips flush against her ass. We both quivered, and I had to stay still for a moment; the stimulation and how erotic the situation was enough to make me come.

When I caught my bearings, I pulled back all the way, then slammed back in, the stimulation to my clit and g-spot sending sparks of pleasure through me.

"You take it so well," I praised, setting a hard and fast rhythm, my hands gripping her hips as I rutted into her.

She rocked back to meet my thrusts, her ass jiggling each time I surged forward. She was beyond words at that point, mewling and whimpering as I took her. Reaching around, I rubbed her clit, making her shatter. Finally, I gave in to the pleasure, coming with a cry as I exploded.

Still, I didn't stop. My hips kept moving, the dildo still buried in each of us. Draping my body over her back, I bit her shoulder before kissing her neck. She looked at me, eyes hazy with pleasure and hooded. It was easy to kiss her, muffling each other's cries as I bullied her G-spot and played with her clit. Our second orgasms built faster, and we rode out the high together, breaths mingling as our lips separated.

Finally spent, I pulled out, admiring the slight gape of her pussy, the creamy slick sliding down her thigh. Turning off the dildo, I pulled it out, tossing it and the harness aside, then collapsed next to her. This time, I took her into my arms. She rested her head on my chest, intimacy wrapping around us like a wrap blanket.

"Behave," I said when she started to suck at the nearest tit

"But they're right there," she mumbled, looking at me with a pout. "And so soft. You want to help me relax, don't you?"

Deciding I liked this side of Denali, pliant, needy, and slightly bratty, I nodded. "Fine. No biting, though."

Humming, she lazily licked my nipples and sucked my areola in her mouth, content to just play with my tits. I'd considered piercing them at one time for some razzle dazzle, and for extra stimulation during times like this.

"I saw Mrs. Milton today," I said causally, trying to ignore the arousal mounting from the stimulation. "Told her about her."

She froze, my nipple falling from her mouth with a wet 'pop' as she stared into my eyes. "What'd she say?"

"She wants to invite you over for our family. It's what I wanted to talk to you about. You don't have to, but it'd make her happy. Me, too."

"Does she know...that...that..."

She trailed off again and looked away. Without being told, I knew what she was trying to say. We were just in tune like that.

"She doesn't know that you went to the slammer, or that you killed someone. She does know you're a biker, though. But she's fine with it, because she knows my cousins are Harlots, too."

Relief swept over her face, and she relaxed again. "I don't want to intrude."

"You won't be. You're invited, remember?"

Sighing, she sat up, much to my disappointment. "You have a fiancé, Estelle, and I told myself I'd stay away from Mrs. Milton. She deserves better—"

"Don't finish that sentence," I ordered, wondering how someone so confident could also be so insecure. "And that woman is eighty-one, with her brain intact. She's more than old enough to decide. Don't take that choice from her, and break her heart a second time. As for Aydin, he already said he won't go to the dinner. We'll tell everyone we're just friends, for now."

"For now?" she parroted.

"I don't know what will happen with Aydin, but if…when…if we break up, I want to give us a proper go."

Her eyes searched my face. Whatever she found made her smile, and she nodded. "Alright, then. I'll go, but no promises that I'll stay for long."

"You don't have to have dessert if you don't want to, but you're at least eating with us."

She snickered. "Forever bossy."

"You like it," I retorted.

"Yeah," she agreed as she returned to my arms. "I do."

Chapter Sixteen

Estelle

"Love, I'm home," Aydin called, just as I was about to start getting ready for my family's weekly dinner.

As soon as Grandma April moved down here, it was something she insisted upon. She wanted us to remain close to one another, and she felt that nothing fostered closeness like food. Nowadays, Vernon earned himself an invite, just because she could no longer cook as she once did, and we all enjoyed his food. I tipped him extra for those family dinners, and we all insisted he eat with us. He declined, an older man with traditional beliefs who believed that an employee and employer should maintain a professional, somewhat distant relationship.

"Hey," I said as Aydin entered the bedroom, not looking at him as I started to braid my hair for the shower.

The sheets that contained the evidence of Denali's presence were in the closet, washed and folded, and replaced with another set. She hadn't been back over since I strapped her, but we texted at least once a day. The more the days passed with Aydin gone, the more I realized how nice it was to not have him around. It sounded shitty, but space allowed me to examine everything that'd occurred between us from the moment we got engaged to when I found out about his drug use. If Tess, Lauren, or Dani were in my position, I'd tell them to leave their partner and look at them crazy for staying. Not only would this hypothetical partner be trifling, but their escalating behavior would make me fear for their safety.

Aydin would always hold a place in my heart, and I wanted nothing but the best for him. However, I no longer foresaw a happy future with him, which meant there was no future for us.

I finished my braids, then turned to look at him. Whatever he saw in my face made his smile drop.

"Estelle...what's wrong?" he asked hesitantly, placing his suitcase by the door.

I'd done some soul searching and came to a solid conclusion about the relationship. Yet, I didn't know how to make the announcement to him. Swallowing, I looked away again, the words I needed to say lodging in my throat.

"Estelle—"

"We're breaking up," I blurted, interrupting him. "I care about you, and I love you, but I'm not in love with you. Our engagement has been toxic, and I don't know if I can just forget—"

"No," he said, the vehemence in which he said that word shocking me into silence.

"What?" I asked, blinking at him.

"No," he repeated, his eyes narrowing. "You aren't leaving. And whoever put that idea in your head, tell them to fuck off, and block them."

"No one put the fucking idea in my head, Aydin," I snapped. "I can think for myself. Since we got engaged, all we've been doing is arguing. You refuse to compromise on a single thing. You get overly clingy and possessive. You fucking cheated and still refuse to get into rehab like I asked."

"I don't have time for fucking rehab!" he exploded, making me jump. "But that doesn't mean things have to end. I love you—"

"I love you, too. I just said that. But I no longer love you in the way you need me to."

He swiped skin care products and books off the dresser, making them crash to the floor. I yelped, my heart speeding up. Looking at him closer, I noticed the pupils of his eyes were unusually large and slightly bloodshot. His body was shaking, and his skin shone with sweat.

No doubt about it, Aydin was high.

Not only was he not looking for rehab, but now, he wasn't even bothering to hide his drug use from me. It reinforced my decision to leave him, but how to get that through his thick skull when he was so unstable was a goal I didn't know how to accomplish.

"Aydin, calm down," I said slowly, terrified that he'd turn that rage onto me. "Please, be rational about this."

"I can't fucking be rational, not when you're trying to leave me!" he screamed, tugging at his hair. "Which one of those sluts put that idea in your head? Dani? She lets anything fuck her, I bet she wants someone else to whore—"

"Shut the fuck up," I snapped, unable to take him talking about my friend like that. "I already said no one put that idea in my head, Aydin. I want to see you get better and to thrive, but not with you as my partner."

"Don't you dare, or—"

I scoffed, crossing my arms over my chest. "Or what?"

His smile was unusually ugly. "Or I'll show the world what a slut you are. All those nudes you send me whenever you go away, videos of you playing with your fucking cunt, bet your simp ass fans would love to see that. They'll go number one on Pornhub in a day."

Immediately, tears stung my eyes at his threat, breathing suddenly becoming a challenge. Even if his threat wasn't serious, it was vile enough to warrant an ass-whooping. But I couldn't manage to move, his words making me freeze, unable to do anything but cry and stare at him in shock.

He nodded slowly as he saw my tears, before swiping them away with deceptive gentleness. "Yeah, that's right. You wanna leave me? I'll show the world exactly what I lost. Brands don't like to work with sluts, you know, and imagine what your family would think. Remember the one with the anal—"

"Shut up," I hissed, finally finding my voice as my cheeks burned. "You can't do that. You won't. It's a crime—"

"Only if they can prove it's me. Otherwise, it's your word against mine."

"And mine will hold more weight, because you're a fucking miserable nobody," I said, my limbs regaining movement, and using that newfound control to take my engagement ring off, and chuck that motherfucker at his miserable, stupid face.

The ring hit his cheek, but he looked at me as if he were bored. "You forget who my family is. They can and will make everything go away, while your fans will always remember you as a cheating whore."

"I haven't—"

"Don't fucking lie, Estelle," he hissed, bending to pick up the ring. "Now, shut the fuck up, put the ring back on, and we'll pretend that today never happened."

He held the ring out to me. I considered tossing it aside and calling his bluff. But that was a risk I didn't want to take. Aydin, to a degree, was right. Those nudes would circulate once posted. My character and appearance would be picked apart by critics, and those who sympathized with me would see me as a victim. Either way, it'd become a defining part of my story, something I didn't want.

Swiping my eyes, I put the stupid ring back on, vowing that the next time I took it off, it'd stay off. The last two attempts to leave him had been a fail, but the third time, as they say, is the charm.

"Good girl," he cooed mockingly, my glare just making him grin wider. "I'm going get some food now. Enjoy your family dinner, my love."

With that, he left the room, head held high as if he wasn't a lowdown, scummy asshole.

DENALI

Somehow, someway, the media had yet to catch onto the war between the Harlots and the bitch-ass Femmes. It'd always been on sight, but recently, we'd been seeking each other out for the sole purpose of violence. Before Eli's death, Ryder had confirmed the Turks were very much involved with the Femmes and Scorpions, before blazing out with permission from Karma following Eli's death. She'd never enjoyed the violence that came with MC life, so it came as a surprise to no one that she didn't participate in the bloodshed.

We'd lost some people on our side, but Eli was the only member they'd gotten. We, meanwhile, had taken out three in a day to avenge her.

"I don't know how I got roped into this shit," I grumbled as I helped Chains lug a Femme's body down the stairs to The Cells. "I didn't help you smoke this bitch."

The basement of the warehouse was huge. The entrance served as storage, with a large space where we grew our weed. It was built before workers had many rights, so the basement also had small, cramped spaces that used to be bedrooms. With some tweaks, they made for a great place to hold someone hostage and to dispose of a body.

"You were available," Chains explained, smirking at my glare. "That's reason enough."

"I'm going to have to shower again," I complained, knowing I couldn't show up to Estelle's mother's home reeking of blood and death.

"Still fucking with that bit—"

"Careful," I growled, kicking open the door to one of the cells. "Karma gave me her permission to monitor her. That's what I'm doing."

Chains snorted, too smart to believe my lie. "Yeah, alright. Just don't get yourself killed chasing pussy, Everest."

Her concern touched me, but it was misplaced. Estelle would never harm me. As long as her fuckhead of a fiancé didn't find out, we were golden.

"Thanks for the concern," I said simply. Dropping the body, I looked at her. "You got it from here?"

"You know I do. Shut the door behind you."

She didn't wait for me to leave before she picked up one of the tools she'd use to dissect the body. When that was done, she'd throw them in a vat of acid, which was stored in a special room.

Showering and changing were a quick process. Kinder and Val had been avoiding me, so when I was ready, there were no further interruptions. I chose my nicest pair of black jeans and one of two blouses I owned. It was a moss green number with long billowy sleeves, with a V-neck framed by lace detailing and ending in a nice little string meant to be tied into a bow. Black slip-on oxfords, hoop earrings, and a gold rose necklace that Karma had given me for my 30th birthday completed the outfit. Mascara, body spray, and clear lip gloss enhanced my looks. For the first time in years, I felt like a regular woman, one just nervous about a date, and not an outlaw biker who'd taken my fair share of lives.

Estelle told me her motherfucker was due to return today. So, she just sent me her mother's address. I rode straight there, arriving twenty-minutes after the dinner started, if they were on time.

Fucking Chains.

Thankfully, when I arrived, they were just sitting down. Estelle was the one to answer the door, looking pretty in an emerald wrap dress, her red curls in a ponytail, her features accentuated by makeup. When she saw me, she blinked.

"You look pretty," I said, leaning in and stealing a kiss, since no one was around.

"Not here, Denali," she hissed, her tone taking me aback. Sighing, she shook her head. "Sorry. I had a fight with Aydin. Just…you look nice."

She walked away without another word. I followed behind her awkwardly, wondering what was going on, if she regretted inviting me.

"Denali's here," she announced, making every eye turn to me, and increasing how awkward I felt.

Although I'd never had a problem with her mom and dad, I came because Mrs. Milton wanted to see me. She wasn't there, and I almost turned and walked out, especially with Estelle's shitty mood. An older black man, Ms. Pratt, Mr. Milton, Kayla, and Harvey, Jr. were sitting at the table, plates in front of them.

I cleared my throat and waved. "Ms. Pratt, Mr. Milton," I greeted.

Estelle's mother smiled kindly. "Hi Denali," she said, then pointed her finger between herself and the handsome black man next to her. "We're married now."

Right. She was Mrs. Pratt-Milton now. I felt like a dumb ass, which was worsened when Kayla and Harvey laughed at my blunder.

"Denali!" A warm, comforting voice called, saving me from more humiliation. Mrs. Milton ambled toward me, much slower than I remembered. She lifted her arms. "Get over here, girl."

The moment she said the words, I hurried to her, bent, and hugged her. She wrapped me in her embrace, warm and comforting. It made me want to cry. She'd helped me through some of my darkest childhood days. I'm not sure where I would've ended up without her. We may not have shared blood, but she was my maternal figure who'd nurtured me more than my parents ever had.

Despite my stint in jail, it was because of her that I was able to leave Chicago and try to do better for myself. My life might not have turned out the way we both expected, but I'd survived and did better than some. I wasn't dependent on drugs or alcohol, had never had to prostitute to survive, never had to steal food, and had never ended up homeless. If Mrs. Milton hadn't been in the picture, my reality would've been much different.

Pulling away, she reached up and took my face between her gnarled hands. "How you become a biker instead of a soldier?"

"It's a long story," I told her quietly. "One I'll tell you about another time."

She looked at me and took in my features. "You tell me when you're good and ready. I'm not going anywhere, not for another nineteen years, minimum. C'mon, baby. I'm hungry."

Not waiting for me to comply, she grabbed my hand and guided me to the table, directing me to a seat that placed me between her and Estelle before she introduced me to the older man. Vernon was

Mrs. Milton's personal chef, but occasionally dined with them because the Pratt-Milton bunch was so cool.

Vernon passed around a bowl of salad. Once we all filled our plates, I reached for the dressing, but Mrs. Milton slapped my arm.

"We still say grace in this family." She gave me a severe look. "You haven't forgotten how to do that, have you?"

I flushed and inwardly cursed myself. I was a grown-ass woman. I never thought anyone could still bring my ass in line and make me feel like a kid, to boot.

Everyone was looking at me, waiting for my answer.

"She isn't a freak show," Mrs. Milton said sternly. "I asked the question, not any of you. Now, answer me, Denali."

"I haven't said grace in years," I admitted, sighing. I stopped in prison.

She looked at me, then waved her hand with a flourish. This little woman still didn't fuck around. I had no doubt she'd take off her fucking shoe and beat my ass.

Annoyed, I clapped my hands together and mumbled a prayer. No one made a move to pick up their forks. I glanced at Mrs.

Milton, and her death stare made me repeat grace immediately, much louder, so fucking loud I'm sure they heard me in the next house.

"Disrespect doesn't become you, chile," Mrs. Milton said, snatching her napkin and laying it in her lap, her words making me feel like an asshole.

We ate in silence, while I stewed in guilt. I shouldn't have been such a bitch, but fuck, *grace*? I'm surprised I remembered the words. The request also caught me off guard. I hadn't thought about any type of prayer in years. On top of that, Estelle didn't open her fucking mouth. Maybe it was my imagination, but I swore she slid her chair slightly over, away from me.

Why the fuck had I come here tonight? I wouldn't stay, that's for sure. As soon as the salad ended, I was making my excuses and leaving.

"Have you had a chance to read any of Estelle's books?" Ms. Pratt asked me while Vernon and Mr. Milton cleared away the plates, momentarily curtailing my plans. Fuck, Ms. Pratt was *Mrs. Pratt-Milton*. I needed to remember that. "Every time she releases a new book, I say it's my favorite."

"I've read Thricebound," I told her. "I thought it was amazing. As soon as I get time, I'm reading more."

Estelle's mother gave me a wide grin. Meanwhile, *Estelle* didn't say a motherfucking peep.

"Mama April was so excited to hear you were coming, sweetheart," she said kindly, easing some of my tension. "Dennis and Edward couldn't make it, but they send their regards. We've been so worried about you."

Usually, I'd call bullshit. Not many people worried about me. My sisters at the club liked me well enough, but half of them considered me a mystery to solve, and the other half preferred my vagueness. But the Pratt-Miltons? They didn't bullshit. If Mrs...*Pratt-Milton* said they'd worried about me, then they had.

"I had a lot going on," I said as Mr. Pratt-Milton walked back in, in time to hear my words.

"That motherfucker got exactly what he deserved, Denali," he told me, and I jerked as if I'd been shot. "I much preferred getting word of his death than yours."

Estelle's mother nodded. "Same."

"What motherfucker and what death?" Mrs. Milton demanded.

"I'm with Grandma," Estelle said, deciding to open her fucking mouth now, looking at me. "You've never told me."

"I googled your name yesterday," Kayla revealed, deciding to stop whispering with her brother. "I showed Mama and Daddy the article that popped up."

"Somebody, answer me now," Mrs. Milton demanded.

If she was going to find out imminently, it was better from me than anyone else.

"I killed a sergeant in self-defense," I said, the silence that descended making me cringe. "He tried to...er..."

Among my sisters, I didn't have to mince my words, nor did I ever open up about my past. Not even Karma knew the specifics. But in this setting, surrounded by a normal family with big hearts who wanted to know what I'd been up to, I clamped up.

"Allegedly, he tried to rape her, but she used too much force, and—"

"Kayla," Harvey hissed, nudging his sister. "This isn't a fucking true crime podcast. It's that woman's life."

"Right," she mumbled, a blush rising to her caramel cheeks, as if she hadn't been happily rambling about one of the darkest moments of my life. "Sorry, Denali."

"I'm…I'm going have a smoke," I said, hurrying out of the room before anyone could stop me, hoping a cigarette would erase the horrible memories rising in my mind.

Chapter Seventeen

Estelle

"What the fuck is wrong with you?" I exploded, glaring at my little sister.

She had a bad habit of being too callous, unable to take anything seriously or consider how her words would hurt people. Her love of celebrity drama and true crime didn't help her empathy, or lack thereof, but being so unfeeling toward someone's trauma was a new low for her.

Fuck, but I felt like a raging bitch. I'd been so caught up in what Aydin had done that I'd frozen out Denali, and my sister had thrown salt into the wound. Everything she'd been through made my drama pale in comparison, and even though I'd extended an invite, I'd been anything but welcoming. She'd been overwhelmed before Kayla blurted that shit out.

"If I were your mama, I'd beat your ass," Grandma said, glaring at Kayla, whose eyes were watering. "You don't talk about people's pasts without their consent, girl, and especially not sounding so goddamn happy."

"I'm sorry," Kayla repeated.

"Go apologize to Denali, and get her back in," Mama ordered, shaking her head. "I raised you better than that, Kayla Marie."

"I'll come with you," I volunteered, owing Denali an apology of my own.

"Okay," she mumbled, rising from her seat, her head down to avoid looking at anyone.

We said nothing during the short walk to the porch. Denali was sitting on the bench, head bowed, her cigarette in the ashtray. When she lifted her gaze, her watery eyes horrified me.

"I'm so sorry—"

Kayla's apology was interrupted by a raised hand. "Don't worry about it, kid. It's over and done with."

Something told me she wouldn't be so forgiving if Kayla were grown. She always had a soft spot for children. I didn't know if she wanted kids, but I knew she'd make an amazing mother if she decided to have them.

"She should worry about it," I snapped, glaring at my little sister, who suddenly found her braids very interesting. "That wasn't right."

"She's a child, Estelle. They aren't known for tact."

Shaking my head, I decided it wasn't worth arguing over. Denali's forgiveness was commendable, but it didn't make what Kayla had done right, and her tears only made me angrier.

"Go back inside, Kayla," I said, wanting a moment alone with Denali.

When my sister was gone, I sat next to her and wrapped an arm around her shoulder. I cupped her cheek and made her look at me, swiping away the tears that had escaped.

"I'm sorry," I said when Denali smiled weakly at me. "For Kayla. And for being such a bitch. Aydin and I…things are rough."

"Then leave him," she replied, then shook her head. "Fuck, forget I said that. I don't think you want to talk about him now."

"You're right about that."

If I had it my way, I'd never talk to or about that asshole again. But I needed a gameplan before I left, as my nudes being exposed to the world was a nightmarish thought.

Sighing, I stood and held out my hand to her. "C'mon. If we don't go back soon, Grandma is going to beat Kayla with her cane." As soon as I said the words, I realized what a bad joke that was, given her past. I laughed awkwardly. "Joking, by the way. Grandma would never actually do that."

"Right," Denali said, lips twitching into a smile as she examined me. "A bad joke won't break me, so don't treat me like I'm glass, babe. I just wasn't expecting what your sister said, but I'm fine, really."

"I really am sorry about her, Denali."

"She's apologized. It's over and done with."

"You're sweet."

She snorted. "I'm anything but."

"Evidence says otherwise," I teased, happy to see her tears drying up, the Denali I was used to making a grand return.

"Whatever," she said with a chuckle. "Let's go back inside. These mosquitoes are about to drive me up a fucking wall."

Laughing, I nodded and led her inside, hoping that the dinner would get back on track and that the rest of the night would go smoothly.

After Kayla's massive blunder, things got back on track. Kayla apologized a dozen more times to Denali, and Harvey tried to engage with her, perking up whenever she gave him a hint of attention. It was clear that he hadn't outgrown finding her pretty, and now that he was older, it seemed like he had a minor crush on her. I didn't have the nerve to burst his bubble and tell her she wasn't only gay, but involved with someone else. Aka, me. Vernon was in the same boat, the old dirty bastard being more sociable than usual. As far as they knew, Denali was just a friend. I didn't blame either one, as Denali was stunning.

While the single males subtly flirted with Denali, Grandma fawned over her. Their reunion was heartwarming, and Mama made them take several pictures together. Denali, for her part, hadn't minded, and Grandma had been delighted and demanded they be uploaded to her digital picture frame.

Once dessert was over, everyone had a couple of drinks. Mama cut me off after my second, which was fine by me. I felt mellowed out, but sober enough to drive. When she finished her wine, Grandma demanded to be brought back to the facility. I said goodbye to my parents, and Denali took Grandma's and Mama's numbers. My siblings and Mr. Daddy had been impressed by Lobster, while the matriarchs of the family worried over her safety. She fit right in, almost better than Aydin ever had, and I longed to be able to bring her to the family dinner as a lover, not as a friend.

Two hours after dinner ended, she and I were tangled in the sheets of a motel, sweaty and sated, each lost in our own thoughts.

"I'm happy I came," she said, rolling her eyes when I snickered. "To dinner, you pervert."

"I'm happy you came, in both senses of the word," I teased, leaning down to steal a kiss.

Despite her being inches taller than me, she was curled into my side, head on my chest as I traced idle patterns on her skin. Having to hide away in a motel to enjoy such intimacy made me resent Aydin even more. Telling Denali did cross my mind, but I didn't foresee that going well. She'd confront him, which would end up with him releasing my nudes out of spite, or him being injured or even dead. The Harlots weren't known for their gentleness, after all, and even now, I didn't want Aydin hurt. Not only could it end with Denali returning to prison, but I just wanted him to accept we were over, get help, and leave me alone.

"You ever wanted to be a biker's ol' lady?" she asked after seconds of silence passed. "Placed on the back of a bike, protected 24/7, wearing a cut proclaiming you belong to someone?"

I tensed. I knew what she was trying to say, without outright saying it.

"Denali...let's not do this now," I said quietly, releasing my hold on her and sitting up.

She frowned, sitting up with me. "It's a hypothetical."

"We both know that's not true. You're asking on the downlow if I'd leave Aydin so you could officially claim me."

Instead of looking ashamed, she shrugged. "Well, would you?"

In an ideal world, yes. It's what I'd been trying to do when Aydin lost his mind and blackmailed me into putting the ring I once loved back on. Now, the gorgeous piece of jewelry felt like a shackle. Not only didn't Denali know, but she wouldn't understand. When somebody had tried to force her hand, she'd retaliated with justified violence.

"It's not that simple," I mumbled, hoping she'd drop the subject and not ruin the stolen bliss we'd found.

"You two aren't married yet. There's no paperwork involved. It's a matter of taking off the ring."

Which I'd tried to do.

Twice.

"And moving out of the apartment we share, and announcing it to my fans, family, and friends, and figuring out what to do with our turtle, and…just…you're oversimplifying it."

"And you're overcomplicating it. Look me in the eye and tell me you're happy with him, and I'll drop it."

She stared at me pointedly, waiting for me to oblige. But I couldn't, because I wasn't a liar. Aydin was making me miserable. Triumph shone in Denali's eyes.

"You can't say shit because you aren't, Estelle," she continued, taking my hands in hers. "I'm not asking for us to run away and get married. Just that you give us a chance. I like whatever the hell it is we have going on and want to explore it without having to hide you."

"I'm sorry," I whispered, standing from the bed and blinking back tears. I began to collect my clothes, unable to look at her and see the hurt written across her face. "I...I can't give you what you want, Denali. Not now."

"Just tell me why," she demanded, remaining in bed as I dressed. "You're sneaking around with me, you've already said you're falling out of love with him, and you can't fucking say that you're happy with him. If you're worried about what others would think, fuck them, because this is about us—"

"There is no us," I snapped, wishing she'd drop the subject. "We're a situationship at best, and I don't know when that would change. Yeah, I've had a crush on you for years, but that doesn't mean you have a claim on me, or get to rush this."

As soon as the words were out, I regretted them. Denali looked crushed. My mouth had gotten ahead of my tipsy brain, grasping at straws to try to shut her up.

"Okay," she said flatly, standing to gather the pretty outfit she'd put together, just to impress my family. "If that's how you feel, I don't know why the fuck I'm here."

"Denali—"

"Save it, Estelle," she barked, whirling to glare at me. "I get it now. I was a childhood goal, and a good fuck, not someone you saw a future with. Have a nice fucking life with the asshole you're trapping yourself with."

"Don't say that," I said, blinking back tears. "You're putting words in my mouth when I didn't mean it that way. I care about you, I do, and I'd love for us to give things a go, but I have to consider more than just my feelings."

"Such as?"

I wracked my brain on what to say, on how to dance around the main reason I was staying with Aydin. Huffing out a breath, I gave her the best answer I could, one that would hopefully placate her until I figured shit out.

"My fans know and love Aydin, even with his behavior at the last signing. He's been a model for several of my covers, and we appear perfect. How would it seem if I just stepped out with not only somebody else, but another woman, and a woman like you?"

She recoiled as if slapped. I wanted to kick myself, but all I was doing was making a mess of things further.

"A woman like me?" she repeated, glaring at me. "Am I not good enough for you and your fucking prissy fans?"

"No, but your lifestyle and mine aren't the most compatible, so—"

A lie, as my lifestyle was more flexible than most, a fact Denali seemed to be keenly aware of.

"Stop talking, Estelle, because all you're doing is making shit worse," she snarled, angrily swiping at her eyes. "If you don't want to be with me, say that, instead of acting like a cowardly bitch who can't stand on business and say what the fuck she means."

"Denali—"

"I thought this was more serious than it was, and that was my mistake," she continued as she finished dressing, grabbed her things, and stormed to the door. "Have a nice fucking life, Estelle."

All I could do was let my tears flow. They didn't move her one bit. She walked through the door and slammed it behind her, leaving me alone with a heavy, regretful heart.

Part Four

Life's a bitch

Chapter Eighteen

DENALI

After Estelle's drunken mind spoke her sober thoughts, I rode around for half an hour before returning to the clubhouse. It was just past midnight, prime hours for debauchery to take place. Sex and drugs were just as common in the Harlots as they were at the Bastards, but most of the women had the decency to fuck in a more private setting, instead of out in the open.

Keyword: Most.

Moans mingled with the music blasting, hang-arounds who wanted to get claimed putting on a show for those who forgot common decency and granted them the attention they so desperately wanted. The smell of sex, alcohol, and smoke was thick in the air, a scent I'd grown accustomed to. I ignored it all, breezing to the bar for a drink, needing to forget everything Estelle told me.

"Whisky sour," I said when Maiden, our main bartender, sauntered to me.

Her green eyebrows rose. She was a natural brunette, but since she patched in, she kept her hair colored and always made sure the hair above her eyes matched her pixie cut.

"Everything okay, Everest?" she asked, knowing my preference for beer and wine.

"Just get me the drink," I grumbled, Estelle's words playing on repeat in my head.

To say I was crushed was an understatement. Not only did her words sting, but they made me feel like a stupid bitch. She and I might not have come from wildly different socioeconomic statuses, but she'd had a loving family who adored her and managed to elevate herself into wealth via her writing. The latter must've given her a big head and made her look down on plebs like me, who had a rough life, and did what they needed to do for survival.

Maiden obliged, saying nothing to me as she fixed my drink. When it was in my hand, she went to tend to another Harlot, one more inclined to chat. Only when my whisky sour was drained did she return, curiosity burning in her eyes.

"I know you have this whole mystery thing going on, Everest, but you're free to talk to me," she said as she slid the second drink to me. "Does it have to do with that Turk's fiancée?"

"I don't want to talk about her," I snapped, my words harsher than intended, confirming her question. Inhaling deeply, I forced myself to calm down. "It's nothing. Just a shitty day."

Her eyes flickered over my face. It was clear she wasn't satisfied with my answer, but she didn't push the issue. Nodding, she walked away again.

My second whisky sour was drunk as quickly as my first. Before I could order another, Valentina took a seat to my left, a blunt in hand.

"Take a hit," she ordered, holding it out to me. "I see you sulking over here, and it's fucking with me, man."

"The fuck do you care?" I questioned, snatching the joint from her and inhaling deeply, exhaling the smoke through my nose.

Aunt Mary began to do her job almost immediately, relaxing me in a way liquor couldn't.

"You're my friend, jackass," Val said with an eyeroll, accepting the blunt when I handed it back to her. "Even if you have your ass on your shoulders right now, I do care about you, and don't like seeing you like your best friend died, when I'm alive and well." I snorted out a laugh, making her grin. "C'mon, Evy. Tell Valentina what's wrong."

I shrugged. "Nothing to tell. Caught feelings when I shouldn't have."

"Forever secretive," she sighed, clapping me on the back and standing. "C'mon, girlie. Let's go for a ride to clear your mind."

She didn't give me a chance to opt out. Despite being shorter, she tugged me up and dragged me out of the clubhouse. I didn't protest. If I really wanted to, I could've escaped her hold, but there was little riding that couldn't fix. The first time might've been a bust, but perhaps some company would undo the heartache Estelle had caused.

Somehow, Val and I ended up on Beale Street, which was buzzing like usual. Instead of going into a bar, we grabbed some finger food at a 24/7 restaurant, eating it as we walked around, taking in the activity all around us. Tourists and locals alike flocked to the famed street, making it crowded year-round. Having been born in one of America's largest cities and living in Memphis for four years, navigating the crowds was light work for me.

"You plan to give me more details?" Valentina asked when our causal chitchat died.

"About?" I said, feigning ignorance as I chucked a fry into my mouth.

She pursed her lips, a piece of lettuce clinging to her chin. "You know what."

I did. She wanted the 411 on Estelle. The entire club knew she and I were involved, due to the emergency Church following Eli's death. Yet, fixing my lips to say that Estelle wasn't the woman I thought she was seemed like a Herculean task. Instead of a sweetheart who could be blunt, I now knew her to be a bitch who could be sweet.

Valentina snapped her fingers in front of my face, making me slap her hand away. She held up her hands in surrender.

"Okay, babes, I won't push the issue. But—"

"Estelle and I are over," I said with a sigh, plopping down on a bench that was somehow free.

Val sat next to me, brows furrowed. "But you liked her."

"I did," I agreed, setting my food on the small gap between us. "But she didn't feel the same way. She was just slumming it with me while she and her fiancé worked shit out."

"The Turkish broker?"

"Yep."

"I'm sorry," Val said after a heartbeat of silence. "It was clear you cared about her, but this is a reminder that the years changed her. It's for the best if you end things now." Sighing, she took the last bite of her sandwich, then chucked the wrapper in a nearby trashcan. "And I'm sorry, too. I've been treating you like a dumb cunt and have been messy instead of minding my business."

"You have, but I'm used to you, Val."

Her jaw dropped, and I snickered.

"I'm not messy," she protested, inspiring more laughter from me.

"And I'm fucking ten feet tall," I said around chuckles, taking the last bite of my Nashville Hot tender, leaving only some fries and nasty-ass coleslaw.

"Your tall ass might as well be," she shot back, making me roll my eyes. Val was 5'5, so I had six inches on her. "You should've been called 'Amazon' instead of Everest, dude."

"I might've been, if you knew geography."

"How was I supposed to know that Mt. Denali and Mt. Everest were fucking thousands of miles away from one another?"

As always, the memory of her ignorance made me chuckle. To say I'd been shocked when she first said that was an understatement.

"If you'd paid attention to elementary geography, you would've known that, babes."

"Whatever," she grumbled, a small smile on her glossy lips.

Standing, I threw away my remaining food and stretched. My heart was still heavy over Estelle, but I couldn't do shit but keep it pushing. Life was a bitch, and even a glimmer of light could be snatched away. Estelle had quickly become a bright spot in my gritty lifestyle, but her true colors dimmed it.

"Let's go back to the club, Val. Thank you for this," I said with as much sincerity as I could muster.

She waved me off. "I didn't do shit. I just listened."

"A rarity, considering how much you like the sound of your own voice," I teased, smirking when she flipped me off. "Did I lie?"

"I plead the fifth."

We began to walk to where we parked our bikes. The crowds were starting to lull. For now, anyway, because they'd surge again when the bars and clubs closed. Music of all sorts floated to my ears, but the blues was still easily heard. The genre may not be on top anymore, but it never lost its popularity on Beale Street.

"Actually, before we go, I wanna stop by the smoke shop and—"

A series of loud bangs cut her off. Gunshots, I realized, all too fucking close for comfort. Screams rose, people panicking as everyone feared the worst. A bullet whizzed past me, and my heart sank. Val and I shared a look of understanding. Femmes had found us, and we were the target. I grabbed her arm and dragged her into an alleyway, intending to hide and call Karma to tell her the situation.

However, just as I got my phone out, three figures darkened the alleyway. Two were Femmes with masks on, though their cuts identified who they were. Their names were unfamiliar; bitches I didn't know. The third was a man who also wore a mask, but whose eyes were eerily familiar.

"Knew that was those Harlot bitches," one of the women said, her lame words making the other girl snicker.

Val and I took out our pieces, just as the shooting started again. I was still in my dinner outfit, but I kept a spare gun and thigh holster in my saddlebags, so I'd never be caught lacking. Never had I been prouder of that decision.

The bitches were awful shots, missing us, and getting dropped within a minute. The fact that this would make the news didn't matter; only surviving did. The man—who I was positive was Aydin—had better aim than those dead cunts and was better at dodging our bullets. I managed to get his arm, and he retaliated by nearly grazing my shoulder. It was a close call, but adrenaline kept me going.

At least, it did, until one of the bullets hit Val in the head.

A scream left me as she dropped to the dirty concrete. Blindly, I fired at him, tears blurring my vision as dread coiled in my gut. He evaded the gunfire easily, flipping me off as he ran out of the alleyway. I considered going after him, but I couldn't leave Val. Letting my gun drop, I crawled to her, praying that by some chance, she was still breathing.

She wasn't.

"C'mon, girlie, wake up," I croaked as I took her in my arms, shaking as I brought two fingers to her pulse point. "Please, Val, open your eyes. We need to get back to the club."

She didn't hear me. Of course, she fucking didn't. The whites of her eyes were showing, already glazing over, confirming what her lack of a heartbeat and non-existent breath told me.

At twenty-seven years old, Valeria 'Valentina' Blanco, my best friend and tail gunner for the Harlots, was dead.

Chapter Nineteen

DENALI

The following day, Church was held to announce Val's death. During the last emergency meeting, Val had sat with me as we learned Eli had died. Now, I was all alone. No one said anything as Karma broke the news. The silence that followed was heavy. Val was friends with just about everyone, a social butterfly well-liked by the entire club. And yet, she'd chosen me to be her best friend, something I'd taken for granted until last night.

But it was too late.

Valentina was a body now, unable to know how deeply I cherished our friendship.

I'd cried all night, mourning her, hating Aydin, and wishing I'd never let my feelings over Estelle cloud what needed to be done. Maybe if she'd been dealt with, Val would be alive.

"What now?" Kinder said, her voice small.

Geri gave her a sympathetic look. Val loved strays and had taken Kinder's bitchiness in stride.

"We strike back," Big Mama said. "Hit them harder, make them wish they'd never been born, and that's a fucking promise."

Her promise rallied some of the members, cries endorsing her words echoing through the room. They weren't enough for me, though. I wanted to avenge Valentina ASAP, to wipe the Femmes from the face of the Earth. And when we were done with them, I'd beg Karma to contact Reign and get him on board with going to war with the Memphis Scorpions.

"We're already on the news," I heard myself saying, thoughts of bloodshed and death dancing through my head.

Nobody involved had been identified. Gang violence in Memphis wasn't uncommon, and when it was clear that there had been no civilian casualties, the media and cops backed off. Our regular donations to the Memphis PD helped them to stay off our backs, too.

"Let's ride out to their clubhouse and blow them the fuck up," I continued, wanting to scream, wishing I had necromancy powers to bring my best friend back.

"Negative, Everest," Karma said woefully, forever a cautious tactic. "We're going to get those bitches, but we need a gameplan first. We run on fucking emotions, we get fucked up, too."

"What do you propose?" Chains asked, sitting with me for once.

She'd been in my shoes recently, when a Femme's bullet had taken away her good friend.

"Aydin was with them," I blurted, causing murmurs to restart. I'd been too distraught last night to share that info with the club, unable to say anything other than 'she's dead'. Taking a breath, I forced myself to continue, blinking back tears. "He fucking shot her. I motion we…we take his fiancée for leverage. Let him wonder if she's fucking dead or alive, and feel the same pain we are."

A week ago, those words would've been unthinkable to speak. But a week ago, I thought Estelle cared about me, and more importantly, Val was alive.

"I second that," Siren said, looking around the room, daring anyone to disagree. "Can I get an aye?"

Karma considered me as agreements rose. Half of the club had wanted to get to Estelle before Val's death. Now, just about everyone wanted vengeance on her fiancé.

"Motion passes," Prez declared when everyone quieted. "We'll develop a plan and get her within the week."

"I know where she lives. I'll put a tracker on her car," I volunteered, Aydin's destruction consuming me.

He had to love her if she was staying with him. If nothing else, his enemies getting the drop on him would drive him fucking crazy.

"I'll get you a tracker ASAP," Tiny said, sounding as distraught as I felt. "That fucker will pay for what he did to Val."

That was all I wanted. If I had to use Estelle to get to her fucking fiancé, then so be it.

Since I lost my virginity, I'd enjoyed sex. It was the most primal way to connect with another human being, and when orgasm was achieved, made you feel a rush of endorphins. Sex with Aydin used to be one of my favorite hobbies. Following our engagement, we fought more than we fucked. Now, I wouldn't dream of touching him with a ten-foot pole. He'd been sent to sleep outside the primary suite, and the bedroom door stayed locked, just for safe measure.

He'd asked for sex twice already. I declined him both times.

One, he was fucking blackmailing me, and out of his mind if he thought I'd agreed.

Two, Denali had ruined me, staying on my mind constantly.

Not only did I already miss her touch, but I longed to hear her voice, and to tell her how fucking sorry I was. Often, I agreed that drunk minds spoke sober thoughts, but what I said four days ago didn't reflect how I felt about her. I couldn't explain why I said what I did, other than wanting her to drop the subject. My only reason for not being with her was Aydin, not any of the false bullshit I'd spewed.

Deciding against rubbing one out to the thought of her, I turned off the shower and stepped out, wrapping a towel around my damp body. I breezed through my morning routine, not having the energy to do the more detailed version. My daily yoga was axed, my hair was thrown into a messy bun, I skipped most of my skincare and just applied my moisturizing sunscreen, and flossing would have to wait until that night. It'd been that way for the past three days and would likely remain that way until I made up with Denali.

Too bad she wasn't answering any of my fucking calls or texts.

When I emerged from the room, I found Aydin kneeling by Crush's tank, frowning as he examined the turtle.

"He isn't eating," he said without looking at me. Standing, he nudged the bowl filled with Crush's favorites closer. He turned his head, so Aydin tried again. This time, the turtle retreated inside his shell. Aydin sighed. "He didn't eat yesterday, either."

"Maybe he senses his parents aren't happy," I replied, sarcasm the only way that I wouldn't break down.

Aydin directed his frown at me. "That isn't funny. We're just going through a rough patch."

"Call it what you want, Aydin. If he doesn't eat tomorrow, we'll call up the vet."

"I'm taking him today," he declared, because why the fuck would he care about what I had to say?

I didn't even care that he'd gotten home late the other night, in obvious pain. He remained covered up, and I didn't ask him what was up. If he'd gotten hurt while cheating on me, that was just karma.

"Cool," I said, going to the door and slipping into some slides. "Keep me posted."

"Where are you going?"

His voice was sharp. I rolled my eyes. My family dinners lasted for hours, a fact he knew, and the reason he hadn't thrown a fit when I was gone for hours the night of our big spat. Since then, he barely wanted me to leave the house.

"I still have shit to do, Aydin."

That was all I said before I left, praying that Crush was okay. As much as I wanted to stew in misery, I needed to make a grocery store run and to get out of that apartment.

Thankfully, Aydin didn't up his assholery further and chase me. Starting up my pink-wrapped 2023 Range Rover with tinted windows, I blasted my favorite radio station, too downtrodden to even connect my phone to the car's Bluetooth. As I drove to the store, I sang along to the classic R&B, my mind going momentarily blank as I focused on driving and staying as on-key as possible.

Instead of immediately going to the store, I just drove around, not quite ready to face anyone. I considered going to one of my favorite walking trails to unwind. Without realizing, I began to drive in that direction. When awareness returned to me, instead of switching course, I kept going. Even if I didn't get out, rocking out alone in my car for an hour or so could be therapeutic. Maybe I could have a good cry. The seclusion meant no one would see me, and Aydin wouldn't question what was going on.

I lasted three songs before I started to second-guess my plan. Still, I wasn't ready to go anywhere crowded or return home, so taking a quick walk it was.

When I exited my car, I kept the door open as I collected my phone and keys and tried to hide my purse somewhere. I lived in a safer area of Memphis, but I'd never take any chances. Before I could lock the door and set off on the trail, the roar of bikes reached my ears. Whirling around, I saw about four bikers trickling into the trail's parking lot, all heading for me. I examined their cuts when they surrounded me, realizing they were Royal Harlots. It gave me some comfort, but didn't erase my anxiety.

Just as I reentered my vehicle to get the fuck, one of the women stopped her bike to approach me.

"What the hell?" I yelled as she yanked open the car door, inching as far back as possible.

Before I could fix my lips to ask her what the fuck was wrong with her, a blow to the head knocked me the fuck out.

DENALI

"You sure you up for this?" Karma questioned as she handed me a black ski mask.

She wanted our identities hidden, at least until Estelle understood how helpless she was. I didn't exactly see the point of it, but I wouldn't question my Prez. Kiwi, Chains, and two probates had been the ones to snatch Estelle when the tracker showed her heading to a secluded walking trail. I didn't know where her head had been, and I didn't care. She should've had better survival instincts if she didn't want to get kidnapped.

Once Estelle was tied up in the backseat, one of the probates drove the Rover back to the U.N. Rainbow removed anything that could trace the vehicle back to us, while Tiny broke into Estelle's phone and texted her family and friends that she needed a vacation. For safe measure, Tiny posted on her story that she'd be MIA for an undisclosed period of time, due to personal reasons. When that task was complete, she made sure the device was untraceable. Chains suggested the device be destroyed, but Tiny pointed out that not answering her family and friends would be more suspicious, so Prez ordered Tiny to text one person once per day.

Karma waved a hand in front of my face, and I blinked. "Hello, Earth to Everest?"

"Sorry, Prez," I grumbled, then cleared my throat, quickly putting the mask on. "Yeah. I'll be fine."

"Just stand in the background and shut the fuck up," Karma ordered. "I don't want you fucking shit up because you're distracted."

"Understood."

With that, me, Karma, Chains, Tiny, and Kiwi filed into the room.

"Wakey wakey, sweetheart," Kiwi called, her accent thickening.

Nothing.

Chains didn't wait for Estelle to stir on her own. Going to the sink, she filled a rusty bucket with water and threw it on her, making her white shirt cling to her curves, and her brushed-out red hair curl up. I pretended that the sight of Estelle sputtering and gasping didn't bother me, just as I tried to ignore how her fear made me feel guilty. Then Val's face popped into my mind, and I only wanted revenge.

Tiny snapped a few pictures of Estelle chained to a too-tiny twin bed and dripping wet, nodded, and walked out. Without being told, I knew those would go to Aydin.

"Welcome, girliepop, to our humble abode," Karma said, lazily gesturing around the room. "If you haven't guessed it, you'll be our guest for the time being."

"What do you want from me?" Estelle asked, her voice trembling as she looked between the four of us.

"Your fiancé," Chains said without missing a beat.

Karma nodded. "You see, girlie, he's been a bad, bad man. Killed one of our own."

Estelle released a choked noise, tears rushing to her eyes. Her breathing became shallow, and she shook her head.

"No. Aydin wouldn't—"

"He would, and he has," I barked, memories of Val's corpse making anger rush through me.

Her eyes widened, then narrowed. "Denali."

Everyone groaned, included myself. Karma turned around and slapped me, a light punishment.

"Great, you fucking blew it," she complained, snatching her mask off. "These are useless, now."

We all followed suit. Estelle began to cry harder, staring right at me.

"Denali, please—"

"Everest," I corrected, crossing my arms over my chest. "And you don't get to ask me shit."

"Everest, stand down," Karma ordered, then placed a hand on her chest and looked back at Estelle. "I'm Karma, your lovely host. That's Chains and Kiwi. They took you, but don't worry. You won't be here forever. Just until the broker behaves."

"Broker?" Estelle parroted. "No, you got it all wrong. He works for his parents business. I've been to their store, I can tell you the address—"

"We know about the fucking store," Karma barked, interrupting her. "He's part time at his parents place. They have ties to the Turkish Mob, and your dumbass fiancé is trying to become an official member of their mafia."

Estelle's mouth opened, closed, and opened, shock momentarily replacing her fear. "W-what?"

"You heard us," Kiwi said.

"Looks like you didn't know him that well, hmm?" Chains added, cruel amusement dripping from her words.

I found nothing funny about the situation. Everything, from Val's death to snatching Estelle, was sad, and only increased my desire to see Aydin's head on a platter.

"H-he'll know I'm gone. He'll—"

"That's the point, dumbass," Karma interrupted. "We're sending him some lovely pictures of you, and giving him our ultimatum. Him for you. Or else."

A sob escaped Estelle. "Please. Let me go. People will know I'm gone. They'll—"

"Covered our tracks there, too, sweetie," Karma said in a saccharine tone. "We texted your folks, friends, and made a post on your IG. Oh, and we have your car. To the world, you've just gone on an impromptu vacation. That's all for now, girlie, but we'll be back."

Her singsong revealed her sadistic side and how she got her name. Cross her, and she'll hit back ten times harder. Her club, man, and children were also off-limits, and got you fucked up quicker than if you just fucked with her.

Karma nodded to us, and we trooped out of the room, but not before Chains turned off the single light in the room, leaving Estelle in total darkness.

Chapter Twenty

DENALI

I purposely didn't see Estelle for two days. As angry as I was with her, I hated her helplessness. When she'd first been snatched, seeing her so humiliated pleased me. But the feeling was so fleeting, it barely registered.

Then, I discovered she was only being given water and no food. That pissed me the fuck off, and I stormed to Karma's office, interrupting her and her ol' man fucking. I didn't give a good fuck. She couldn't starve Estelle.

Perhaps that's why she didn't give me much pushback. The shock of seeing them fucking helped bring sanity back to me. If I had run up on Prez, that would've gotten me beaten. It might've also gotten Estelle killed as part of my punishment. I'm almost certain she was still alive because of me.

Val was dead because of this feud. That heartbreak called for in-kind retaliation.

"Estelle needs to eat, Prez," I said, ignoring the daggers her husband directed at me. I'm sure that motherfucker wished he had real knives. "Can I bring her a plate?"

Not only had I interrupted them, but it was an open secret that Prez and I fucked before, something he'd always held against me.

"Yeah, Everest," Karma said irritably, unconcerned that she was naked and her husband's cock resembled an angry red snake. "A knock would've been nice."

"A locked door would've been better," I retorted, my nerves shot.

She glared at me and pointed toward the hallway. "Out!"

Turning, I stalked to the door and turned the lock on the knob. "You're welcome," I flung over my shoulder before slamming it shut.

She'd hand me my ass later. Right now, getting her pussy off took precedence.

Val's death had sucked the joy out of us. *Me.* I regretted so fucking much how we'd been so distant the last weeks of her life. As I walked to the other side of the bar to where the door led to the kitchen, I avoided looking at her picture on the wall with the officers. Hers now had a black sash on it. Soon, it would be moved to the Free Bird wall, and that just broke my fucking heart.

The kitchen was deserted. We'd eaten a couple of hours ago in joyless companionship, each of us as miserable as the next. When I returned to my room, I sat on the side of my bed, so fucking down and dejected. I'd thought about calling Mrs. Milton. She'd help to guide me back to the right path.

Then, I remembered we were holding Estelle hostage. Mrs. Milton didn't know it, but *I* did, and I knew it was a gross betrayal. I might not have cared about Estelle any longer, but her grandmother did. I'd intended to bring her an extra blanket and sneak her some snacks. We only fed our hostages once a day, but Kinder had caught me raiding the kitchen and informed me that Estelle hadn't eaten since we brought her to the U.N.

Now, as I carried a tray heaping with fried chicken, baked macaroni, stewed green beans, and a tall glass of lemonade, I couldn't wait to lay my gaze on Estelle again. Just to reassure myself that she wasn't being mistreated, on behalf of Mrs. Milton, of course.

I set the tray on the table outside of Estelle's prison, fished my keys out of my pocket, and unlocked the door. A sniffle greeted me as I carried her food in. Her chains clanked, and I could barely make out her sitting up on the small bed since it was in the corner, stuck in the shadows.

Being kept in darkness was a special type of torture. Humans needed light to thrive. If someone feared the dark, they broke faster. If darkness wasn't a concern, it took a little longer, but eventually disorientation would set in, and they'd only want to feel safe again.

The light from the hallway allowed me to see one of the two chairs in the room. I set the tray on it, then turned and flipped on the overhead light before closing the door.

"Denali?"

Estelle sounded as if she'd cried buckets. Instead of facing her immediately, I heaved in a breath and remembered everything she'd told me, how she actually felt about me. It was enough to bring my anger back, and I spun around, ready to fucking order her to shut up. What I didn't expect was her busted lip and nose caked with dried blood, teary, blackened eyes, and disheveled hair.

Of course, they'd beaten her. What did I expect? She was a fucking enemy. We broke our enemies before we killed them. Estelle couldn't die, though. That bitch had to live so I could properly hate her. The first opportunity she got, she'd shit on me.

Glowering, I snatched the tray, stalked to her, and set it in front of her on the bed. I'd warmed the food for her and everything, forgetting how treacherous she was.

"Eat," I directed, spinning around and going to the more comfortable chair, the one for the interrogator. "You have ten minutes."

"Even a dog has more time!" she wailed.

"Stop being a boujee bitch and eat the fucking food, Estelle," I barked.

"No! And I'm n-not boujee," she said around pitiful sniffles.

Debatable, but arguing that point would only waste more of the time I granted her.

"Eat the fucking food," I told her again. "I didn't have to bring you a plate, so don't make my fucking efforts go to waste."

Her shoulders slumped, and she gave me an accusatory gaze. "Who are you? I thought I knew you."

"No, you didn't. You weren't interested in getting to know me, so tell that lie to a bitch who'll believe you."

She contemplated the food. I halfway expected her to swipe the fucking tray off the bed. I would've been mad as hell if she'd been that much of a brat, but she gave in and grabbed a piece of chicken.

"Eat slowly," I reminded her. "I don't want you to fucking hurl."

Sidling a glare at me, she sank her teeth into the meat. "I'm sure allowing me to wallow in my own vomit has a place on your torture menu."

"Nope, sure doesn't. Making you clean it and threatening you with more dire consequences does."

Her face crumpled. She set the chicken leg back on the plate and licked her lips, then sucked her fingers, reminding me of how her mouth had felt sucking my nipple and lapping my clit.

"Help me," she begged, her eyes huge and vulnerable. "Please? If you can't do it for me, then do it for my grandmother—"

"Don't you fucking dare!" I fumed, annoyed she was playing on my sympathy for some of the same reasons I'd already considered. I was doing it out of genuine concern for Mrs. Milton. Estelle was doing it to be a sheisty bitch. "I'm not fucking good enough to be a part of your family, so don't try to use them to get your way."

Fuck, those words slipped out, but they were true. In essence, that's what Estelle said to me. I'd be a charity case to the Pratt-Miltons.

"I never said that," Estelle told me. "I didn't mean any of what I said, the way you're taking it."

"Then what the fuck did you mean?" Lifting my brow, I folded my arms and met her gaze. "I'm all fucking ears."

"Please, just trust me."

I had. That was the fucking problem. She'd once again reminded me why I was better off not letting my guard down.

"You don't deserve my fucking trust," I spat, hating her because of how her current state affected me and because of how she'd crushed me so deeply that I'd actually cried.

"You must care just a little if you kidnapped me."

Estelle's words echoed in my head and, at first, I smiled. But her assumption was so ludicrous that I laughed my ass off, so hard that tears rushed to my eyes.

"You think too highly of your fucking self," I said when my chuckles died away. "I'm insulted that you think I'm that fucking desperate." Pretending to think, I snapped my fingers. "On second thought, it tracks. You think I'm just a piece of shit, so of course I'd be so heartbroken I needed to fucking snatch you."

"You're twisting my words around, Denali," she said, a soft, miserable sob escaping her.

I fucking hated seeing her so devastated. Despite what she'd done to me and how she felt about me, I'd always wanted Estelle to be happy. If I didn't make her happy, then she shouldn't be with me, but she could've let me down more gently. Blowing out a heavy breath, I lost some of my attitude.

"Eat, babe. You must be starving."

She froze at my sudden change, then lowered her lashes and swept me with a sweet, relieved gaze. "Actually, I'm not. I was on the first day. Now, I'm just exhausted. It's so dark in here and…and…" She pointed to the door that led to the toilet. "I have to stretch my arms out to reach the toilet, and then it feels as if I'm going to fall off. I can't see in front of me, so I hold my pee in for a long as possible."

"The light is on now," I said gruffly. "Why don't you piss now?"

Estelle shook her head. "No! No! Please, just help me to escape. Please. I'll pay you—"

"No," I said with real regret. "You can't offer me any amount of money to make me betray my club."

"Then do it because of what I mean to you."

I heaved in a breath, counted to three, and heaved in another breath, trying to cool my fucking temper. It didn't work. "That would be nothing," I told her. "You don't mean shit to me."

I thought flinging those words at her would make me feel better, but they only made me feel worse. I hurt her.

"I mean something to you," she croaked, reaching out to touch me, her face crumpling when I recoiled. "Because you mean something to me. Much more than I can ever explain."

"Even if I wanted a fucking explanation, no amount of words could take back what the fuck you said to me the other night."

"I was only trying to make things better."

"Shutting the fuck up would've worked. You didn't have to keep opening your fucking mouth. But you've never known the beauty of silence, so I shouldn't be surprised that you fucking yapped, until you exposed your feelings."

"That isn't true," she insisted.

"I'm done talking about us, Estelle. Eat your fucking food. Your ten minutes are long past." Moreover, her food was probably cold. I could've saved myself the fucking trouble of warming it.

"We don't have to talk. Just leave the door unlocked and release me from my chains."

"No, Estelle. *No.* You're the club's prisoner. Not mine. Even if I wanted to let you go, which I don't, I couldn't. I'm not betraying my club for you."

"I won't tell anyone that you helped me if I'm caught." She drew in a deep breath. "I can't be locked up in here. Those girls beat me up. I thought you—"

"You thought I was such a fucking lowlife that I'd have you abused to get my lick back?" I laughed bitterly, even as I worried for her safety. "That's fucking rich that you think I'm so pathetic."

"I don't! I think you're gorgeous and brave, everything I want—"

"Shut up," I snapped. "If you wanted me, you wouldn't have thrown me away."

"I didn't throw you away. I swear. If you touch my pussy right now, you'd see how soaked I am for you."

I snapped my brows together at the sudden lewdness, trying to pretend the offer wasn't tempting. "No," I pushed out.

I wanted nothing more than to find out, but doing so was wrong for so many reasons. Even overlooking the power dynamic, it'd be the definition of insanity. Doing the same shit and expecting a different result. Maybe how we ended was my fault because I'd expected more from her. If I'd known I was just a fuck, I could've kept my feelings in check, and her offer wouldn't have been so upsetting.

"Fuck no," I added for good measure.

She licked her lips again and studied my mouth. "It's just the two of us," she said, suddenly throaty. "Let's make each other feel good. If they come down and see us together, they won't bother me."

"Who comes down here?" I demanded, intending to tell them to keep their fucking fists to themselves.

"Their names don't register. I'm too busy trying to protect my head."

"I'll take care of it," I promised, hating that I still had the urge to protect her.

"You won't have to, babe," she said huskily. "If you let me go. If you won't take cash, enjoy my body as payment. You know how much you enjoy fucking me. I'm offering you no-strings-attached sex if you help me to escape."

Any desire I felt evaporated, and I stiffened, offended. I couldn't believe her nerve. "I'm not for fucking sale with money or pussy."

"But—"

Jumping to my feet, I stalked to her bed and grabbed the tray. At the door, I flipped off the light.

"Wait! No," Estelle cried. "Don't leave me in the dark, please. Please? I'm sorry. I—"

"Shut the fuck up," I ordered, and slammed the door, plunging her into darkness.

Breathing heavily, I stood there for a moment, her sobs traveling through the door. I flinched.

Mrs. Milton's face popped into my head. Terrorizing Estelle was a shitty way to repay her.

"Hey, Everest." Siren's greeting scared the shit out of me. "Karma's looking for you."

I set the tray on the table. "Karma knows my location," I said flatly. "It sounds like your excuse to get me away so you can beat Estelle again."

She'd want to avenge Val, which I understood. If Estelle hadn't been my…whatever, I'd want to make her suffer, too. It didn't matter that Siren and Val were frenemies, who competed over everything and argued about so much—from who had the better bike, to whether Cuban or Venezuelan Spanish was better, and more shit I couldn't think of at the moment. At the end of the day, they were sisters.

Siren shook her head. "I haven't seen Estelle since we brought her here," she swore.

Another sob traveled through the door, and I glanced over my shoulder, gnashing my teeth together.

"What's up?" Siren asked, nodding toward Estelle's door. "Why all the racket?"

"I brought her food, but she said she isn't hungry. When I left, I turned off the light, even though she fucking begged me not to."

"If it's bothering you that much, turn the fucking light on, Everest. That's simple."

My pride suggested otherwise.

Rolling her eyes, Siren took her key out of her pocket. Aside from the officers and the enforcers, only a select few were allowed keys to the holding cell. She cracked the door wide enough to stick her hand in and flip on the light before closing it again.

"Feel better now?"

I did, but I refused to admit it, so I shrugged, picked up the tray, and sauntered off.

After returning the tray to the kitchen, I walked back into the clubhouse. A lot of the girls had left their dorms to come for the evening socializing. Usually, Val was at the center of everything. That woman had never met a stranger.

"Everest!" Kinder called, forever seeking my attention.

I didn't want to be bothered. My thoughts were all jumbled. I wasn't in the fucking mood to be sociable, let alone with Kinder.

"Karma's probably in her office," Siren said, breezing by me and heading to where Chains, Kiwi, and Kinder sat.

I sighed and went to Karma's office, remembering to knock.

"Come in," she called.

When I walked in, the scent of smoke hit me full-force. She blew out a plume of smoke from her nostrils, then set the cigarette in the ashtray on her desk.

"Sit," she ordered, fully clothed now that Greg was gone.

"I didn't mean to interrupt you and him," I said as I took one of the seats in front of her desk.

She waved her hand. "My pussy and me are fine. The interruption didn't affect us. I have a job I want you to go on. It's very lucrative, and it gives you a chance to clear your head."

Something I sorely needed, but that meant leaving Estelle to fend for herself. I kept myself away from her for two fucking days, and look how that turned out.

"Kiwi told me to offer it to you."

"Why?" I asked suspiciously.

"What the fuck do you mean, why?" Karma demanded. "Because you're sisters and she's looking out for you."

"Estelle is all beat up, Prez. It sounds to me like sending me on a fucking run is a convenient way to get me out of the way, so she can be finished off."

"I'll ignore that," Karma said evenly. "You're acting like Kiwi isn't always giving you fucking runs. You're her favorite because you get shit done."

"I'm passing on this one, Karma."

"Are you really allowing a piece of pussy to interfere with your bag, girl?"

"She's all fucking beat up, and she hasn't eaten in two goddamn days."

"Which you saw to. You brought her a plate."

"She took one bite of chicken, then said she wasn't hungry."

"Angel is next up on the roster for runs. If you don't take the job, I'm telling Kiwi to send her."

Angel wasn't my favorite person. She'd joined the year before me. From the moment Karma brought me to the club, Angel had been up my ass. Nowadays, we keep our distance from one another, the result of my beating her ass during a party.

"Congrats to her," I said sourly.

Karma cackled, picked up her cigarette again, and took another drag. "If that's your final answer, then there's nothing more for us to discuss."

"Actually, there is," I said, remembering Estelle's battered face. "I'd like you to give me permission to move our prisoner to my room."

"Any particular reason why?" Karma said, her expression closing. She knew how to hide her thoughts, especially when she disapproved. "I think she's perfectly fine where she's at. It doesn't matter how you know her; she's our enemy. Our prisoner."

"I know, Prez. I promise I won't give her any special treatment. I—"

"Just by allowing her in your room will be special treatment."

"Until we prove her guilt or innocence, she doesn't deserve to be starved and beaten."

Karma scowled. "If I agree to this, you better not let her out of your fucking sight, Denali," she snapped, pissed with me.

Never before had she used my real name. It came as a shock, and I was silent as I considered her words.

"Does that mean I'll have to bring her with me to eat?"

"If she has to be in your sight 24/7, you tell me what it means."

A lot of fucking fights, unless I stayed in my room with her. That wasn't the worst idea, except for our close proximity. I didn't want her to get in my fucking head with her bullshit. The moment I moved her, she'd think her pussy held power over me.

"I expect you to make sure she doesn't escape."

"I will." Hope soared in me. It had nothing to do with sleeping next to Estelle. "Is that a yes, then?"

One curt nod lifted my spirits, and I grinned, standing with new energy invigorating me. "Thank you, Prez."

"I'd better not regret this."

She'd never regretted her favors to me before. I saw no reason that would change.

Chapter Twenty-One

Estelle

Even after days, my face ached. The bruises had just started to fade, but I was still swollen and achy. Denali, for her part, protected me from further abuse, keeping me confined in her room. It was nicer than expected, with an industrial metal and wood four-poster bed, a small sitting area, posters, a large wardrobe, a mirror, and a wall-mounted TV, with a speaker and some books on the shelves below it. It was a visually appealing room, and seeing Thricebound on the nightstand would've brought me joy if I were there on my own freewill. Likewise, if I were there on my own freewill, being tied to her bed would've been thrilling, if it wasn't to keep me confined whenever she left.

The claims made against Aydin had yet to leave my head. The worst part was that I believed them. He'd changed so much, on a scale that couldn't be explained away by occasional drug use. It was easy to believe he was involved with a mob, but hearing he murdered someone was hard to wrap my head around. But part of his changes for the worse were his increased selfishness, remorselessness, and cruelty. If what I'd been told was true, and he was a part of an enemy set, why wouldn't he target the Harlots?

Just one more thing I didn't know about him, and one more betrayal to add to the list. I wasn't a Harlot, or even a hang around, but he knew I adored Michelle and her sisters, all of whom were Harlots. And yet, he took a stand against them by aligning with enemies.

Fucking asshole.

Even so, I'd rather be in our shared apartment than tied up at the clubhouse of the Memphis Royal Harlots. I'd been good, not trying to escape, knowing it'd be futile, but I was starting to go stir-crazy. If I could leave the room, maybe I could run outside, hop the chain-link fence, and get the hell out of dodge. It was a risky plan, but they needed me alive, and even after everything, I knew Denali would protect me. She'd moved me to her room, after all, to prevent me from enduring more beatings, and had tried to feed me when no one else had.

The door opened. Denali walked in, carrying a tray of whatever the hell was served at the club today. Seeing lasagna and garlic bread, my stomach growled, but I ignored the urge to eat. It was a skill I perfected in my teenage years, and one I revived as an act of protest.

As had become typical, Denali didn't say a word as she unlocked my chains and shoved the tray into my lap. Once I accepted it with a quiet 'thank you', defying her order to be silent once again, she went to her en suite bathroom. It shocked me that she didn't watch me eat as she had been, but my behavior must've been good enough for her to trust I'd be okay unchained and alone for a little while.

Her mistake.

I took a few bites until I heard the shower start up. Then, I made my move.

Setting the tray aside, I dashed to the door, my feet pounding against the old wooden floor. Just as I opened the door, the shower water stopped. My adrenaline surged, and I ran faster, thankful no one was in the hallway that doubled as a game room with some office space. Just as I made it to the stairs, strong arms wrapped around my waist, making me yelp. Denali's scent enveloped me as she clamped a hand over my mouth, dragging me back to her room.

Maybe I was a tad fucked up, but her show of strength was so damn sexy.

Dropping me onto her bed, she returned to the door and slammed it, the lock clicking. I tried to pretend her towel-clad body didn't affect me, even as my eyes longed to follow the stray droplet of water that rolled down her perfect body.

"What the fuck is wrong with you?" she asked when she whirled to face me, her eyes narrowed. "Are you trying to get us killed?"

"You wouldn't let me get hurt," I whispered, unable to meet her angry gaze. "You—"

"Would be fucking incapable of saving you if my Prez whooped my ass for letting our hostage roam free. What the fuck don't you get about the fact that I'm not calling the shots?"

"You are," I protested, motioning to her room. "You have me captive in your room, feeding me, chaining me, telling me when to bathe. You're controlling my every move and protecting me. How isn't that calling the shots?"

She huffed in frustration, pinching the bridge of her nose, the raising of her arms making her towel ride lower. "Estelle, fucking listen to me. Everything I'm doing, I got permission from Karma to do. If she declined my request to bring you here, I would've had to keep you in the cell. I'm. Not. In. Fucking. Control."

"You'd—"

"Shut the fuck up," she snapped. "I wouldn't do shit. Even if I could, if you escaped and got punished, I'd let your ass get beat, because you know the risk."

"Stop acting like I mean nothing to you," I snapped, getting to my feet. "I know you're loyal to your club, okay? But you wouldn't do any of this for a regular prisoner, so stop bullshitting and acting like you don't care."

Her jaw clenched, and she looked away, allowing me to admire her perfect side profile. "You're being held captive, and your biggest concern is how I feel about you?"

"Third biggest. Number one is getting the hell out of here, which you just fucking prevented. Two is staying alive, which is easy since you're protecting me."

"It won't be easy if you try dumb shit like that again," she said, grabbing my wrist and dragging me to the bed. "Since you can't fucking behave—"

"Denali—"

"Can you please shut the fuck up for once?" she snarled, shoving me onto the bed. "Your fiancé killed my best friend, and you stomped on my fucking heart. I should cut your tongue out and mail it to him, but instead I'm protecting you. Instead of being grateful for that, you wanna test the limits more and more, because you want to act like a dumb heroine of a stupid novel instead of someone with a brain. Try to escape again, and you won't have to worry about anyone else beating you, because I'll do it myself."

Her voice cracked, and I knew deep down that her words were just a threat to keep me in line. Swallowing, I reached to take her hand, but she stepped out of my reach.

"I'm sorry about your friend," I said quietly, looking down at my lap. "She didn't deserve what happened to her. I didn't think Aydin was capable—"

"Save it," she ordered. "This conversation is over."

"No, it isn't," I snapped, getting to my feet and planting myself in front of her. "We have nothing but time right now, so lets fucking talk so you stop acting like a bitch to me?"

A disbelieving laugh escaped her, and she scrubbed a hand over her face. "Acting like a bitch?" she finally said. "Did you already forget that my best friend is dead because of your man, Estelle? Did it slip your mind that you basically called me fucking gutter trash too good for you, when I wanted to make things more serious?"

"I didn't say that, and you know it. I'm sorry about what I said, but—"

"Nothing will excuse it, so stop fucking torturing me, and shut the fuck up and behave."

She guided me to the bed, then clamped the chains around my wrist. Instead of going to finish her shower, though, she opened one of the nightstand drawers and pulled out a sock. Approaching me again, I quickly figured out she was going to gag me, or at least try to. That thought panicked me more than anything else. I didn't want to be silenced, and I longed for us to reconnect again, for me to be able to comfort her for the pain she was experiencing. That wasn't possible if I were gagged.

"Aydin was blackmailing me," I blurted, just as she was about to shove the sock into my mouth. "The night of the family dinner. He…I tried to leave him. Tried to break off the engagement. He told me he'd leak my nudes if I left."

She recoiled as if slapped, anger darkening her features. She searched my face. Whatever she found only pissed her off more.

"Don't be mad, please," I whispered, tears filling my eyes as I worried she was angry at me.

What if she thought I was trying to manipulate her, when I was just explaining the situation?

"Okay," she said simply, the word clipped.

She dropped the towel. Out of respect, I closed my eyes, letting my tears fall as she got dressed and left the room.

DENALI

I was going to fucking kill Aydin. Slowly, to inflict as much pain as possible. I'd ask Chains for pointers and make him pay for all the harm he caused, but most especially to avenge Valentina and eliminate the threat to Estelle. When she was released, I'd dip into my personal savings and buy her silence. Aydin wouldn't be around to terrorize her anymore, and she'd be compensated for her trauma. We could go about our lives, and I'd breathe easier knowing that the motherfucker of all motherfuckers was dead.

I'd had my hands full with one Ms. Estelle Pratt-Milton. Not full per se. I've been overwhelmed by her nearness. When I got her out of the cell and marched her to my room at gunpoint, her chains dragging the floor, her walk of shame achieved what I'd wanted. I ordered her not to fucking talk to me. She didn't listen because she loved to talk. I tuned her out; just happy she wasn't on her own and vulnerable to whoever. Most of the time, I ate in my room. During the times Karma insisted I join everyone, such as today, I chained Estelle to my bed.

A nice thought under other circumstances.

Even though she'd remained a chatterbox, she hadn't argued with me until today, nor had she revealed how awful her fiancé was. It explained her behavior at her family's dinner and made me reconsider my harsh stance on her. But what was done was done, and regretting the past would do no good.

Instead, I'd apologize to her by taking her fiancé's head.

I badly wanted to take Lobster to ride out to Estelle's apartment, but a motorcycle drew more attention. So, I took one of the five Dodge Grand Caravans Karma had purchased two years ago. Models made before 2017 could be purchased for less than ten grand, and those made before 2015 could be purchased for less than five. I drove over the speed limit, trusting that the ghost license plates Rainbow had outfitted the van with would protect me from detection. I wore all black, and a black face mask hid my features. If I moved quickly, I'd never be identified.

It was the middle of the day, so the apartment building was deserted. I got to Estelle's floor with no issue, and jimmying the lock…wasn't fucking needed, because the door was already unlocked. My brows furrowed, and my hand went to my piece. As I carefully pushed the door open, I listened for voices, footsteps, running water, anything, but heard nothing.

When I was inside, I carefully closed the door, then scoured the apartment for that slimy fuck bag. No real man made a sport out of hurting women, and Aydin's crimes against women ranged from blackmail to fucking murder. Fuck him, fuck the Turks for tapping him, and fuck the Femmes for working with him.

Memories of sex with Estelle ran through my mind as I crept around. We'd made love—no, wait, scratch that. We *fucked* in just about every room. I ignored the heat rushing through me, instead focusing on the things that were out of place, or missing…

Motherfucker.

With a snarl, I stormed to the primary bedroom. It was a mess, and half of the clothes in the closet were gone. Aydin wasn't simply not home, but he'd evaded us. Instead of trying to get Estelle back, he ran like a pussy, leaving her to her fate.

She deserved so much fucking better.

Hating that I couldn't get my hands on him, I left the room with my fists curled, wanting to scream, wanting to teleport to Aydin and gut him.

Just as I was about to leave, movement caught my eye. Turning, I came face-to-face with that big ass terrarium, where Estelle's turtle was looking back at me, because the motherfucker couldn't even take his pet.

"You're fucking kidding me," I muttered, my conscience tugging at me.

I'd never been one to hurt innocents. Sure, I sometimes made a hobby of hunting creeps when they weren't an active threat to me, but animals and children were never harmed at my hand. If I left Crush, if I remembered correctly, I'd be condemning the thing to…fucking something. I didn't know diddly shit about turtles, but it felt wrong leaving Crush all alone.

Sighing, I took a moment to figure out how to open the thing and scooped the turtle up. It retreated into its shell, which was fine by me. Hopefully, Estelle would be happy to have some extra company.

When Denali returned from her sudden detour, the last thing I expected to see was her carrying Crush. I'd been so worried, deep down knowing that she'd gone to confront Aydin. If he'd killed her best friend, why wouldn't he kill her? Seeing her return safe and sound was a relief, and seeing Crush made my jaw drop.

"Here's your fucking turtle," she said, placing him next to me, then unlocking my chains. "Get a list together for him. And you, too."

Finally, I noticed the shopping bag she carried. She pulled out a pen and paper and handed them to me.

"Why is he here?" I asked as I accepted the items, a confusing mix of grief and relief flooding me at the thought that she'd killed Aydin.

Grief, because I still shared many good memories with him, and years of my life. Relief, because he wasn't the man I thought he was. I didn't know if he'd always been an awful human being, but he'd certainly become one. If he hadn't been an asshole, I would be Denali's, her friend would be alive, and most importantly, I wouldn't be a hostage.

"Your fiancé is gone," she said calmly, pulling out a Lego set, making my brows furrow. "He left the turtle. Thought you'd want him."

That motherfucker. Sure, turtles could survive a while without food, but they needed loads of water, plus an occasional tank cleaning and a bath when they shed. He claimed to care about our reptilian son, yet he'd left the poor boy to fend for himself.

"You're lying."

"The fuck I am," she snapped, my lips forming an 'o' as I watched her scatter the Legos around the room. A laugh bubbled up when I realized she was trying to deter me from escaping. Her glare silenced me, though I struggled to fight my smile. "If you step on one of these—"

"It'll hurt like a bitch, I know," I said, unable to hide my amusement.

The situation was dire, but using a children's toy to keep me trapped was hilarious.

Her lips quirked into a smile, and she nodded. "I'm going take my shower now. Don't fucking leave the bed."

With that order, she navigated to her en suite bathroom, cussing whenever her sock-clad feet stepped on one of the plastic bricks she placed. I struggled not to laugh at her. When the door clicked shut, I turned my smile to Crush, who was crawling toward me. I helped the little guy along, placing him on my lap and rubbing his shell as I wrote down everything we needed. His presence made me happy for more than one reason.

Most of all, it showed Denali still cared about me, even if she refused to admit it.

Chapter Twenty-Two

DENALI

On October 12, 1810, Bavarian Prince Ludwig married Princess Therese von Sachsen-Hildburghausen, or Princess Therese Charlotte Luise of Saxony-Hildburghausen. I couldn't remember all the particulars of her actual name. Chains, Angel, and some of our other members with German roots usually started the club's Oktoberfest with a brief history of why we created a beer garden and ate different types of Allgau cheese, tangy pickles and sauerkraut, frankfurters, bratwurst, liverwurst, Bavarian-style pretzels and noodles, Bee Sting cake, and a bunch of other regional foods.

We hung blue and white decorations, used a big wooden barrel to set up a tasting station for all the different beers, and hired an authentic Polka band that specialized in Oompah music. Every year, we did The Chicken Dance because what Oktoberfest could go on without that staple?

Karma was really good about celebrating our diversity. America's Independence Day preceded Venezuela's by a day. She left it up to Siren if she wanted to add her country's flags to our celebration or if she preferred hosting a party to celebrate Simón Bolívar's birthday later in the month. I'd learned a lot about different cultures and vowed to visit some of those places one day.

We charged non-members a fee to attend whatever holiday party we threw. Most of the time, the money we earned was donated to some charity, although sometimes we used the funds to help a sick member.

Over the past couple of days, Karma suggested I allow Estelle a little more freedom. The grounds were secure with cameras and guards everywhere, so she was able to roam around. I didn't particularly like it. After our half argument, half heart-to-heart, and the return of Crush, Estelle hadn't tried to escape again, but her good behavior didn't mean the members liked her. Moreover, a condition of Estelle's release into my care was keeping her by my side 24/7, so I really wondered what the fuck was up. However, I didn't want to test my luck. It wasn't my place to question my president. She could always throw Estelle back into a cell, so I held my tongue.

What I didn't hold back on was my fucking drinks. I knocked back more than a few, as did my sisters. We toasted Val, each of us trying to outdo the other. The more we drank, the longer the toasts went on, and the more our tears flowed until our normally rowdy celebration became a drunken memorial.

In death, as in life, Val was the center of attention.

That reality set in as I was called up for another toast. Lifting my stein, I swayed, so drunk that everything blurred in front of me and then doubled or tripled until special awareness wasn't my strong suit and dizziness was my frenemy.

"Valentina!" I yelled, just a fucking wreck. "Bitch, I love you. Why'd you have to die? Why couldn't you duck?" Somehow, I took another sip of my lager, then raised the stein again. "She was a good woman. My friend," I sniffled, pounding my chest. "A social butterfly who accepted me for me. It was none of that I'm-too-good-for-you shit. Or you don't fucking measure up to me, blah, blah blah." I smacked my lips together, searching for saliva because my tongue was so fucking dry. A second pound I gave to my chest tipped my stein and almost knocked me the fuck out. "She shouldn't have died. I shouldn't have seen her die." Blubbering, I jerked my hand high, sloshing beer over my head. "Death to those fucking Bloody Femme cunts! Death to the Turkish Mafia."

As my sisters cheered in agreement, I tipped my head back and raised my stein a couple of inches from my lips, determined to do a trick Val perfected. Instead, the last of the beer rained over my nose and chin, every fucking where except my goddamned mouth. Annoyed, I threw the fucking mug aside. "Why'd you have to be extra tonight, Chain…Chains? Val was the only one allowed to be extra. A stein's a mug and a mug's a stein."

"Alright, girlie," Karma said, planting herself at my side and hooking her arm through mine. "Let's get you to your room so you can sleep this shit off."

Big Mama appeared at my other side and mimicked Karma, holding me tightly, her face kind.

"I told her to open her eyes, Mama," I said, too tired to say her full name. I was too drunk to hold back my grief and too emotional to try to hide it. "She wouldn't listen to me. Why wouldn't she open her fucking eyes? I wanted to run after that motherfucker and fuck him up, but I couldn't leave my Val. Tell her to come back. Please. Please don't take her from me. Tell her to open her fucking eyes."

We rarely showed emotion, especially in public. But for the first time ever, Big Mama hugged me and allowed me just to cry. Throughout my life, I'd lost a lot and had few people who cared about me. Valentina had been one of them, and she'd been stolen away.

"Are you ready to get to your room, love?" Karma said gently, stroking my hair while Big Mama continued holding me.

I nodded, the beer churning in my gut. Out was better than in, but I really didn't feel like dealing with vomit.

"C'mon, Everest," Chains said, replacing Karma. "Let's get you to bed."

Too drunk to resist, I stumbled between the two women as I half walked and they half dragged me from the clubhouse to the dorms.

"We know you did everything you could," Chains told me as cold air washed over me. "And, remember, I can never out-extra Val. She was special like that."

"Yes," I agreed miserably, unable to stop the twirling in my head and the churning in my gut. "Vomit."

Big Mama held onto me as I doubled over, releasing the contents of my stomach in wave after wave of sour beer, sauerkraut, bratwurst, and Bee Sting cake. The stench drew the last bit of goop from my gut.

"I'll hose that away," Chains promised. Normally, we had to clean up our own mess.

"You'll feel better quick now that you don't have fifty gallons of beer inside you," Big Mama said, hauling me to my feet.

"I'd been dead if I'd drunk that much," I grumbled, allowing myself to be pulled along.

Neither of them responded to me, and we fell silent the rest of the way. Once we reached my room, they guided me in, my quiet surroundings as overwhelming as the alcohol and the toasts had been.

"Where's Estelle?" Chains asked.

I shrugged. "Dunno. Don't care," I added petulantly. "Karma said she could walk the fucking grounds. I guess she's *walking the fucking grounds*."

"I'll look for her," Chains swore, her second promise of the evening, when normally, she didn't make one to anyone but Prez. "Now that you're here, I'm sure Karma expects her to be also."

"Probably," I agreed, plopping on the edge of my bed. "Just leave the door unlocked. If I'm sleeping, I don't want her to fucking disturb me."

"With the way your eyes are dropping, you'll probably be asleep as soon as we leave you alone," Big Mama said.

"Why don't we test that theory?" I said, adding, "bah-bye."

Chains pulled my comforter back. "In bed now."

"As soon as I tuck you in, we'll leave," Big Mama promised.

"Not even my mama tucked me in," I revealed, back to being a whiny, slightly less drunken bitch. I leaned my head against her stomach and hugged her. "Thank you."

"No problem, baby," she said, showing me the depth of her maternal side. "Lie down, Everest."

"Okay," I mumbled, falling back so hard, I swore stars dropped from the sky for a personal dance revue. My head fucking hurt so badly. I closed my eyes, Estelle's scent comforting me despite how much I wished it wouldn't. "Miss Val."

Those were the last words I remembered until I woke up, dying of thirst. I didn't know how long had passed. Vomiting had minimized the risk of hangover, but left me with an awful taste in my mouth. Coupled with the realization that I still wore my stupid fucking costume, I got my ass up and stumbled to the bathroom. The bright light hurt my eyes, but I soldiered on. Stripping down, I started up the shower. While the water warmed, I brushed my teeth, then hopped in to smell less like vomit, sweat, and party.

Less than ten minutes later, I was emerging, fully nude since I dried off in the bathroom. One of my deepest, darkest secrets was my love of moomoos. They were comfortable, and I enjoyed going commando. I threw one on, braided my hair, then crawled back in bed, intending to pass back out.

The door creaked open. I didn't pay attention to it, since I figured Estelle was finally returning from wherever the fuck. The thought that she'd been with another biker crossed my mind, and I ignored the anger I felt at the possibility. I had no claim on her, so what she did with her pussy wasn't my business.

All thoughts were forgotten when lips nuzzled my neck, so I tipped my head aside, allowing for easier access, thinking it was a certain redhead.

"Estelle," I whispered, torn between pushing her away and pulling her closer. "What are you doing, babe?"

A giggle reached my ears, one that definitely didn't belong to Estelle. "Wrong girl, Everest."

My eyes flew open, and I scrambled away so fucking fast I fell out of the goddamn bed. When I raised myself on my knees, her bare fucking pussy greeted me, thanks to her open robe, where she wore fuck all underneath.

"What the fuck are you doing in my goddamn room with your pussy out?" I demanded, jumping to my feet and reaching for her. I grabbed each end of her robe and jerked them together. "Tie this motherfucker and then *leave*."

Instead of complying, she snaked her arms around me and pressed her lips against mine, horrifying me, bad memories populating my head. "No, I want you, and you want me. I know you do. I've seen you checking me out."

"You've seen me…?" Too outraged to continue, I shoved her away and backed up, convinced she was fucking drunk, although I didn't smell alcohol on her. "Get your fucking ass the fuck out of my room."

"But—"

"No fucking buts," I snapped, trying to keep my breathing under control, remembering that Kinder was a barely legal teen still finding her way. "I don't want you. Get that through your skull."

"Stop lying to yourself—"

"Get the fuck out, Kinder," I repeated, pointing to the door, my tone letting her know I meant fucking business, resisting the urge to lay her out.

That'd cause a problem with Geri, and right now, unity was needed. Estelle's special treatment already had some members pissed off.

She got off my bed and paused in front of me, trying to reach for me. I slapped her hands away, the urge to throttle her becoming harder to resist.

"My pussy is yours, Everest," she breathed, looking at me through her lashes. "I touch myself to you every night. I've never been with anyone else, you know. I want you to be my—"

"I won't be your anything!" I yelled, at my wits' end. "So stop being a brat, and get out."

"We're both grown women—"

"No, you're a child cosplaying as an adult, and who has an issue with boundaries. I'll tell you one more time to leave, before I take this as disrespect."

Disrespecting an officer meant a beating, once I was eager to dish out.

She studied me, then smirked, misreading my anger as something else entirely. "You'll fold, eventually," she cooed and sashayed away, taking my silence as her fucking victory.

"Crazy bitch," I grumbled when she closed the door, massaging my temples.

The situation—the entire fucking night—was so fucking unbelievable and ludicrous, I had to laugh. No, I forced myself to, focusing on the slight humor of the night instead of memories of Sergeant Motherfucker. Kinder was lucky I saw her as a misguided child, instead of a would-be rapist. Otherwise, she would be dead for violating my space, then taunting me. If she'd been aggressive, instead of killing her, I would've just beaten her ass for disrespect. Shaking my head, I lay back down, glad Estelle hadn't walked in and gotten the wrong idea.

I understood why I wasn't invited to Oktoberfest, but I thought Denali would stay a little while and then return to her room. When she didn't, I couldn't bear to remain alone a moment longer. Not even Crush's presence helped me, so I placed him in the small tank that she'd gotten him—too small to be used 24/7, but containing the water he needed—and left the room, deciding to go for a walk. Retrieving Crush was a kind gesture, but my son wasn't enough to keep my thoughts at bay.

I was so hurt and upset by what Aydin did. I hated my thoughts, but I despised my guilt even more. If Denali hadn't seen me in the bar that night, her friend would still be alive. Most of all, I loathed that she didn't trust me enough to let me in. I wanted her to forgive me, so I'd soothe her through her grief. Instead, she kept her walls up, resulting in me feeling little else but guilt and regret.

"How fucking long are you going to be out here, woman?" the guard dogging my steps asked at one point, to which she was ignored.

Sounds of a good time peppered the air—laughter, music, and chatter—along with the scent of food that watered my mouth.

But I'd already eaten, so I doubted Denali would bring me any party food. Dejected, I found a bench tucked against a wall toward the back of the property. Usually, when I looked around and took in my surroundings, ideas flowed, and I couldn't wait to get to my computer. I'd save a note on my phone to refer back to it later. Now, all I saw was a place, muted surroundings where I just existed.

I'm not sure how long I sat there before I decided to return to my *slightly better* prison than that fucking cell, prompted along by the same guard on duty.

"Everest won't be happy, you know," she'd said, making me huff, get my ass up, and return to Denali's room.

Just as I arrived, Kinder walked out of the room, her robe open, revealing her nudity.

She met my gaze. "Call me whenever you're ready for me again, Everest."

Denali's laughter floated to me. Smirking, Kinder threw me a kiss and sailed away.

I stood in heartbroken silence, remembering my mortification when I discovered Aydin's cheating. Yes, Denali and I had a lot between us, but I never expected to discover she was a cheater, too.

Livid, I stormed into the room. Her eyes flared in surprise, before they narrowed.

"Where the fuck have you been?" she demanded as if she had the fucking right, ignoring the fact that a mostly naked woman had walked out of her room.

"Fuck you. I don't owe you an explanation," I said, speaking out of anger and betrayal. "You should've been happy I wasn't here. My presence would've cramped your style."

"I didn't fuck Kinder," she said in warning. "Now, answer my question. Where were you? You should've brought your fucking ass back in here the moment you saw me come in."

Of all the fucking lying ass nerve. "I didn't see you walk in. I was too fucking far back, Denali. I don't believe you didn't screw her."

"I don't give a damn what you believe," she retorted. "It's the truth."

"In your dreams! I've heard this before."

"Too fucking bad you were naïve enough to believe it. Oh, that's right. He was from the right side of the tracks, so anything he said you believed."

"That isn't fucking fair! Before he fucked over me, I had no trust issues. If I take you at your word, how would that make me look?"

"Like you were fair and had a fucking brain to realize I'm not him. You have trust issues? Take it somewhere else. I've never given you a fucking reason to doubt me. If anything, that shit's reversed, so fuck you."

"You—"

"Furthermore, you're still my responsibility. If you want to wander around, you tell me where you're going. How would it look to Karma if I fucking lost you?"

"Like you put pussy before your responsibilities."

Her laugh lacked humor. "If that was the case, you wouldn't be here, because nothing is more important to me than my club, and I'm sick of you forgetting that."

"I wish I could," I yelled. "You kidnapped me because of your club. That's something I'll never forget or fucking forgive."

Even as I spoke, I knew I didn't mean my words. Already, I'd forgiven her, as insane as it sounded. It was as if I speed ran Stockholm Syndrome. If only she could develop Lima Syndrome, and we could live happily ever after as a fucked up but loving couple.

"No, Estelle, you got kidnapped because of what that motherfucker did to Val. I kidnapped you to protect you. If they couldn't get to him, they'd fuck you up as a message."

"You're a liar."

"Oh, I was the one who suggested we take you as leverage," she said evenly, and gave me an ugly smile. "He killed Val in front of me on the same fucking night you crushed me to my fucking soul."

"You're lying," I croaked, unable to believe her, that she'd intentionally put me through something so traumatizing.

"What did you expect me to do?" she asked quietly, the venom seeping from her tone.

In her moomoo and braided pigtails, those doe eyes looking so fucking sad, she looked so much younger than her thirty-two years, and reminded me of that lost teenager from all those years ago.

"I expected you to...to make them see reason, to—"

"I wanted revenge, but this," she said, motioning to the chains on her bed and back to me. "Protects you. Nothing would save you after Val died, and quite frankly, I didn't care if you were free or not. Only that you were alive while Aydin suffered."

I wasn't in the fucking right headspace to hear her honesty or see her pain. I was so fucking angry, I wanted to scream and opened my mouth to blast her. Instead, the night of my family's dinner replayed in my mind, all the cruel words I'd said to Denali, making me shut my mouth. Because of Aydin's behavior, I'd lashed out then, too.

He was a wrecking ball, destroying anything he came into contact with.

I didn't have to rewind back to the night I'd seen her in the bar. All I needed to do was change how I'd behaved that night, and Denali would've been with me, not Val. But how could I express that when she'd forever blame me for Aydin's crimes?

Hurt and confused, I drew myself up. "I'm tired," I said coldly. "Do I have your permission to take a piss, or will you count every minute for that, too?"

"Fuck you," Denali said, crawled back into bed, and turned her back on me. I suppose I had my answer.

Chapter Twenty-Three

Estelle

Despite having a smaller tank and being in an unfamiliar environment, Crush was doing just fine. Whatever had been afflicting the turtle had blown over. Maybe Aydin's evil energy had sickened him. Out of his father's presence, Crush was back to normal, much to my happiness. It would've been awful to have a sick turtle, on top of being held captive.

The door opening interrupted my watching Crush. I turned to face Denali, my stomach growling as the scent of coffee, egg, and bacon wafted to me. She carried it to me without a word, then turned to leave.

"Wait," I said, breathing a sigh of relief when she stopped, her back still to me.

After last night's confrontation, I wasn't sure if the final coffin nail had been placed in our relationship. The fact that she was even willing to consider me told me I still had a chance.

"What, Estelle?" she asked, how tired she sounded, making me feel so fucking low.

"I'm sorry," I stated, seeing no point in beating around the bush. "About what I said at the motel. About last night. About Aydin and your friend. Just…I'm sorry."

A heartbeat of silence passed before she said anything, still not looking at me. "You haven't done anything wrong. Aydin is the issue, and how you feel about me—"

"I care about you so much, Denali," I inserted, cutting her off.

Some may even call what I felt love, but I decided it was too soon for that emotion to be applicable.

"What I said at the motel isn't how I feel. Aydin was blackmailing me, and I was grasping at straws. And last night, I felt slighted that you'd chose another woman over me."

She huffed out a breath, finally turning to face me. "I didn't choose anyone over you, girl. Kinder came onto me, and I kicked her out. She's young, and even if she wasn't, I don't want her. I only want you, even now, but—"

"Stop with the buts," I ordered, stepping closer. "You want me. I want you. What the hell is the issue?"

"I had you kidnapped," she reminded me, the tiredness in her eyes giving way to something softer and more vulnerable. "You're my hostage. The club's hostage. That's the issue."

"I don't care," I said, stepping forward.

Studying me, she closed the distance between us, her hands finding my waist before her lips crashed into mine. It was hungry and desperate, the pent-up frustration and weeks of distance pouring out. Her tongue slipped into my mouth. I moaned softly, my hands tangling in her curls. We stumbled toward her bed, our mouths never separating. Denali's fingers dug into my hips, making sure I stayed close, her firmer breasts smushed against my softer ones, our nipples pebbling at the friction. I broke the kiss to nip her jaw, then trailed my mouth down her neck, sucking on the pulse point.

"Missed you," I mumbled against her, my hands yanking at the hem of her shirt. "Take it off."

She lifted her arms, allowing me to peel it off, and exposing her bare skin. I copied her as she finished undressing. Our clothes were shed quickly, and it wasn't long until we were both nude. Her eyes darkened as she took me in. Leaning down, she captured one of my nipples, sucking hard and swirling her tongue around the sensitive bud, sending jolts of pleasure through me. I arched into her, my hands finding her breasts as she sucked mine. I pinched one nipple, rolling it between my thumb and forefinger.

Soon, she was pulling away and picking me up, tossing me onto the bed. I squealed with laughter, which was silenced when she draped her body over mine and kissed me again. Our bodies aligned perfectly, and disappointment went through me when she broke the kiss. It evaporated when she trailed her lips to my throat, nipping at my pulse point, before she went lower. She switched between nipples, sucking them with fervor. My hips bucked when teeth grazed the bud, grinding my pussy against her thigh.

"Denali, please," I begged, something I was unused to doing with other women. But if she wanted to be in control, I'd welcome it. "Go lower, please."

She hummed, her hand tracing the curve of my hip before delving between my legs. A gasp left when she parted my folds, finding my clit with ease. She rubbed firm circles with her thumb, driving me wild with desire. Pressure built until I was panting and writhing, wanting more and needing her.

"So fuck wet for me," she praised, looking me in the eyes as she played with my bundle of nerves. "You've missed me, baby?"

I swallowed, my cheeks flushing. "You know I have."

My voice came out in a desperate whimper, a sound that made her release a low growl, before two fingers were plunging inside my dripping cunt. My pussy clenched as I cried out, the feeling of her digits pumping in and out of me, her thumb continuing to play with my clit, driving me wild. After weeks of not being touched or not touching myself, it was overwhelming. I moaned when she curled her fingers towards my belly button and hit a particularly sensitive spot.

She smiled against me as her mouth returned to my neck, sucking hickies into my skin, a visible claim and reminder of what we were getting up to.

I rocked against her hand, chasing my hand. My nails scraped her back as she fingers me, a loud mewl bouncing off the brick walls of her room when she added a third finger. Crush's tank gurgled in the background, but the mildly annoying noise wasn't a concern to either of us at the moment. Everything faded away as she fucked me with her long fingers.

"That's it," she breathed into my ear, before nipping the lobe. "Come all over my hand, Essie."

Her command pushed me over the edge. My pussy pulsed as ecstasy rippled through me, my name falling from her lips, and thighs trembling as she worked me through it, drawing out my pleasure. When she finally withdrew her fingers, she made a show of tasting them, sucking them clean as she held eye contact with me. A quick kiss allowed me to taste myself, before her mouth was descending my body, bypassing my breast, not stopping until her head was between my legs.

"I need to taste you," she said, her voice husky with desire as she hooked my legs over her shoulders.

That was all she said before she buried her face in my mound. Her tongue was relentless, gliding through my folds to drink as much of my arousal as possible.

"Fuck, yes," I whimpered, gripping the sheets as my toes curled.

She smiled against me as she moved to my clit. Sucking hard, she gripped and kneaded my ass cheeks, her shoulders keeping my legs wide open for her. Her mouth was working magic, licking, sucking, nibbling all the right places and in the right order. It was enough for me to forget our dynamic, her as my captive, and me as her captor.

If anything, being her hostage only made her want hotter.

Two fingers plunged back inside my pussy as her tongue flicked against my clit, pumping fast as pleasure coiled low and tight in my belly. I ground helplessly against her tongue, unable to do anything but chase that high, my body slick with sweat and my breathing labored. A sob of pleasure left me when she sucked my clit particularly hard, some unintelligible plea escaping my lips. Whatever I said made her hum against me, the vibration throwing me over the edge. I shattered, a scream leaving me as my body trembled, my release gushing into her mouth. She drank it all down, licking me through it until I felt like a boneless sack of flesh.

Even so, Denali wasn't done.

She shifted next to me and intertwined her legs. She guided my hand to her pussy, and hers to mine. A choked moan left as her digits reentered me, the sound resembling more of a gurgle.

"I love how you feel," she whispered as her fingers slid deep. "Fucking soaked, and all for me." Our foreheads pressed together, breaths mingling as our fingers explored the other's depths. "Just fucking perfect."

Her praise made me flutter around her, the room filling with the wet sounds of our arousal, our moans blending together. Her fingers curled, going straight for my G-spot. I mirrored her, my index and middle fingers feeling her velvety walls clench tightly, and the heat that radiated from her.

Denali's breath hitches, and she leaned forward, her lips brushing mine in a teasing almost-kiss.

"You feel how wet I am for you?" she murmured, scissoring her fingers within me, sending sparks racing down my spine.

"Yes," I breathed, thrusting my fingers in further until her cunt welcomed my knuckles, twisting them slightly to tease her.

Our bodies rocked in sync, both chasing our pleasure. Sweat began to make her beautiful brown skin shine, and I leaned forward to lick a bead of sweat that rolled down her neck, enjoying the saltiness of her flesh. Her free hand gripped my hand, holding me close as she pumped her fingers fast, her thumb returning to my clit. I gasped against her throat, copying her as I began to thumb her swollen nub, giving it the attention it desperately needed.

"You're so tight," I whispered, my voice breaking as she focused on that spongy spot deep inside me.

Denali's eyes locked with mine, her chest heaving as she slid a third finger into me. I cried out as I was stretched wider. Not to be outdone, I did the same, relishing the feel of her hot and pulsing cunt. We got lost in the intimacy of the moment, our free hands roaming. Mine found the curve of her hip, while her hand returned to my tits, teasing my nipples and adding to my pleasure. A familiar heat spread through my limbs. Denali sensed it, her pace quickening. Her fingers would withdraw, only to dive back in, thumb never leaving my clit.

"C'mon, Essie, give me one more," she urged, her own body shaking as my fingers curled and thrusted with fury.

With a pinch to my clit, my third orgasm crashed into me. I screamed her name as my pussy contracted, my body contorting. A few lazy thrusts of my fingers was all I could manage, but luckily, it was enough to trigger her own release. Her head fell back, a low moan leaving her as she ground against my fingers, her juices coating my hand.

Even after we both came down, we let our fingers stay buried in one another, waiting until our breathing returned to normal. The air was thick with the scent of pussy, our bodies keeping close, and everything feeling right once again.

Part Five

The Curtain Call

Chapter Twenty-Four

DENALI

When I woke up, I hightailed my ass out of my room before Estelle awakened. I didn't want to look at her and feel either guilt or doubt, which I'd been plagued by both ever since we made love the other night. A part of me felt used, a little voice saying she was fucking me to get some leverage. Maybe if that was the only thing bothering me, I could've brushed it off. However, it was my guilt that almost ate me alive.

If Estelle thought she had no choice but to sleep with me, I didn't know how I'd respond. I certainly couldn't send her away, and I didn't want her back in The Cells. Therefore, I thought it best to keep my distance rather than to have my suspicions validated.

Because if they were, that'd make me no better than all those who tried to take advantage of me.

Arriving at the clubhouse bright and early, I walked to the buffet, grabbed a plate, and served myself a little of everything in the warmers. Scrambled eggs, grits, buttermilk biscuits, sausages, bacon, and grapes. Once I carried my plate over to the table where Kiwi and Chains sat, already chowing down, I took a seat. A swear fell from my lips when I realized I forgot a beverage and utensils.

"If I don't have fucking brains, I'm thankful to have legs," I grumbled, shoving my chair back and getting to my feet.

I stomped back to the buffet table, poured myself a glass of OJ, grabbed a fork and napkins, then returned to my seat. Before I dug in, I frowned at my plate and squinted. I'd had four pieces of bacon when I left my plate. Now, I only had one. I scowled.

"Which one of you bitches stole my fucking bacon?"

Grounds for bloody war. Bacon wasn't only an American classic, but one of my absolute favorite foods. Nothing hit the spot like strips of greasy fried pork.

"What are you on about, mate?" Kiwi asked, her expression as innocent as Chains'.

"You have to the fucking count to three. Either give me my bacon and get the fuck up and get me the bacon you stole."

"Fine," Chains huffed, popping to her feet. "I'll get the bacon."

She was back before she was missed and dropped three pieces on my plate to replace what had been stolen from me.

"Want to talk about anything?" Kiwi asked.

When I finally made it to the clubhouse the day after Oktoberfest, everyone had been quite solicitous of me, inquiring after my well-being and mental state. I wasn't used to such concern, and it made me want to be swallowed up by the Earth. I could handle indifference, but being the center of worry? Yeah, that was a little too much for me.

"Yeah, babe, how are you feeling?" Chains asked, stuffing bacon into her mouth.

"I'm fine. I have one fucking meltdown, and suddenly I'm everyone's patient."

Kiwi sectioned off her stack of pancakes, then shoved it into her mouth, butter and syrup sliding down her chin. Once she swallowed, she grabbed her napkin and dabbed her lips.

"You're about ready to have another one," she said. "This one will be sober. That'll make it worse."

"I'm fine," I insisted, catching sight of Kinder piling her plate with food.

Since the incident, she'd kept her distance. She hadn't even taken her meals with us. I hadn't forgiven her fucking ass for causing such a major rift between Estelle and me, so I hoped she didn't come to the table and try to make small talk.

Thankfully, she didn't. She trudged by the table, slow enough for me to stop her if I wanted to. I'll bet if there'd been rocks in front of her, that bitch would've kicked them. One day, I'd forgive her, but that wasn't today. I wasn't in a particularly forgiving mood. Nor was I feeling social, so

I was happy to eat in silence. However, that ended as soon as the food was gone.

"What's on your agenda for the day, babes?" Chains asked me, pushing her plate aside and throwing her napkin on top of it.

Avoiding Estelle. "I have a payment to pick up from the auto shop," I said casually.

"Do you need company?" Kiwi asked me.

"Karma may have other jobs for me," I said, standing. I'd beg her to. "I wouldn't want to tie up your entire day."

Before they responded, I turned and headed for Karma's office.

Following our mind-blowing sex, I thought Denali and I had gotten back on track. Instead, I woke up to an empty spot as usual, and she barely spoke a word to me over the next three days. When she returned the morning after our sex with a plate of food, she was back to the annoyed, distant woman she'd become since I was taken hostage.

By the fourth day, I was about to lose my mind. I ate alone, awakened alone, and usually went to sleep alone. I suspected she was sneaking around with Kinder, but I couldn't prove that point, so I kept that thought to myself, although arguing was better than a complete shut-out.

After waiting until my normal early evening, hoping she'd return, I changed my routine. Instead of walking around the grounds, wandering aimlessly like the ghost of a Victorian child, I went to the clubhouse. No one had told me specifically to stay away, although as the 'fiancée' of the enemy, that was a reasonable assumption. Therefore, it wasn't surprising when I walked in, and sudden silence descended.

Groups of women sat at tables, either finishing or nearly finished their supper. I hadn't eaten since breakfast. When Denali wasn't around, I usually had one or two meals, depending on which guard tailed me.

Two women stood behind the bar, one leaning against it, while the other halted with a bottle in hand.

While I adored my fans, I hated being in the spotlight, which was insane considering I was a well-known author. But usually, I was already seated or standing behind a podium. The way they stared at me made me feel exposed and judged.

I'd spent years in therapy, learning body positivity. However, I couldn't compare to some of the gorgeous women in the club, including Denali.

"If it isn't the author," Kinder sneered.

Unnecessarily, in my opinion. Everyone knew my identity, and most of them didn't like me. If I'd ever doubted the extent to which I was hated, it was crystal clear now. In the heat of our argument, I'd blocked out the beating I'd gotten from women whose identity I still didn't know.

"Can we help you, Estelle?" a woman with deep auburn hair asked. She was older, but quite pretty. She pinned an inscrutable green gaze on me.

"I'm looking for Denali."

"She isn't here," another woman said. Dark-haired and stunning, she looked me over, then turned and whispered to another chick at her table.

They cackled.

I lifted my chin. "There's no reason for rudeness," I said crisply.

"There's no reason for you being here either," Kinder said, jumping to her feet. "Except to come between Everest and me."

"There is no Everest and you," I snapped, having enough of her bullshit. No, enough of all their bullshit. I'd done nothing wrong. For everyone to pin Aydin's crimes on me was so fucking unfair. "Stop already. She already told me."

"Do you think she'll tell her side bitch about her main one?" Kinder asked, chuckling.

"Kinder, give it up," one of the women said. "Everest doesn't want you. Everyone knows it."

"She will," she snapped, glaring at the woman, before focusing on me. "You're stupider than I realized."

"I'm not stupid at all," I said, the stress of the past few days and just everything getting to me.

"Am I the one who lived with a motherfucker and didn't know he was a killer?" Kinder replied. "You're either a dumb cunt or a liar."

"Kinder," the redhead said coolly. "Enough. Estelle gets your point."

"Clearly not, if she's still fucking here," Kinder said with a prissy little sniff.

The redhead ignored her and looked at me. "Go back to that fucking room, and if you ever bring your ass in here again, you're going back to The Cells."

"But I didn't do anything. I didn't know Aydin was such a motherfucker or a drug addict. I guess I didn't give a fuck enough to really pay attention to him. I don't know." I looked at Kinder, unsure of anything. "If you and Denali, Everest, are a couple, you can have her. I'll step out of the way. I refuse to be anyone's seconds. That's why Aydin was blackmailing me. I discovered he was fucking over me, and I wanted to leave him. He just wouldn't let me."

No one cared. I was the usurper who'd come between Denali and one of their own. Her withdrawal from me made sense. They might not have been official, but who knew what happened between them before I moseyed my ass along?

"I want to go home. To my grandmother," I continued, wanting to let Grandma know I was alive and well. "She's an elderly woman, and she knows I'd never go so many days without calling her. Suppose she worries herself to death? I didn't fucking do anything!" I yelled, not moving anyone.

Kinder's satisfaction at my falling apart added insult to injury, so I turned and started for the door. I wouldn't linger where I wasn't wanted.

"Stop." I recognized the redhead's voice. I halted, too tired and confused to disobey. "Come here."

Swiping at a rogue tear, I turned and stumbled to the table, finally able to see her president's patch and her name.

She nodded to an empty chair, next to a dusky-skinned woman. "Sit."

"I didn't do anything," I repeated, stuck on that truth.

"Sit," Karma said again.

It wasn't as if I had a fucking choice, so I followed her order.

"How'd you and Aydin meet?"

"In school. He was so sweet then, but everything changed when we moved in together."

Karma's expression gentled. "What's your grandmama's name?"

I bit my lip, suddenly afraid I'd revealed too much, and they'd hurt her. Grandma was fearsome, but she'd grown frail, and even the strongest person in the world couldn't fend off a bullet.

Leaning forward, I grabbed Karma's hand, uncaring that one of the women next to her tensed. "Please, don't hurt her. She is even more clueless about Aydin than I was. I'll do anything to protect her, even give my life if it means saving her."

"And Everest?" she asked, not responding to my heartfelt plea. "Would you give your life to save her?"

It really didn't matter since she had someone else. Once again, I was the second choice, but I loved Denali. My hope for her had always been that she was happy. If I didn't make her happy, then I had to step out of the way for someone who did. However, that didn't mean I wouldn't die to protect her.

I nodded, exhausted. "I would."

She squeezed my hand gently, then tugged her own away. "Your grandma's safe, babe. Tiny, our Tech, has been texting some of your family and friends to keep suspicion down. When your grandma started blowing up your phone, she used a program to mimic your voice. She's none the wiser."

"I suppose my voice is all over the internet," I said, the thought making me uneasy. "It was easy enough to feed into some stupid AI program."

"AI will be the downfall of our civilization," Karma added, a sentiment I agreed with. "It's all bullshit."

"It is," I agreed, longing to hear my grandmother's voice. She understood me better than my mother did at times. Even though my thoughts were shit and I couldn't plot a micro story at the moment, let alone an entire novel, I missed sitting at my desk and seeing where my characters led me. "I want to write. And...and...and Crush needs his terrarium. And...I want to go home."

It was unbearable, especially thinking about Denali and Kinder together, flaunting their relationship in front of me. I'd be powerless to do anything, even leave. I started to cry because it was all too much. The shitshow my life had turned into, the loss of Denali, and missing my grandmother, devastated me. Maybe I had no pride to cry in front of women who didn't give a fuck if I fell off the face of the fucking earth, but I couldn't stop.

"What the fuck happened?" I heard someone bark.

Suddenly, I was being gathered in arms and hugged tightly. Denali's scent washed over me, and I nuzzled into her as she stroked my hair.

"Calm down, Estelle," Denali said with uncertainty, the concern in her voice washing over me and making my tears turn into sobs. She swore, hugging me tighter. "Can somebody tell me what the fuck happened?"

"Kinder," a woman said, making Denali groan.

"You're a fucking snitch ass bitch, Maiden," Kinder barked, having an attitude with everyone.

"Unlike you, I won't piss off an officer," Maiden replied, the conversation fading away as I tuned out every other voice to focus on Denali.

"Babe, it's okay. Shhhh," she cooed as I continued sobbing. "I got you, Babe. You're alright."

I buried my face against her leather cut. Her touch was soothing, but I knew it would be temporary before she returned to her main bitch, as Kinder had so eloquently put it.

"I didn't do anything," I repeated. "Let me go. Please? You can live happily ever after with Kinder. She told me the truth."

Denali's stiffening barely registered; I continued to wail and ramble.

"I've only ever wanted you happy. If you want to be with a barely legal teen with an attitude problem—"

"Estelle," she crooned, cutting me off as she crouched in front of me and tipped my chin up. "What are you doing inside the clubhouse?"

"I was l-looking for you," I mumbled, the incredulous look on her face making my cheeks heat even more. I was so overheated. "I just wanted to talk to you."

"What exactly happened?" She shook her head and stood before I gathered my thoughts. "Never mind," she continued, her tone reeking of barely restrained anger. "I fucking know already. Come with me."

"I want to go home."

"You can't," she said gently. "You aren't safe with Aydin."

"Fuck him," I growled, so tired of hearing that name, still so hurt over his many betrayals. "I wish that motherfucker would fall off the face of the fucking earth. I wish I were a dragon rider so I'd incinerate his fucking ass, starting with his big, stupid, lying fucking mouth."

"Well, goddamn, girl, I didn't know you were so bloodthirsty," Karma said, laughing.

"Creatively bloodthirsty," Denali crowed. "I like it."

"If you want him, use me. Let me be the bait that lures him," I said wildly, imagining how easy my life would be with him out of the picture. I could go home, and maybe with him gone, Denali would give me a chance. "Then I don't care what happens."

"You can't do that," Denali said, though I knew it wasn't her decision to make. It was the president's. "He will kill you. He'll believe you gave up secrets."

Still sitting, I stomped my foot and slammed my palm on the table like a petulant child. "I don't know any fucking secrets to tell, goddamn it."

"Let's go, Estelle," Denali said, thrusting her chin toward the door, not giving me much of a choice but to follow her orders. She guided me toward the door, her hand at the small of my back, but halted us near the exit. "Wait a sec."

Again, I had zero say-so. Turning, she stalked to where Kinder sat, punched her— no, knocked her out *with* a punch—and kicked her side. She looked around the room. "If any dumbass wants to lie on an officer again, I'll personally shoot them."

Silence followed the announcement. Satisfied, she returned to me.

"Now, we go," she said, and held the door open until I walked into the cool evening, too stunned to comment.

Inside her room, she locked the door. "Sit," she ordered, going into the bathroom and coming out with a cold towel. She sat next to me, then tenderly wiped off my overheated face. "I'm not involved with Kinder, and I don't appreciate her fucking games. She'd better thank you for saving her from a life-threatening ass-whooping. Lying and disrespecting an officer could be a death sentence."

Her words chilled me, and even though I didn't like Kinder, the death of someone so young being on my shoulders would haunt me.

Instead of saying that, I settled for, "I-I didn't do anything," a refrain I was stuck on, although I meant it in an entirely different context here.

"You're my priority, babe. Walking into the clubhouse and hearing your teary voice wasn't pleasant. Seeing to you was more important than dealing with Kinder."

"I just…everything is all jumbled, but I miss you. I don't know why you barely want to look at me."

"Real shit, Estelle? I didn't know how to take our sex. Did you feel coerced, or were you trying to coerce me? Talk about a fucked-up jumble. Look into my fucking brain, and you'll see all kinds of fucking wires crossed."

"Never," I said fiercely, leaning into her and pressing my lips against hers. "You're brilliant."

"You're so fucking good for my ego."

I laughed, my first genuine one in days. "I only speak the truth."

She drew me into her arms and hugged me, then gave me a light kiss. "I want you, Estelle. But I want you to want me to. Not under any pretenses, or for a bid for revenge or survival. But because—"

I silenced her with a deep kiss. She moaned into my mouth, arching into me as my hands found her hair. When I cupped her breast, she grumbled and pulled away.

"Not now, babe," she said gently, almost shyly. "Why don't you join me in the shower? No strings attached."

Her rebuff stung, but her counteroffer soothed me. "I'd like nothing better," I responded without hesitation.

Chapter Twenty-Five

Estelle

Denali and I didn't make love in the shower. I felt no disappointment over that fact, as the simple intimacy of the moment deepened our connection. Roaming our hands over each other's bodies to lather the soap and then using the shower to wash the suds away. Massaging each other's scalps once we poured shampoo onto our hair. Drying each other off before Denali led me to her bed and took me into her arms.

Her mouth had covered mine, and soon, we were getting sweaty all over again. Our kisses were languid as our hands explored each other's bodies. When my fingers brushed over her slit, she pulled away, her eyes hungry as she shifted on the bed.

"Remember when we bumped pussies?" she said with a small smile, her description making me snicker.

"How can I forget it?"

"Been thinking about it, too. Never thought that shit could feel good, but I was wrong."

I got what she was saying immediately. Taking the clue, I guided her legs apart with gentle hands, positioning us until our thighs were intertwined. Heat radiated from her core, mirroring the ache I felt in my cunt.

"I want to feel you, Estelle," she whispered when I didn't immediately move.

Who was I to deny her?

My hands found her hips, and I pulled her closer. Our bodies aligned perfectly as our wet folds met. The slick glide sent pleasure racing down my spine, intensifying when we began to move. Denali rocked her hips forward, her clit nudging mine as I lifted my pelvis to meet her. The friction was intense, and our juices mixed as we ground together.

"Feel so good," I murmured, my breathing growing labored as we sped up. "Missed you so much, Denali."

She hummed as she braced her hands on my shoulders, her nipples hard as they grazed against my chest. I leaned back and cupped them, fingers teasing the pebbled peaks until she moaned.

"Fuck, Essie," she whimpered.

Our hips rolled in unison, clits swollen from the pressure the other's body was applying. The bed creaked below us, the sound of our ragged breaths echoing through the room, mingling with the sounds of our wetness and the noisiness of Crush's tank.

"Feels good, baby?" I said, thighs trembling as my pleasure mounted.

Her answer was a kiss, her tongue exploring my mouth as she ground harder against me. I angled us so our clits aligned perfectly, the sensation toe curling. The coil forming in my lower belly tightened, every nerve alight.

"Keep going," she murmured against my lips, her husky voice strained.

"I don't plan to stop."

Her pace quickened, hips snapping forward with more urgency. I bucked up to match her, my fingers digging into her ass as I ensured she stayed flush against me. Sweat beaded on her skin and trickled down, adding to our slickness. A second shower would definitely be needed, but neither of us cared.

The coil unraveled, and I came with a cry, pleasure pulsing through me as my pussy clenched around nothing. Seconds later, Denali was joining me in bliss, her grinding becoming erratic jerks as groans escaped her. We rode out the pleasure, and when the aftershocks faded, we collapsed in a tangle of limbs.

"You're so fucking perfect," she mumbled against me, her voice husky with satisfaction.

I smiled, my forehead resting against hers. "I'm anything but, Denali."

Her answer was another kiss, before we shifted so we could cuddle. Her head was on my chest, a familiar position that relaxed me.

Just as we were about to drift off to sleep, gunfire and screams filled the air.

"What the fuck?" she said as she jolted.

I was too shocked and scared to say anything. Whatever was happening, the commotion was drawing closer. Growling, she hopped off the bed, throwing on her moomoo from last night.

"Stay here," she ordered as she grabbed her gun. "Don't leave this room. I don't know what's happening, but if it's a breach and they get in here, *hide.*"

"But—"

She didn't give me a chance to respond, turned, and rushed out of the room.

DENALI

We were indeed being breached. As soon as I left the dorms, it was chaos. Bloody Femmes and suited men I didn't recognize were wreaking havoc, attacking my sisters as if they had the fucking right. I shot as many as I could, navigating through the mess as I searched for Karma. As SAA, it was Siren's job to protect our Prez, but grouping up would be less dangerous than being scattered around the U.N.

"How the fuck did they get in?" I heard Karma bark as I entered the clubhouse.

"I don't know, Prez," Siren replied.

I shot two fuckers trying to sneak up on them, catching their attention and securing the area, for now. "Hole in the chain link, near the back," I guessed, wishing we'd gotten that repaired when we first noticed it two weeks ago.

The location was surrounded by trees, and the hole wasn't even big enough for a raccoon. However, it provided an easy location to cut the chain link, providing entry to enemies.

Karma groaned. "It was going to be repaired this fucking weekend." She shook her head. "What the fuck ever. Move out, ladies. Kill as many of those bitches and bastards as possible, and don't get shot."

Val rose in my mind, but I pushed her away. Now wasn't the time for grief. Nodding, I turned to leave, ready to follow my Prez's orders. I could only hope Estelle had listened to me, and that I could return to her in one piece.

We moved out, mowing down dozens of intruders. Every Memphis chapter Femme bitch must've been present, and I knew that there was a high chance the Harlots were going to take some losses. The thought pained me, but kept me going. The more Femmes that died, the more of us that lived. Siren, Karma, and I made for an efficient unit, killing the enemies and protecting each other. Hope that we'd make it out of this mess alive blossomed within me.

That hope crashed and burned when I noticed a man and a woman moving toward the dorms. Estelle flashed in my mind, and without a second thought, I broke formation and took off running. I ignored Karma's shout, my only concern being protecting Essie. When we got out of this mess, I'd take my beating for disobeying her, but I'd be damned if I left my woman defenseless.

As soon as Denali left, I didn't waste time finding an outfit and shoes in case I needed to run instead of hide, as she'd instructed me to. The gunfire was nonstop, sounding like what I imagined a warzone might. Piercing screams, loud pops, sonic booms, and an acrid scent that burned my nose.

I lost track of time, but it all seemed to last an eternity, until it finally calmed down, and silence fell around me. Shoving my hands under my thighs to keep from wringing them, I waited anxiously for Denali's return. When five minutes ticked by and she didn't walk in, my imagination began to conjure up her injured or dead.

The amount of gunfire I'd heard wasn't child's play. In my heart, I knew there were casualties.

Suppose Denali was one of them? What then? I didn't want to consider that.

The doorknob turned, and I smiled, relief flooding me. It crashed and burned when the door swung open, and Aydin strolled in, a big gun in his gloved hands. He was dressed all in an all-black suit, cosplaying a stock villain from an old cartoon.

"Well, if it isn't my precious fiancée," he started.

"Aydin—"

He cracked me across my face, and I reeled onto the bed.

"Shut up, Estelle," he snarled, lunging for me.

Thanking my quick reflexes, I darted out of the way. A scream left me when he wrapped an arm around my waist, forcing my face down on the bed.

"All I've fucking done for you, and you decide to slum it with a Harlot slut," he spat, ignoring my cries and struggling as he straddled my waist. "You're lucky I didn't leak your fucking nudes. No, I have a better idea. I'll chain you to the fucking bed, and if you leave me again—"

A bullet whizzed between us, barely missing me and interrupting Aydin's villain speech. He flipped over the side of the bed, and I rolled over quickly. Denali stood there, an angel of death as she aimed her gun in Aydin's direction, not caring what a mess her moomoo had become.

She squeezed the trigger. "Run, Estelle," she ordered me before a kick sent her reeling.

A tall woman stood in the doorway, smirking at Denali and raising her gun. "Karma's pet, no?"

Somehow, I recognized her. Her bleached blonde hair and scarily blue eyes were familiar, but I couldn't put my finger on where I'd seen her before.

"Fuck you, Luce," she snarled as she regained her bearings.

Luce...fuck, no, wait...Luce was Alex. Whatever, that didn't matter. What mattered was that Luce was aiming her gun at Denali's head.

"No!" I screamed, the shock of my voice drawing her focus away and giving Denali just enough time to fire her own weapon.

Luce dropped like a sack of potatoes, a pool of blood forming beneath her.

Before Denali could regroup, Aydin came at her. If he'd fired his gun, she would've been dead. Instead, he swung his fist. She sprawled onto the floor, her gun slipping out of her grasp.

He tried to kick her head, but she rolled out of the way before his foot landed. I wouldn't watch my woman die, so I searched for a weapon of my own, something I could use to knock him out. Where did Denali keep all her guns?

Grunts, curses, and flesh connecting with flesh broke through my panic.

"Fucking bitch!" Aydin hollered.

Abandoning my search, I turned and screamed. He had his hands wrapped around Denali's throat.

"No! Stop, Aydin," I called, hoping to break through his rage, but he ignored me.

Spying Denali's gun, I scrambled to it and didn't pause because I didn't have time to hesitate. I aimed it, wishing I could close my eyes, but knowing I couldn't since he was too close to Denali for me to risk blindly firing.

The first shot stunned him, and he released her immediately. She fell to the floor, coughing and sputtering, holding her throat. I'd shot him in the shoulder, leaving him mobile. He brought his other hand to his waistband and yanked out another gun.

I didn't wait to see who he'd aim at first. Raising the weapon, I aimed it at Aydin's head and pulled the trigger.

Chapter Twenty-Six

DENALI

More Harlots than I cared to admit ended up dying in the siege, but in the end, the Turks and the Femmes took the heaviest losses. Once it became clear that we weren't to be fucked with, they'd retreated, their numbers a laughable portion of what they started with. Luce was dead by my bullet, and Aydin had gotten shot by Estelle. I was so fucking proud of her, but I knew your first kill, no matter how justified it was, could be a traumatizing thing.

I thrust a bottle into Estelle's hand. She was still in shock, that much was clear. After I'd killed Sergeant Motherfucker, nothing felt real. Even now, that period of my life and my prison stint felt more like a hazy dream than something I lived.

That didn't fucking matter, however. What mattered now was Estelle and getting her to feel better.

"Drink," I ordered as we sat in the clubhouse, where the bodies had already been removed by Dusty—our cleaner—and other sisters.

"I killed him," she mumbled, eyes dazed. "I killed another human being."

"It was him or me, babe," I said gently, taking her hand in mine. "You chose me, and I'm so fucking thankful for that."

She nodded, took a big swig of liquor, looked at me, and took another. It stung that she might regret saving my life, but at the end of the day, she was a civilian, and such violence could traumatize them. Compared to most of the other Harlots and me, Estelle had lived a sheltered life. Violence was something she was aware of, but not something she lived and breathed. I'd stopped believing in a higher power long ago, yet I prayed this incident wouldn't leave a permanent mark on her psyche or soul.

"I'm proud of you, Estelle," I said quietly when she set the bottle down. "What you did took a lot of courage."

"I'd do it again," she replied after a heartbeat of silence, a haunted look still in her eyes. "But I keep remembering Aydin as alive. Laughing. Happy and sweet, before he became…him. Now he's dead. I met his parents, laughed with his family, and I took their son away."

The pain in her voice made my heart ache. Unsure of what else to do, I squeezed her hand, searching my mind for what to say.

"You know about my first kill, since your sister exposed me. You know I knew him, and—"

"He tried to rape you. He got what he deserved, just like Aydin did," she interrupted, the sharpness in her voice hinting that she was starting to process the events. "I just wish my stupid brain—"

It was my turn to interrupt her. "What you're feeling is completely valid, Estelle. When I killed my Sarge, I was in shock. It felt like my whole world had been uprooted, and I didn't even like the bastard when he was alive. You loved this man, so I can only imagine how hard it is for you."

"But—"

She was forever argumentative, but I couldn't let her continue to beat herself up for her decision. As she said, Aydin got what he deserved, and when I walked in, the motherfucker was on top of her. That was reason enough for him to die. If I hadn't been worried about hitting Estelle, he would've been shot immediately.

"I killed my second man six months after I got out of prison," I continued. "He was a hang-around at the Bastards. When I was prospecting, I went to their clubhouse a lot. Zapper was a drug dealer, wanting to prospect. He just got out the pen, too. We became tight. Then I caught him spiking my drink. I beat him to death with a bottle, same way I killed my Sergeant. Karma almost called me Bottle for the incident, but decided it was a dumb road name." I took a deep breath as I remembered that night, the betrayal and fury I felt. "I wondered how someone I'd become so close to could be such a snake. How I was able to take his life, when I'd met his daughter and mama. It fucked with me, even more than my Sarge's death."

"He was a predator. He deserved it."

"Exactly, Estelle," I said. "If I didn't kill him, he would've hurt more women. If you didn't kill Aydin, after he killed me, he would've hurt you. He deserved to die, but that doesn't mean you can't mourn him."

"I shouldn't, though."

"There's no 'should' or 'shouldn't' in situations like this one. Only what could happen, and what does happen."

She nodded and tugged her hand away to take another drink of alcohol. Even with my words, I knew she'd need more time to process. I'd give it to her. Aydin was dead, so she'd be free to go. I ignored my fear that she'd ghost me, telling myself that she wouldn't do that. Even if she ended things, she'd at least give me a heads up.

Maybe I could convince Karma to keep Estelle here a little longer.

"Move in with me," she said suddenly, making my eyes widen. "I...my apartment has more than enough space, and I make enough to cover rent. I...I'm used to waking up with you, and used to living with another human being. You can bring whatever you want, and—"

"How are you two doing?" Karma said, interrupting our conversation.

Never before had I been more unhappy to see my Prez.

I shrugged, ignoring the ache in my heart at the losses we took, and at Estelle's pain. "Good as we can be, Prez."

She dug into her coat, pulling out Estelle's phone and car keys. "Your motherfucker is dead, girlie. You're free to go."

"I want Denali…er, Everest to move in with me," Estelle blurted again, looking at Karma like a child asking for a puppy. "Can I take her with me? Please?"

Karma and I exchanged a look, then laughed. Prez looked back at Estelle, a smile on her face. "That's up to her, girlie." Switching her gaze back to me, she clapped me on my shoulder. "You did well today, Everest. But if you ever disobey me and run off like that again, I'm pistol-whipping you."

Her threat issued, she walked away, leaving Estelle and me alone again. All-in-all, I got off light.

I looked back at Estelle. "We can go whenever you're ready."

"I don't want to leave you," she said, her bottom lip wobbling. "But I miss my mom and my siblings and Grandma and—"

"And you're free to see them again, babe," I replied, taking her hands again. "I'm just a phone call away. You have a nice ass apartment. Better than my old raggedy room at the club."

"That's why you should come with me." She took a deep breath, speaking again when she was more composed. "With Aydin, I moved in with him before I saw him at his worst. Up until that point, he'd just been a good man, and I could count on one hand the times we argued. It isn't like that with you. You've shown me every side of you, and I want to live with all of them, good or bad. I want to wake up to you in the morning, go to sleep with you at night, and spend time with you in between. Neither of us is the easiest to live with, but we mesh well together. So, please, come with me."

Her words left me speechless, in the best way possible. She made it hard to refuse, even if that stupid voice in my head was telling me moving in with her would be a mistake. Everything between us had happened so fast, in a manner that spat in the face of tradition. Moving in with her was a big step, especially because she'd just lost her fiancé, and we weren't even a couple.

"I'll come over daily, and you're welcome at the club, but I'm not living with you yet, babe," I decided. As hard as the words were to push out, they needed to be said. "You just lost your fiancé, and we aren't even a couple."

My words made her look even more dejected. I felt like a bitch, but *it needed to be said*.

"Heal a little. Let everyone get used to you without Aydin, and we'll go from there."

"Fuck everyone else," she hissed, slamming her fist on the table. "They don't know the half of it, and they never will. If you don't want to live in that apartment, I'll get us a new one. If it's because we aren't official, I officially declare you, Denali Bernard, as my girlfriend. There. Problem solved."

I chuckled at her sarcastic petulance, even as my heart did somersaults. "Well, I take thee as my girlfriend and bestow the same honor upon you."

At my words, she reached over and kissed me. I wanted nothing more than to scream from the rooftops that Estelle was mine, but now wasn't the time. The club had just taken so many fucking losses in a day. We had families to contact, things to repair, blood and bullets to clean. Besides, it was already known that Estelle belonged to me.

I had a goofy grin on my face when she returned to her seat, one that slipped into a small smile when she spoke again.

"Are you sure you're not moving in with me?"

"Positive."

She huffed out an annoyed breath, her slight pout adorable, but nodded. "Fine. But when it's our three-month anniversary, I'm asking again, and not giving up until you say yes."

I laughed at her vow. "Wouldn't expect otherwise, babe.

And this time, when she asked, I'd happily accept. It may be too soon, but I already knew I was going to spend the rest of my life worshipping Estelle Pratt-Milton.

Epilogue

Estelle

A year later…

At the start of last year, I was positive that I'd be walking down the aisle with Aydin, ready to live happily ever after with the man of my dreams. But that man turned out to be a myth. Instead of Prince Charming, he was the villain of my story, one who'd been hellbent on…well, I didn't know. I had no clue what his goal was. I knew he wanted to keep me with him, but that was all I was sure of. Beyond that, I didn't know what drove him to make bad choice after bad choice, and I didn't care. All I knew was that they got him killed, and he deserved it.

It'd taken me a month to accept what I'd done, and by the time Denali moved in with me into a new apartment around our sixth month anniversary, I was over it. It'd been him or her, and I knew from the jump that I'd made the right choice. She'd respected my wishes and, minus the kidnapping incident, never crossed my boundaries. In fact, she made my healing more of a priority than even I did, and it was one reason I loved her. She was everything Aydin wasn't, and I couldn't ask for a better partner.

It was why I was marrying her, and by this time tomorrow, she'd be my wife.

Actually, in twenty-four hours, we'd be wife and wife, heading to…somewhere. I didn't fucking know. She allowed me to plan the wedding of my dreams, in exchange for her planning the vacation.

"You look beautiful, baby," Grandma said, sitting on her walker and sipping a glass of champagne. "Should've known you'd be marrying Denali. As soon as you saw that girl as a child, you were smitten. That fucker running out was a good thing."

I pasted on a smile. As far as the rest of my family knew, Aydin had broken up with me and left Memphis.

"Don't mention that man today, Mama April," my mother said, misreading my strained smile. "He brings up nothing but bad memories. God, I can't believe how well he fooled us."

Michelle, Lake, and Juno gave me a knowing look. As Harlots, they knew what had really gone down during the day of the siege, even if they were still in the dark about the fact that the Memphis chapter had held me hostage. Karma had told them my 'vacation' had been a willing one, where I'd spent the weeks at the United Nations to sneak around with Denali. I endorsed the story, not wanting the sister chapters to feud.

"I wish I could've gotten my hands on him," Lake said, a frown tugging at her lips.

"Seconded," Juno added.

"Thirded," Michelle said, making Mama's lips purse as she looked away.

Bad blood ran between the two. Years ago, Michelle had nearly gotten Mama arrested by claiming a police report she made was false, to protect her raggedy parents. I understood why she wouldn't want to back up the story, but Mama had never truly forgiven her for it.

"Enough about Aydin," I said, carefully sipping my champagne, not wanting to mess up my painted lips. "He's my past. I want to focus on my future with Denali."

"I'll drink to that," Michelle said, raising a glass, encouraging her sisters to do the same.

"Where are your friends, baby?" Grandma asked.

"Dani is picking up the cupcakes, Tess had a less-minute errand, so she'll be arriving just when the wedding is starting, and Lauren is on her way."

While Denali and I cut a cake, cupcakes would be served to our guests. A delay meant that they weren't ready before the wedding, but I didn't care. A benefit to a local ceremony—I'd chosen my dream location of Memphis Botanic Garden for the venue—was that things coming up last minute weren't the end of the world.

Grandma pursed her lips. "They should've left earlier, then."

I refilled her glass, hoping more champagne would placate her.

Kayla, who'd appointed herself as my hair and make-up artist, slapped my shoulder. "Stop moving, girl, before I burn you with the straightener."

After learning at twelve how much in-demand beauticians could make, she dreamed of opening her own beauty parlor one day. She was on track to meet her dreams. Even if her customer service demeanor could use some work, the soft glam makeup look she'd done for me was gorgeous and accentuated my features nicely.

"You will do no such thing, Kayla Marie," Mama said, giving my little sister a look of warning. "If you do, I'll send you by your daddy and finish her hair myself."

"Sorry, Mama," she grumbled, making me stick my tongue out at her.

She stuck her tongue out right back, and I giggled. Mama gave both of us another look, putting an end to our exchange. Even though I was twenty-seven, she knew how to gather my ass up quickly.

Lauren arrived soon after Kayla curled my hair into ringlets, wearing a forest green gown like Kayla's. My only rule for my bridesmaids was that their dresses be formal, and the shade of yellow or green I selected for my wedding colors. Everything else was up to them.

"The cavalry has arrived!" Dani announced as she strolled in, her golden-yellow gown the same color as Tess's, who was right behind her.

With their arrival, all four of my bridesmaids were present.

"What's all this?" I asked with a smile, accepting the bag Tess handed me.

"You have something old," Lauren said, gesturing to the pearl jewelry set Grandma had given me to wear.

"You have something blue," Dani continued with a knowing wink, making my cheeks heat when a chorus of 'Oohs' echoed through the makeshift dressing room.

She'd helped me pick out blue lingerie, just for Denali's viewing pleasure.

"And something borrowed," Tess finished, referencing the veil my mother had worn when she'd gotten married to my biological father, a decade to the day before his death. "The bag has your something new."

A grin on my face, I eagerly removed the tissue paper. Three things were inside, each from one of my best friends.

"The perfume is from me," Dani said with a proud grin. "I know you've been wanting it, and that shit smells good, so you'll smell like a dream for your lucky lady."

"The champagne glasses and the case are from me," Lauren said. "You two need something special to toast with."

"And the scrapbook is from me, so you and Denali can always have pictures of your wedding day and vacation," Tess continued, smiling softly as I examined all the items my friends had gotten me. "They put me in charge of bringing the gifts, but I kinda sorta lost mine, and took for-fucking-ever finding it. So, sorry about that."

I laughed, tears pricking my eyes at the love surrounding me.

"Don't you dare make my sister cry and ruin my hard work," Kayla ordered, grabbing a fan to fan my face, looking at me. "Don't cry, woman. Stay composed."

"She could cry all she wants to," Mama said, tearing up herself. She looked at my friends, holding her arms open. "That's so sweet of y'all. My girl is lucky to have friends like you three."

"I'm lucky to have all of you," I whispered, blinking rapidly to stay composed as Kayla ordered.

All the love surrounding me made that more difficult. I was blessed to have such a support system, and even more blessed to have Denali as my fiancé.

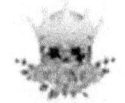

DENALI

"I don't think I've ever seen you look so girly before," Chains noted, inspiring murmurs of agreement from my bridesmaids.

Kiwi, Chains, and Siren, were the sisters I selected. Valentina was flying free, so Karma was going to be my best woman. To honor Val, I asked Estelle if we could have a memorial easel wreath in front of the podium where Glory would be officiating. She agreed without hesitation, because she knew how important that was to me. Since I had no family in attendance—I never reconnected with any of them once Daddy kicked me out—Big Mama was my fill-in parent, sitting in the first row, where my birth givers should've been. The rest of the Memphis chapter would be in the audience to cheer us on.

Mrs. Milton offered to split her time between Estelle and me, but I didn't want to tax her in such a way, so I declined, telling her Estelle would be so disappointed if she wasn't with her the entire time. It was a lie, as Estelle had suggested the same thing weeks ago, and I told her that Mrs. Milton may not mesh well with my club sisters. She'd laughed at that, but dropped the subject.

"You look real good, baby," Big Mama said, passing the blunt to Karma.

They could handle their weed, but Kiwi, Chains, and Siren were iffy, so I'd forbidden them from puffing on anything until I got my woman back to our home. Once we were gone, they could act a fool all they wanted.

I smoothed a hand over my jumpsuit as I examined myself in the mirror, inclined to agree with my VP. "Thanks, Mama."

While I still had a veil, I wore an ivory jumpsuit with a deep V-neck instead of a dress. The cap sleeves gave way to a cape, and the waist was cinched, making me look extra snatched. My favorite part, however, was the deep pockets.

"You welcome, Everest."

"Stop showing favoritism," Chains complained to Big Mama, her painted lips frowning.

We all snickered at her petulant tone. Since Oktoberfest, when I got absolutely plastered, she gave her permission for me to call her 'Mama,' no Big needed. It was special treatment, and I was glad to flaunt that privilege. They all had some blood relatives who gave a damn about them. I didn't, so it was only fair that Big Mama let me use a special nickname for her.

"You excited, mate?" Kiwi said, looking at the blunt longingly, when she was the worst offender.

Blunt mellowed most people out, but it got Kiwi too hyped up.

"More than I can describe."

"Estelle's a good woman," Siren said, a sentiment I more than agreed with.

"I agree," Karma announced, standing from the folding chair that had been dragged in.

Her forest green dress matched her eyes beautifully and made her hair pop. It, too, had pockets, which she was digging in. She swore at something, but I didn't pay her much attention, too busy examining my appearance for any flaws. I wasn't an insecure woman, but I wanted to look perfect for Estelle today.

"You look fine, girl," Siren said, reassuring me slightly.

She wasn't only a looker, but also dedicated time to her appearance, something I couldn't say. The rest of my sisters agreeing with her helped boost my ego. I also thought I looked damn good, and I hoped Estelle would feel the same way. The only thing she hadn't picked out for our wedding was my jumpsuit.

"It's almost time to get out there and wait for your bride," Karma said.

"This calls for a toast," Chains said, already turned up even without hitting the blunt.

"Everything calls for a toast with you," Kiwi told her.

"What's a celebration without at least fifty?" Chains replied, with a grin.

We all laughed, even though she was completely serious. Just as Val had been, Chains was a big partier.

"Since we're pressed for time, let me say this, then you can fucking really toast," Karma said cryptically. "I talked to Duchess recently. She sends her congrats, by the way."

"I will be sure to call and thank her," I promised, not wanting to disrespect the Founder of the Harlots and National President by disregarding her well-wishes.

"She knows you'll be otherwise preoccupied for the next several weeks," Karma said. "Just remember to do it when you return."

"I will."

"Can you get to the part where we have to toast, Prez?" Chains whined. "I've been sober for twelve hours."

Grinning, Karma walked to where she'd left her purse and opened it, pulling out a piece of paper. "Got permission from Duchess to do this. A reward for helping to bring down Aydin and his motherfuckers. More importantly, you killed that bitch, Luce. Here." She handed me the paper.

At first, the words didn't register, then it slowly dawned on me that I was holding a deed to a plot of land on the club's grounds, big enough to build a house on.

"I've been talking to Duchess about building homes that we can rent to members who are interested. Rent would be discounted, and we'd bring in money. Hopefully. Duchess and Jamison are still crunching numbers and running projections. But she said I could divide the area I chose with you. You can add Estelle to the deed. Jamison gave his permission when Duchess explained the situation. Once your home is built, if it's approved, you'll help us oversee the experiment, and receive a cut."

Unable to find any words, I ran to Karma and hugged her. "Thank you," I said sincerely, the gift enough to make my eyes misty.

"You're welcome, girlie. You're a damn good member. You deserve a reward for everything you've done," Karma said, pulling away and swiping at a stray tear. "Now, we can toast."

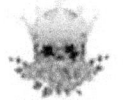

Estelle looked stunning in her designer gown. She had the money to pay for it, but I insisted I foot the bill for the wedding, including the gown. Being an officer who did regular runs meant I made good money, but before her, I had little to spend it on, so it went into a savings account. Five years of earning thousands a month meant I'd accumulated a lot.

Whereas my jumpsuit cost around five-hundred dollars, Estelle's *Vivian Westwood Elisa* gown cost thousands. The dress had an open back and revealed the sides of her breasts, but the asymmetrical halter neckline meant she wasn't showing too much skin. The leg slit originally showed a glimpse of her thick thighs, but she had it outfitted with white lace for extra modesty. I was a tad disappointed, but her dress, her choice.

As her father escorted her closer, I admired how the jacquard crepe material clung to her beautifully. As it should, as we flew out to New York for a fitting.

She was less than two feet away from me now. I fidgeted with the bouquet I held, eager to have her by me and make her my wife.

Karma nudged me. "Chill out, girlie. She's almost here."

Her tone was teasing. Nodding, I forced myself to still, looking at the decorations to distract myself. Gold and green ribbon lined the pews, with different yellow flowers decorating most of the area. It was a botanical garden, and Estelle wanted to honor that. She'd done an excellent job, blending the formality of a wedding with nature.

It didn't take long for me to get bored looking at the decorations, but by then, Estelle was there. I grinned at her. Her father nodded to me as I took her hand in mine, his eyes moist, before retreating to a front pew and sitting next to his wife, my soon-to-be parents-in-law looking beautiful together.

"Hi," she said shyly.

"Hey, babe," I replied, so in love that it felt like my heart would burst. "You look gorgeous."

"So do you."

With both brides at the altar, Glory began to speak. Neither Estelle nor I was very religious, but Mrs. Milton was, so we opted for the traditional Baptist script.

"Dearly beloved, we are gathered here today in the presence of God, to witness and bless this union, as Estelle Pratt-Milton and Denali Bernard join together in holy matrimony," Glory began, smiling at me as whispers arose.

Before today, my full name wasn't known, only my first. Not that it mattered. Soon, I'd be Denali Pratt-Milton. My father's name was a reminder of him, and his memory carried nothing but hurt and pain.

"Denali and Estelle will mark their transition as a couple, not only by celebrating the love between them, but by celebrating the love between everyone present. Without that love, this occasion would be far less joyous."

I rolled my eyes as some of my sisters hooted and hollered at the acknowledgment. Those bitches didn't know how to act, and luckily for them, Estelle giggled.

"This holy bond is not to be entered to lightly, but reverently, thoughtfully, and in accordance with the purpose for which God created it," Glory said, looking between us, then at the audience. "If anyone present knows of any reason why this couple should not be joined in holy matrimony, speak now, or forever hold your peace."

Estelle and I both looked at the crowd. My eyes sharpened into a glare, daring someone to open their mouth to try and fuck up our wedding.

"We're not going to do that shit, Everest," one of my sisters called, inspiring laughter.

"Behave, everyone!" Karma ordered, silencing the noise. "This is a special fucking occasion."

Normally, their antics didn't bother me, but today, I was a tad mortified. Estelle just rolled her eyes, but Mrs. Milton was glaring at the side of the church that was so rowdy. Estelle's younger siblings laughed, while her older brothers whispered to their partners, just like their parents were. I swallowed coarsely, trying to hide my anxiety.

Estelle squeezed my hand. "It's okay, Denali. I warned my family that there'd be some…incidents."

I nodded, and before I could reply, Glory began to speak again.

"If y'all are done acting like fools, we may proceed," she declared, relieving me. "Who gives Miss Estelle away?"

Harvey Sr. stood. "I do."

Estelle smiled at her stepfather. He grinned back, quickly wiping at his eyes.

Glory looked at us again. "Estelle and Denali, as you stand here before friends, family, and God, I ask that you declare your intentions to join each other in the sacred covenant of marriage." She looked at me. "Denali, if it's in your heart, please repeat after me."

"In the name of God, I, Denali Bernard, take you, Estelle Pratt-Milton, to be my lawfully wedded wife."

"In the name of God, I, Denali Bernard, take you, Estelle Pratt-Milton, to be my lawfully wedded wife," I parroted, my voice cracking as my emotions started to get the best of me.

I blinked rapidly to contain my tears, a feat, but I had to get through my vows before I allowed myself to cry.

"To have and to hold you from this day forward," Glory continued, waiting until I repeated it before she went to the next part. "For better or worse, for richer or for poorer, in sickness and in health."

"For better or for worse, for richer or for poorer, and in sickness and health, I will love and cherish you, Estelle," I said, going a little off script.

Glory gave me a sharp glare, but continued with the prepared words. "To love and to cherish you until we are parted by death. This is my solemn vow. Don't go off script this time," she ordered, inspiring more laughter, including from Estelle and me.

When I finished my vows, Glory had Estelle repeat the exact same ones. By the end of it, some tears had escaped both of our eyes and rolled down our cheeks.

"Estelle and Denali will now exchange rings as a symbol of their commitment and endless devotion. May the Lord bless these rings as you bless this union, in your infinite wisdom, today, tomorrow, and always. Amen."

"Amen," everyone echoed as glory held out the pillow containing our rings. I grabbed mine, anticipation buzzing within me.

"Estelle, I give you this ring to symbolize my love and devotion. With all that I am, and all that I have, I promise to honor and cherish you, or you can take my gun and shoot me," I said as I slipped the ring onto her finger.

She released a teary laugh as she grabbed her ring. "Denali, I give you this ring to symbolize our love and devotion. With all that I am, and all that I have, I'll honor and cherish you, in this life, and the next."

With the rings snugly on our fingers, it came time for the final portion of the ceremony, the part I'd been waiting for since we began.

"Denali and Estelle, having witnessed your marriage in the eyes of God and before all who assembled here, by the authority vested in me by the State of Tennessee, I pronounce you Denali and Estelle Milton-Pratt, wife and wife. You may now kiss—"

She didn't get a chance to finish before Estelle was flinging herself into my arms and kissing me. I wrapped my arms around her waist, happier than I'd ever been. Twenty years after a chubby-faced little girl stumbled into my life, she'd grown into a beautiful woman and was now mine, until death do us part.

Author's Note

Thank you for reading Estelle and Denali's story. When I first had the idea for Melting Point, I had no clue it would turn out the way it did. Denali and Estelle were supposed to be strangers with no prior history, and the meat of the story was going to start a year after they had their one-night stand. Clearly, it didn't pan out that way, because my thoughts wanted the book to pan out differently. Who am I to refuse the voices in my head that give me the power to write? Though different from the original plan, I'm happy with my story, and I'm very satisfied with the end product. Abuse and domestic violence are major themes of Melting Point. If you or anyone you know is experiencing DV, the number for the American National Hotline is 800.799.SAFE (7233). You can also text 88788 or chat at thehotline.org. The website for the National Hotline also has resources available. You are not alone.

I highly encourage you leave a review if you enjoyed Melting Point. Or, even if you didn't, leave a review. My only request is that you keep things constructive and respectful. If you want to contact me, shoot me an email at nev.ryn.writer@gmail.com. You can also message me on one of my socials, linked below. The TikTok is looking a little rough right now, as I'm merging my author and personal account, because I'm a lazy bitch who can't be bothered to run two accounts.

Thank you again for reading, and have a lovely rest of your day.

Contact Nevaeh

Instagram:
https://sqr.co/Neveah-Ryn-Instagram/
Threads:
https://www.threads.net/@nev.ryn
Facebook:
https://sqr.co/NevaehRynFacebook/
Goodreads:
https://sqr.co/Goodreads-Neveah-Ryn/
TikTok:
https://www.tiktok.com/@that_thick_author
Website:
https://www.nevaehryn.com/

Books by Nevaeh Ryu

The Mesmerized Saga
Mesmerized (The Mesmerized Saga, #1)
Bewitched (The Mesmerized Saga, #2)

Royal Harlots MC – Memphis, TN Chapter
Melting Point

About Nevaeh Ryn

Storytelling has always been Nevaeh Ryn's passion, and since she was young, writing has served as an escape. It shapes her, and she hopes to have a positive impact with the stories that she weaves.

Nevaeh pursued a BFA in Creative Writing at Full Sail University to hone her craft. She's a first-generation graduate, and she finished school in April 2025 and completed a four-month marketing course in November 2025, with plans to pursue further education in the future.

Her debut novel, Mesmerized, was unleashed onto the world on May 26th and served as an entry into the world of fiction writing. She has several more stories slated for later this year, including the second book in the Mesmerized Saga, Bewitched, which will come out on the first anniversary of Mesmerized. In addition, Melting Point, a story a part of the Royal Harlots MC, will drop on December 26th, and will be Nevaeh's first MC romance novel.

When she isn't lost in her own world, she spends her free time gaming on her PC, cooking up new recipes, and, of course, reading and writing. She's an avid Sims player and expresses herself through an ever-growing collection of tattoos.

Excerpts

Dr. Feel Good Blurb

Opposites attract has never been truer than when a hotheaded biker chick with a target on her back crosses paths with a stuffy physician whose reputation means everything to him.

Michelle 'Athena' Mitchell is president of the Royal Harlots MC - Kansas City, KS. After the Royal Bastards eradicated the local chapter of the Bloody Scorpions, things have been smooth sailing for all concerned. In the dead of winter in a remote stretch of woods, completing a job for the Bastards should've been a breeze for Athena. Instead, members of the Kansas City Bloody Femmes use it as an opportunity to avenge the Scorpions, ambushing her and leaving her for dead.

Athena collapses on Felix Good's property. On vacation in his secluded cabin, Felix is one of the best in his field. When he sees her motorcycle cut with the president's patch, he wants to leave her there, but his oath prevents him from ignoring the stranger. With the roads closed and the woman bleeding out, he takes her to his place to patch her up.

Has fate smiled on Athena or cursed Felix?

Chapter One – Felix

Snapping the folder shut, I pushed away from my desk and got to my feet, hours away from the start of my weeklong seclusion at my cabin with only the forest, wild animals, and much-needed silence surrounding me.

Whistling softly, I threw my stack of mail into my briefcase, then grabbed my coat and shrugged into it before glancing at my wall clock.

5 PM. Too late to stop at Ally's and work out the details of our agreement. She'd just have to wait. Patience was not only a virtue but one of my requirements. Her training would begin earlier than expected. At this point, the contract was a mere formality. I'd taken her out to dinner and evaluated her three times. She'd make an excellent pet.

Without warning, my door opened, and Ian Purdue walked in. He was my best friend and an OB/GYN, with an office in the same building where my practice was located. Unlike him, I opted for a field that brought me the most money and prestige. Plastic surgery to people who would and could pay top dollar to improve themselves. I promoted high-maintenance beauty standards and a luxury lifestyle.

Originally, I wanted to be a trauma surgeon, urged on by Iris, my ex-wife, until she ruined my fucking life and turned me against her and everything her type represented.

"Glad I caught you," Ian said. "I wanted to talk to you about Kali, Felix."

Tightening my lips, I nodded to the folder. "I've finished drafting her disciplinary report. Her *third*," I said with meaning. "I'm terminating her. If she ran to you, she's really out of her mind. I don't like gossips, and I especially hate mayhem."

Ian visibly gritted his teeth, not a stickler for rules like me. Without law and order, chaos descended.

My family created enough of that. My hedge fund father with mistresses, bastards, and scandals. My attorney sister with six ex-husbands, no children, and a string of lovers. My CEO brother with seven children, no wives, and no morals. And my assistant DA brother with a wife, a mistress, a friend with benefits, and no conscience. Of course, I couldn't leave out my mega-preacher mother, warped, flawed, holy, and narcissistic.

"After we cleared up her last mishap, you agreed that if Kali was written up three times in twelve months, you'd let her go," Ian started. "She has two weeks left before that timeline resets."

"She could have a day, and I wouldn't give a damn," I stressed.

"What did Kali do?"

"Scheduled three patients at the same damn time. And one, *one,* is a nitpicker about time and chewed me out that she had to wait an hour over her appointment time."

Ian opened his mouth, closed it, and opened it again, finally settling on scratching his jaw. "Can I talk you into giving her one more chance? She must've had a good reason for the overbooking. I got her the job. I feel responsible for her."

"Her 'reason' that two of the patients are constant cancellers doesn't excuse her insubordination."

"Kali can be a little flaky," Ian said, deciding to cop to the woman's issues. "But she isn't unruly, your staff and patients like her, and she tries to do better."

Turning away, I walked to the mirror on the other side of my spacious office and adjusted my tie. "Tell me you're not sleeping with her anymore."

"I'm not," Ian said without hesitation. "She is very happy with the man she met six or seven months ago."

I took my comb out of my coat's interior pocket and neatened my dark hair.

"I want to go on vacation with no loose ends. Leaving Kali in her position definitely counts as one."

Ian released a frustrated growl, and I sighed, meeting his gaze in the mirror.

"She has two little kids."

"Out of wedlock and by two different men. Maybe if she'd married, she wouldn't have such a challenging time."

"Can you get off your fucking self-righteous soapbox for one fucking minute?"

Abandoning the mirror, I turned and faced my friend. Ian—my opposite in every way—was also my conscience, the bleeding heart who opened his practice to the morally and financially challenged. He didn't believe in commitment; I didn't believe in love and preferred business arrangements with defined expectations and financial rewards.

"If you insist on letting Kali go, I'm writing her a letter of recommendation, *you're* providing references, and *we're* giving her a severance package."

"Absolutely not! She doesn't even work in your goddamn office."

"I can't have an ex-lover working in my fucking office, Felix."

If he asked me, I'd tell him he had feelings for Kali. Since I didn't believe in love or marriage and he hadn't asked, I kept my opinion to myself.

"Your roaming cock isn't my damn problem. You aren't fucking her now, so hire her yourself."

"I don't need that drama. She might get the wrong idea."

"Didn't you just tell me she's happy with whoever, fuckhead?"

Ian shrugged. "She is, but why rock the boat?"

I squinted. "What aren't you telling me? What crazy woman are you fucking now?"

He smirked at me. "None of your fucking business. Now, about Kali."

Ian didn't intend to let this go. Unfortunately, he knew my cabin's location. If I walked out, he'd follow me there, not caring about the travel time.

Frustrated, I thrust my hand through my hair, ruining the neatness I'd just achieved. "If I give in, she doesn't get a reset for twelve months."

"That isn't fair."

"Neither is your request, Ian. You know it was shoddy work to schedule three patients at once, no matter the reason. At least admit that."

"Fine," he gritted. "She didn't make the best decision in this instance."

"Thank you." Shifting my weight, I buttoned the top button on my coat. "Do you accept my terms?"

"I could drive to your cabin and convince you of all the reasons you're a fuckhead for this ultimatum and harp at it for the entire weekend. By the time I left Sunday night, you would've changed your fucking mind."

"I intend to hunt. Which you don't like. Remember?"

"I don't have to stalk the woods for poor, indefensible creatures. I can relax at your cabin while you kill them."

"My patience is wearing thin," I said. "You aren't changing my mind on this."

"Fine. I accept your terms, asshole."

"Lovely. Anything else?"

Ian eyed me and pursed his lips. Immediately, I knew he had something else to tell me that I wouldn't like.

"Are you familiar with the Royal Bastards?"

"Who isn't?" I scoffed. "A passel of lawless thugs." As was their sister club, the Royal Harlots. An even worse travesty for women to go down the path of rack and ruin, violence, and viciousness.

"I wouldn't say that around them. They may not take too kindly to it."

"Luckily, I won't have an occasion to be in their presence."

"Arthel got me to see one of her sister's daycare workers. The father of her baby is a Royal Bastard."

My mouth fell open in cartoonish shock. If my jaw could've unhinged, it would've hit the floor. I couldn't believe Ian allowed one of those criminals into our building. If he wanted to risk his law-abiding patients, that was between him and his clients. Mine were high-brow and high-class. "You're kidding me."

"I'm dead serious. His name is Reese Sinclair. He's the club's sergeant-at-arms."

"And you accepted her as a patient?"

"I didn't know about her connection to the club until her first visit. Apparently, Arthel didn't either. Her sister and brother-in-law intended to pay for the girl's care."

"That sounds like Tess and Big Poppa." I liked those two, a God-fearing couple who attended my mother's church.

"I agreed to match their money and had intended to talk to you, Shawn, and the others about pitching in."

"I'm not part of your fucking practice," I growled for the umpteenth time.

"Yeah, but you are my fucking friend."

"Let me guess. This biker woman isn't married to the motorcycle man?"

"Stop fucking focusing on wrong shit," Ian snapped. "I like her. She's twenty-one years old and in need of help."

"I'm not a damn charitable organization. Neither is your practice. We're for-profit businesses. Yet, in the last twenty minutes, you've stood there and pleaded the case of a woman because she has two small kids and another woman who is young, unwed, and pregnant. Neither of which is your problem. Unless you want to fuck her."

Ian glared at me. He wasn't one to cross that ethical line. "The girl is my patient. Nothing more. Nothing less. Reese Sinclair opened an expense account for her. I don't know what he thinks, but he deposited enough to cover three pregnancies."

Annoyance robbed me of air, and I drew in deep breaths. When I returned, I'd start the search for a new location. I couldn't remain in a building that allowed the likes of Reese Sinclair and his one-percenter outlaw club. It would be too tempting to alert my brother, Brandon, and bring those lowlifes down.

"Reese Sinclair isn't a man to be crossed, Felix," Ian warned, knowing me well. "Whatever is going through your fucking narrow mind, toss it the fuck out."

What could I say? Ian had already accepted money from criminals. He kept my secrets, so I'd keep his.

For now.

"I'm headed to the hospital to check on her. She was admitted yesterday after an altercation of some sort."

"And so it begins," I sneered tightly. "Anything else?"

"Just be careful on the road. Heavy snow is expected overnight."

Too livid to respond, I snatched my keys from my desk, my overcoat from the rack, and stormed out.

Athena

"What's the old coot doing?"

I followed the direction Fendi, my VP, nodded to where Razor, the president of the Kansas City chapter of the Royal Bastards, stood, chatting up one of their bike hoppers.

Halloween decorations hung around the Devil's Pit. Fake cobwebs crisscrossed the ceiling with plastic spiders of assorted sizes. Skeletons, witches, and bats hung from the rafters. An animated witch standing in front of a steaming cauldron stood in the pool table area. Crystal balls and bowls of peanuts lined the bar, and orange lightbulbs replaced the clubhouse's infamous red ones.

Leaning over, I grabbed a handful of peanuts from the bowl on the bar and popped as many as possible into my mouth, then swigged deeply from my beer. "He's hoping his Viagra doesn't go to waste."

We snickered.

"That chick's twenty, if she's a day, Athena." Fendi had a thing about age. Now that she'd soon hit forty, she was even more insecure. Instead of celebrating her hard-earned wisdom, she insisted laugh lines were wrinkles and a shaved pussy was better than one sprinkled with gray hair. "He'd never look twice at me nowadays, although I was once his favorite fuck."

"It tracks. I just turned thirty, so I'm out too," I said mildly, gulped more beer, then glanced around. "Besides, you don't want Razor and never have."

It had been, and still was, Louisiana. And Warrior. Distaste ran through me, but I shoved it aside. Meanwhile, I almost pitied her obsession with Louisiana, a man so in love with his wife, he forgot other women existed the moment he met Jinx.

As for Warrior...yeah. *No. Fuck no!* I wasn't going there, so I stood on the footrails of the stool to see above the press of bikers, hang arounds, wannabees, club property, and bike hoppers, and made a production of looking around.

"I'm trying to scope out Reese and Louisiana in this crowd. Maybe, they'll know where Jinx has gotten herself off to."

Fendi smirked, never a fan of Louisiana's ol' lady, blaming Jinx for him throwing her over. "Maybe, she's knocked up again," she sneered. "That bitch should stop trying at this point. She's old as well. Thirty-one."

"Enough," I warned, tired of Fendi's cattiness, especially toward Jinx.

If Razor's summons hadn't come just as we were returning from a weeks-long run, I would've had my entire crew with me. Razor insisted it was so important that we couldn't go anywhere else before we checked in with him. Personally, I would've finagled a postponement of the meeting until tomorrow, but my VP talked sense into me. I could enjoy the reunion with my little sisters and our dog without the meeting hanging over my head. Besides the last thing I needed was cuddle with Bob the Biter and catch up with Lake and Juno only to have Razor send me on another run, so instead of enjoying our annual Halloween party at the Haven, our clubhouse, not too far from the Devil's Pit, with our club members, we had to wait until Razor arranged his fuck.

Once I became president, I negotiated the separate Halloween parties with Razor. Which had *absolutely nothing* to do with Warrior. I'd die on that fucking hill, too. I couldn't weasel out of our mixed celebrations for Thanksgiving or our joint Christmas charity runs.

Unfortunately, Razor had outsmarted me, got me to his clubhouse on Halloween, *and* left me stuck with Fendi and her bitterness, fueled by her lack of confidence.

"You've discussed what a good fuck Louisiana is, but there are other motherfuckers out there who lay good dick," I continued, hoping she'd get my words through her thick skull.

"I've had my fair share," Fendi confirmed, "but I'm waiting for my man to come back to me."

Maybe I was the dumbass for continuing to waste my breath on advice she refused to take.

"He *isn't* your man," I gritted. "He belongs to Jinx and has, legally, for the past ten years. You're turning forty next month." Tempering my annoyance and ignoring our complicated history, I laid a hand on her arm. "I know you want kids. We've talked about it—"

"I *wanted* kids. *Keir's*," she said, referring to Louisiana's given name. "Without him, my pussy is a one-way passage. Dicks go in, but babies don't come out."

"You're fucking disgusting," I said, shaking my head and laughing despite myself. "Come on. Let's find one of the guys. They'll point us to Louisiana. It's just so fucking crowded tonight, so he and Jinx probably haven't spotted us."

"You're fucking insane! I'm not hunting that motherfucker down. *I'm* the queen. He comes to me. Always has and always will."

I clenched my jaw to keep from cursing her out. Louisiana *did* come to her, but not for the reasons she made it sound, and usually with Jinx. He loved the fuck out of that woman and didn't want bullshit with her, who (guiltily), I preferred over Fendi.

Jinx could be a royal bitch when provoked, but Fendi was a fucking cunt on a good goddamn day. Again, it had nothing to do with Warrior, even if she'd fucked him for months not long after he and I split.

Water under the fucking bridge.

"Keir will be forty-three. I'm sure he's ready for a kid," Fendi chirped. "*Mine*. That's why my womb is closed to anyone else's seed."

Snorting, I rolled my eyes. "Are you sure you haven't convinced yourself of that because *you* don't want children?"

"I'm not getting into a great debate with you about this." Fendi's sea-green eyes narrowed. As a child, she'd been a catalog model, but she fell in with the wrong crowd and everything went to shit, turning her into the hardened, cynical chick she was today. I understood. My fucking life hadn't been roses and sunshine, but I chose to still believe in happiness. To look for the good. Not every fucking situation was a competition or meant as an affront. "We all know *you* dream of a knight on steel and chrome to put a ring on your finger and resurrect the kid you lost."

Ouch.

Since I didn't have extra money for dental bills, I didn't clamp my jaw any tighter and risk a fucking tooth. Somehow, I managed not to answer her. If I clocked that bitch, Razor wouldn't be happy. He didn't like his brothers fighting. He definitely wouldn't tolerate it from me and my sisters. In certain situations, I kept a certain facade in place, knew when to shut the fuck up, and followed most protocols and rules.

However, if anyone had heard her say that disrespectful shit to me, she'd be due an ass-beating when we returned to The Haven.

While I'd recently added diplomacy to my set of skills, violence was required in this life, and I'd never shied away from it. Years ago, as a hang around, I quickly gained a warlike reputation, and Fendi—president of the KC chapter, until I unseated her two years ago—pegged me as the goddess of war.

I suggested Morrigan, although the Celtic goddess tended to turn into a crow, and I *hated* fucking birds. *Almost* as much as I hated hard liquor, seclusion, pumpkin *anything*, doctors, cops, lawyers, Bloody Femmes, Bloody Scorpions (except one), cooking, housework, jellybeans, and circus peanuts.

It didn't matter. Fendi shot down Morrigan, Enyo, and Bellona, all more fitting in my estimation. And Fendi outright laughed when I suggested Freya.

"She's the goddess of love and beauty, Athena. Neither of which are associated with *you*. That's your sisters' calling cards."

Never mind that Freya was *also* the Norse goddess of war. As a prominent figure in their pantheon, she occupied several roles. I didn't correct Fendi, though. At the time, I hadn't been able to without consequences.

Almost a decade later, and those fucking words still left me salty. Like

Fendi, the Harlots and their sisterhood came before any pettiness for me.

A hand landed on my shoulder, and I turned partially.

"Razor's ready to see you," Warrior murmured.

He was the club's treasurer, mean as a fucking snake to enemies, and as beautiful as Lucifer was rumored to be before he fell to Hell. Where Warrior belonged, in my estimation.

I'd worked at the strip club for two fucking weeks before the fine motherfucker blazed into Memphis on Royal Bastard business, came into the joint for a lap dance, and fucked me to within an inch of my goddamn life.

Back then, I needed a better way to help Mama and Daddy make ends meet. Fast food work hadn't cut it. On my eighteenth birthday, Mama introduced me to her johns, although she didn't tell Daddy. As her pimp, he wouldn't have liked being cut out of our arrangement, but the stupid motherfucker just drank away the money she earned for our rent and utilities. We had to do *something* so we wouldn't end up on the fucking streets.

Just a few weeks in, and Mama and I decided the risk was too great. If Daddy discovered our duplicity, he would've fucked us up. Lake and Juno, then thirteen and eight, were still oblivious to shit, still happily in school during the week, and at Aunt Sheron's during the weekend to play with our cousins.

My sisters were the reason I hadn't moved away and got my own place. When Mama wasn't around for them, I made sure I was. I didn't want them to go through what I had, and if left up to my father, their virginity would've been sold to the highest bidder as soon as their tits started coming in.

With our joint decision that I leave streetwalking behind, Mama got me into a high-end strip club. We both thought prostitution within that framework would be safer. In the end, she regretted that decision because Warrior took me away.

I fell in love. Though Warrior later proved he was a motherfucker, he took care of my parents and little sisters so

Lake and Juno would have chances I never did. And when our parents were killed when Lake was sixteen and Juno was eleven, he brought them to live with us.

We'd been so good together, him and me. I saw forever with him. Until forever came with conditions.

"Snap to it, babe," Warrior ordered, ending my trip down memory lane.

Shrugging his hand away since he hadn't moved it from my shoulder, I made a face at him. Defying him wasn't always an option, although when things had become too intense and I threw out my safe word, he'd stopped instantly. "Don't fucking touch me, fuckhead. You lost that goddamn right five years ago when you told me to choose." And then began sticking his cock in Fendi. If not for her, maybe we could've found our way back to each other.

Sighing, Warrior squeezed the bridge of his nose. "And you chose, Michelle," he snapped, inflaming my temper further. That fuckhead knew better than to call me by my name. "Wrong, in my fucking estimation, but do you see *me* with hard fucking feelings?"

I jumped to my feet and brought my booted foot down onto his. He barely flinched. "If you ever use my name again, you'll be sorry," I swore. "I'm Athena to you. From now until the end of the fucking world."

"Fine," he gritted, turned, and began weaving through the crowd, expecting me to fucking follow.

Knowing I had no choice burned my fucking ass.

###